BONEMAN

BONEMAN

Lisa W. Cantrell

A TOM DOHERTY ASSOCIATES BOOK
NEW YORK

BONEMAN

Copyright © 1992 by Lisa W. Cantrell

This book is printed on acid-free paper.

A Tor Book
Published by Tom Doherty Associates, Inc.
175 Fifth Avenue
New York, N.Y. 10010

Tor® is a registered trademark of Tom Doherty Associates, Inc.

Library of Congress Cataloging-in-Publication Data

Cantrell, Lisa W.
    Boneman / Lisa W. Cantrell.
        p.   cm.
    ISBN 0-312-85307-6
    I. Title.
    PS3553.A548B66   1992
    813'.54—dc20   92-24636
                                                          CIP

First edition: November 1992

Printed in the United States of America

0 9 8 7 6 5 4 3 2 1

for best friends

ACKNOWLEDGMENTS AND THANKS

The author would like to acknowledge, for technical advice and assistance, the following experts: Special Agent Shirley L. Burch, North Carolina State Bureau of Investigation; John H. Burton, M.D.; John Lamont, Crisis Intervention Associates. Any errors in interpretation or use of the information provided by these fine professionals are entirely my own. And a special thank you to Burton Whicker, Leanne Johnson, Barry Cantrell.

De Boneman come
De Boneman go
Nobody know what de Boneman know

—Old Haitian children's rhyme

ONE

Someone was coming.

The alley loomed dark and silent in the midnight pall. A waste-land in a sea of city noise, city light. An oasis of shadows amid the flash.

Someone was coming.

Dampness overlay the gloom. The dank, predatory scent of mildew, decay. It clung to the air with a tenacity that not even the fresh morning sunlight would dissolve. Sunlight never quite reached this place.

Someone was coming.

The mist knew, and rolled slowly back and forth, searching for the darkest corners, the deepest crevices to hide in, sliding up against the cracks as though it could seep through them and disappear.

Back up State Street, the night was rife with laughter and music, people on the roam. Glitter lit their eyes, and their steps were full of pagan energy and thrust. And if beneath the surface of that vigor lurked a quiet desperation, a wellspring of concern that all was not as it should be, in fact something was very, very wrong, they hid it well. For the street was their talisman; the glitter, the noise their bead on life. Things not surrendered easily.

They went about their nightly rituals determined to ignore the fear, ignore the darkness at the other end of the strip—and what it might hold. Because their world was safe, *wasn't it?* Their space was full of light and life. As long as they stayed inside their space, the shadows couldn't touch them.

Within the alley, the world was far away. Darkness was the talisman here, and close-kept secrets a paramour of the night.

There was no laughter. No music or glitter. Only the wind held life.

At the moment it, too, was still. Watching. Waiting.

Someone was coming.

The darkness stirred. A shadow shifted briefly in the silence.

The skittish mist crept closer to the walls, hugging the corners and edges as though trying to clear a path through the passage-way, trying to escape.

No one walded the silent street beyond, but the echo of a single footstep sounded in the secluded alley.

Someone was coming.

Coley Dean gripped the knife nested in his right jacket pocket and jerked a quick glance up and down the cheap, neon-lit strip.

"Bastards." He spat the word, scowling as a garbage truck ambled by. "Think they can cut in on me, but I'll show 'em," he muttered. "I'll show 'em."

The moon cast a sullen sheen on the oily, rain-streaked city streets. The drizzle had let up earlier, but dankness still clogged the air like the smell from the Dumpsters out back of Mel's Diner where Cannibal Bob liked to hang out. Cannibal Bob would eat anything.

A few cars cruised by, a smattering of pedestrians. But traffic was mostly light, about par for a late-night Monday.

Coley waited impatiently for a cab to pass, then crossed on over and headed up State Street, past Julio's Pizza, past Trader Jeans, past the Master's Touch Massage Parlor that promised rubdowns from Jim and Tammy look-alikes. (He went there occasionally and always asked for Tammy Lee, who looked the least like the Bakker broad but had nice hands.)

Gaudy neons—red, yellow, blue—dabbed color on the murk. A mixture of dingy whites and yellows spilled from streetlamps, windows, and doors of still-open joints.

Traffic noise vied with music, conversations with curses and laughs. All merged to a dull background roar that sounded oddly at times like somebody moaning; the city, he guessed. The mishmash of night-shine and street-loud lit State Street from Wilson to Greer, Monday through Sunday, eight P.M. till two.

Not much of a place, maybe, but his place, his little corner of the world. And nobody was gonna fuck it up. Nobody.

He fondled the knife in his jacket pocket, letting its hard length caress his palm.

Sometimes people laughed at his hands—the ones who didn't know him, the kids growing up. "Girl's hands," they'd snicker, "Practice mitts for junior tits."

Coley's hands *were* small. Extremely small, even for his size—a few inches over five feet, a hundred and twenty-eight pounds.

But with the blade . . . with the blade. His hand reached new proportions holding the blade. It expanded then. Grew. And nobody laughed.

"Hey Coley, got something for you, sugar. Best on the block, and you know it."

A prostitute Coley had dorked a few times for the price of some crack sauntered up. She was trying to look sexy and looked like shit. Rock candy not agreeing with her.

"C'mon, baby," she whined. "Make you a special deal."

"Get a case," Coley said, then ignored the curses she hurled after him as he walked on by.

After crossing the next street, he picked up his pace. The crowd began to thin, giving him room to indulge the cocky swagger he'd adopted long ago to compensate for his lack of stature. Made him look tough.

The crowd did seem a little sparser than usual, he thought, as he cast a narrow-eyed glare at a couple of street lice who quickly moved out of his way. But then most people hung out at the upper end of the five-block strip, where the main action was.

Farther on, the razzle-dazzle faded quickly, bright lights and crowds giving way to shadows and the barricaded doorways of daytime businesses closed for the night. There was some action to be found here, true, but it kept mostly to the alleys, deals done better in darkness than in light.

He crossed another intersection, the last big one before the blocks of strictly daytime businesses that led into warehouse row. Here, most of the traffic was turning right, heading out to Glenwood or circling back to cruise the main strip just one more time. This intersection marked the end of the rainbow, so to speak.

It was as if he'd stepped out of hyperspace.

Behind him, the traffic noise was a background drone, punctuated by an occasional horn blast or the squeal of locked-down brakes. Before him, the street lay silent and dark.

Some doorways ahead were shielded by iron bars and padlocks strung on chains, others were protected by roll-down steel mesh gates that totally encased their display windows and safety-glassed doors.

A sudden gust of wind teased some litter from the sidewalk in front of him and swept it into the gutter, as though clearing a path for him to walk.

Coley strode on, unconcerned by the deserted street. Better this way. With what he had planned, he didn't need prying eyes.

The sound of a car approaching from behind . . .

Reflexively, he ducked into the shadows of a recessed doorway, then turned to see, tensing at the thought that it might be the heat. They did drive-bys from time to time, shining their spotlights on the darkened storefronts. He'd been zapped by those spots a time or two, and it always made him feel like a roach. Like in his kitchen at night, when he'd go in and turn on the light and the damn things would scuttle back underneath the cabinets and sink.

Damn pigs. Had no right making you feel subhuman. No right.

A run-down Ford with one headlight came junking by, radio on full blast. Coley let out his breath. Couple of his sometime customers; he recognized the car. He watched it slow at the next corner, ease on, then stop at the mouth of a narrow alley that ran between two darkened warehouses about midway down the next block. The radio clicked off.

Coley moved up a few doorways to get a better look.

The guy on the passenger's side had leaned out his window and was talking to somebody, Coley couldn't tell who, the dude kept to the shadows. But it was obvious what was going down.

Sonofabitch! Willie Dee had been right. Some bastard had moved into his territory. *His* territory, by God. Like it was okay for somebody to just pick out a corner and go to dealing. Like just because Coley had been out of town a couple of weeks it was open invitation for some independent pavement pusher to move on in.

Well he'd show the fucker "move in." He'd carve his initials on the dude's face.

More verbal exchange. The kid climbed nervously from the car and entered the alley, pulling out his money as he went. Coley frowned. Bad business making a customer get out of his car like that on the street, smacked of a setup. But within moments, the kid was back, jumping into the car which quickly took off down State.

Anger rekindled. Coley fought it down as he resumed walking, letting it seethe just to the boiling point where he felt juiced. If somebody had set up shop in an alley Coley considered his turf, he'd set them straight in a heartbeat. No sweat. They just didn't know who they were dealing with here. He'd show them.

He fondled the knife. Came to the end of the block.

Darkness cloaked the area ahead, a vivid contrast to the carnival atmosphere he'd left behind. Away from the lure and luster of the main strip, this space was generally shunned, even by the street lice.

Warehouses mostly, empty black faces with their eye sockets boarded up. Coley began to feel a little edgy. No people roamed these sidewalks, no traffic cruised by. Nothing stirred.

Nothing.

He fingered the knife in his jacket pocket, nested it against his palm. Its cool, hard presence reassured him. He knew what he was doing, how to handle himself. He and the knife had their routine.

Stepping off the curb, he crossed the street.

Darkness closed in around him as he walked, as though it opened as he approached, then folded back together behind him. The faint babble of nightlife seemed suddenly to recede even more, sounding hollow and very far away—like the roar of the ocean far from the beach.

Coley fingered the hilt of the knife, running his thumb down the length of the slit. He liked doing that. It felt good, the way it slid smoothly against his hand, warmed to his touch. That first instant when steel kissed skin.

Any dumb-ass could use a gun. It took skill to use a knife. And guts. Not many people could walk right up to a guy and stick him, look him straight in the eye and never flinch. It took steel.

Another time, Coley would have laughed at his joke. Right now, he fondled the knife, kept walking.

Was the dude standing in the alley watching him? Probably. Did he have a piece on him? Probably. Chickenshit little bastard, they all carried them, thought it made them hot shit. But a gun didn't particularly worry Coley. He knew how to handle himself in a tight situation, and besides, the dude wasn't apt to shoot a potential customer right off the bat, was he? And that's what Coley would pretend to be—until he got close.

He felt primed for the confrontation. Eager, in fact. Whatever it took, he wasn't about to give over an inch of his territory, not an inch—except the five that came with the knife, of course. Those the dude could have full measure. With his blessing. All for free.

Taking a couple of steadying breaths, he headed for the alley. Time to deliver the message: Nobody was moving in on Coley Dean's action. Nobody.

The mouth of the alley was a narrow slit. Down here, darkness was king. And silence. Silence was its queen.

Coley hesitated again as he neared the darkened entrance, well aware that some of these guys could play rough.

He'd heard the rumors being bandied about, felt that odd sense of unease that had been spreading through the streets even before he'd left town—that something was coming, they didn't know what, only that it was coming and it was bad.

Junker gossip! Coley spat in disgust.

He wasn't buying it. Was he some two-bit juvie, frightened off by the first little hint of trouble on the street? Hell, no. He was an established businessman with connections in high places. If there was anything worth knowing, he'd have heard.

Still . . .

Suddenly Coley felt his skin crawl, remembering what some of those rumors had involved: drug cults, ritual sacrifice, voodoo.

Bullshit. He fondled the knife. He didn't believe all that stuff, wasn't buying into that line of crap. It was just those goddamn Haitians from the south side trying to throw a stink into the works.

Well let 'em try. He wasn't about to back off and let the fuckers waltz right in on him. No way. He'd spent a lot of time, taken a lot of grief to build up this territory. He wasn't about to let some

14

stinkin' drum-beaters with their island mumbo jumbo scare him off.

Actually he did smell something rotten, getting stronger the closer he came to the alley. That must be what was bothering him, that smell of alley filth. He hated it.

He curled his nose, scrubbing at it with his left hand.

Maybe it was just the silence that was spooking him. It was very quiet here. No sounds came from the alley, not the rustle of clothing, not the scrape of shoes on cement. Not even the sound of somebody breathing. Just that garbage stink. Had the dude left, then?

The image of that kid earlier, making his buy, came back to haunt him. The kid had been nervous, twitchy. Maybe it was just having to get out of his car—enough to cause some major concern. But what if it were more?

Just what *was* the deal here?

He looked at the dark, silent alley, fondled the knife.

What was the matter with him? Was he turning pussy?

Shit!

He stepped forward, maintaining his grip on the blade he was ready to pull at the slightest wrong move.

"Hey." For a moment nothing happened. Then the soft rustle of movement. Coley focused on the tall black man who materialized in the thin light that trickled in from the street. The warehouses formed solid walls of darkness on either side, but toward the front and rear of the narrow slit, pale light filtered in and framed the shadowy form Coley judged to be standing about six or eight feet away.

"Hey, you," he said, more aggressively.

No answer.

Coley stepped forward. "You got a mouth, asshole?"

"You buy?" The soft, raspy voice sent an unfamiliar shiver scurrying across Coley Dean's skin with the prickle of spider's feet. Who was this dude? Why didn't he show himself?

"Yeah, man. I buy. I buy all you got."

The dude moved another step forward, catching more of the light. He was tall, well over six feet, with a dumb, shiteating grin plastered on his ugly face. Coley wrinkled up his nose again at the stink that went beyond not taking a bath. Goddamn filthy pavement pusher.

The dude reached into his pocket.

Coley's hand spasmed around the knife, almost jerking it out. But the dude was only after his stuff.

"Twen'y pop."

Coley couldn't quite tag the accent; some sort of pidgin. He glanced at the hand extended, palm up—and big, that sucker was *big* like a catcher's mitt, with fingers that stretched out like they'd been melted and sucked through a straw. He counted eight vials.

"Twenty a pop. That's one-sixty, right?" Coley made like he was pulling out his roll, looking into the eyes that stared blankly at him—

—and something about those eyes, something dark, and smooth, and empty, made him hesitate again, stay the motion that would have brought out the business end of the blade.

This wasn't some crack-house kid trying to support his habit like Coley'd assumed. This dude was older—*colder*—with the kind of eyes that looked through you like you didn't count. Haitian maybe, or—*Jamaican*? Shit! *Was this one of the posses moving in?*

Now, that thought gave Coley real pause. Those dudes were bad. Big-time bad. They'd joint you in a heartbeat, scatter your pieces from here to D.C.

The dude didn't blink. He didn't blink at all, Coley realized as he stared into the glassy eyes fixed on him. And he didn't say anything else either. Just waited, hand held out, shiteating grin still pulling his ugly face.

And just how long can a person hold a grin? Coley wondered, fingering his knife.

Suddenly he wished he was somewhere else. Wished he'd let Snarky or Leo or one of those other cats handle this for him. This dude was Spook City.

Instinct said back off.

But that was sure suicide.

Things had gone too far, and Coley had his reputation to think of. Back off now and he'd have every pavement pusher in Phoenix City moving in on him by dawn.

The glittery eyes continued to fix on his. He felt almost afraid to look away, as though if he jerked his head aside, his eyes might be pulled from their sockets.

16

He blinked. His lids felt gritty and dry, scraping across his eyeballs like sandpaper. His eyes burned. He wanted to close them—

—and maybe he did for a second because when he looked again the man in front of him had moved. The air seemed filled with lights, tiny white lights, dancing like swimming dust particles, shimmering brightly, shifting and swirling and brushing his face.

Everything was slowing down. He thought the pusher was lowering his hand—but it was taking forever. Coley was having trouble focusing his gaze.

What was going on?

Coley's skin tingled as though bathed by fine mist. He breathed in; his nose and throat felt dry. His vision blurred.

He blinked several times and shook his head. His vision cleared somewhat, enough to see that the big dude was still standing there, staring at him, still grinning that stupid, shiteating grin.

Whatever had happened for an instant was gone.

"Buy this, cocksucker." Coley yanked out his knife, blade licking forward quickly, like the tongue of a snake—

or did it take forever?

His hand suddenly felt thick; fingers numb and cold.

The dude didn't move. Didn't even flinch. Just grinned.

Rage erupted in Coley. Who did this fucker think he was? *Who?*

"I'll show you, asshole. I'll show you."

Coley hadn't originally intended killing the dude. Just freak him out a little. Maybe do some minor damage, enough to leave a lasting impression.

Now he wanted to kill.

Spittle flew from his mouth as he rammed the knife forward, bringing it up at groin height for maximum shock value, then pivot, thrust, follow-through, an expert's impeccable routine. Like great choreography, it should be put to music. He visualized the blade entering the soft tissue just below the rib cage, angling upward through the liver toward the heart.

He thrust forward again and again, maximizing the wound so the fucker would bleed to death if nothing else.

There should be blood, where's the blood?

Still the dude didn't move. Didn't back off an inch.

17

Long arms hung limply by his sides, big hands weighting them down.

Grin in place.

Coley's rage evaporated. Fear rushed in.

What was happening here? What the hell was going on?

He was still trying to comprehend as the dude raised his huge hands and fastened them around Coley's throat.

It was so unexpected that at first Coley didn't react. Then he let go of the knife. It spiraled down . . . down into a deep, dark hole that was suddenly spinning around him; he kept waiting to hear the blade hit but it just kept falling . . . falling . . .

His head felt thick and heavy, as though it, too, were about to fall off and go tumbling into that pit after the knife. He tried to lift it, but he couldn't, tried to raise his arms, but they were cold as ice. He kept reaching . . . *reaching* . . .

trying to scream . . .

trying to breathe . . .

Most of all trying to breathe as the huge hands began lifting him by the neck until his feet were dangling midair.

The last thing Coley saw as he passed into the Great Beyond was the shiteating grin.

At the opposite end of the alley, a shadow stirred. Tendrils of mist oozed away from the movement, slithering like silent, pallid worms across the ground.

A figure emerged from the darkness. The man stood there, silhouetted by dim light falling on his back. He was a handsome young man, of medium build, dressed in a dark, tailored business suit; he made no further moves.

A moment passed.

Up at the mouth of the alley, the tall, grinning black man released Coley Dean's body. It flopped to the ground. Swinging around, he slowly began walking toward the well-dressed figure waiting silently beyond.

When he reached that end of the alley, the silent figure turned and disappeared back into the shadows from which he'd come.

The grinning black man followed.

TWO

J. J. Spencer studied the computer screen, rereading the words he'd just typed. Blackness surrounded the yellow letters—all caps—making them seem at once an intrusion on the pristine surface, *to be wiped away at the earliest possible moment like a smear on his great-grandmother's cherry sideboard,* and an incursion into enemy space. Always a scary prospect making that first entry on a new piece of work.

Retain or erase? The eternal question.

He continued his perusal of the screen. For a brief instant, the ebony field seemed poised like an army of spiders ready to gobble up the meager words, the bobbing cursor at the end of the G winking on and off like a fly caught in their web screaming "Help me! Help me!"

Then the image dissolved, along with his indecision. He gave the screen a nod. "Yeah. Good title." Sat back in his chair with a satisfied grin.

This was going to be a most excellent series. He could feel it in his finger bones.

Now to get down to the real nitty-gritty.

He flexed both hands, spaced down several lines, and started on the text:

```
In the beginning God created the
heaven and the earth. And it was all
downhill from there.
```

Stopped typing. Reread it.

First sentences were so important. You had to hook the reader in, get them committed right from the very start.

He reread it again.

Not exactly original. But hey, if it was good enough for the Big Guy . . .

He moved on to sentence number two, studying this one a bit more critically.

"Get rid of the 'and,' " he muttered. "Not supposed to start a sentence with 'and.' "

He tried it without.

"Nah. Better with."

Put it back.

"Yeah."

Anyway, this was a short story, not a newspaper article. Creative license (and bad grammar) could be indulged.

"Okay. Now what?" He sat there lightly tapping his index finger against the spacer bar and tried to get in touch with his muse.

Apparently she was sleeping late this morning.

A cool breeze wandered in through the open window at his back and roamed around the living room, stirring papers and dust and the hair on J.J.'s neck. It smelled of springtime freshness—and somebody's breakfast bacon.

J.J. took a good whiff. Lord, didn't that bacon smell good. He wrinkled up his nose and tried to pull his mind back on line. No time to fool around here, and besides that, bacon was bad for you. Full of fat and cholesterol.

He tried to imagine the wrinkled strips squirming around in the pan, looking like grayish-pink globs of half-congealed whale blubber loaded down with salt and chemicals and swimming in thick, clotted grease, tried to imagine how that would taste. And it worked somewhat.

But Lord, didn't that bacon smell good.

Oh, well . . .

Returning his hands to the computer keys, J.J. held them poised, waiting for the next inspiration to strike.

It didn't.

"C'mon . . ."

No dice. Apparently this was going to be one of those mornings.

He leaned back again and sighed. The first time in six months he'd actually been able to take some time off from work to devote to his writing—his *real* writing—and here he was, stuck after only two sentences—*plus a killer title, don't disregard the importance of that.*

"Great."

Outside, bright May sunshine beamed serenely down. Birds were singing. Bees were buzzing. He could hear every one of them. Every. Single. One.

He flexed his fingers once more and sat up straight, trying to refocus his concentration. If he didn't get to work soon, the entire morning would be shot.

Across the street a car door slammed; an engine started. In the house next door a baby wailed.

J.J. stared at the near-empty screen. Why was it so easy to pop off a two-thousand-word lead story for the Phoenix City *Review* and so bloody hard to write fiction? He could have written his daily column in the midst of a rock concert, but just let him sit down to work on his novel or a short story and there came every sound, every irrelevant thought, every movement divebombing in.

It was a kamikaze conspiracy to take out his muse. "Unfair."

Sighing again, he leaned back in his chair, clasped his hands behind his head, and reread the opening pair of sentences a couple more times, hoping that would jump-start his stalled brain.

And he'd thought these stories would be easier to write.

When he'd first come up with the idea for the Jehovah Jones adventure series, he'd thought it would be duck soup. After struggling for six years trying to write a spy novel (still unfinished), doing short stories would be a piece of cake. Right?

"Yeah."

The blinking yellow cursor sat there leering at him.

"DoDo." He glared at it.

Reminded him of a theology professor he'd had at State.

The man would ask you a question the pope couldn't have answered in five million words or less, then just sit there staring at you and snap "We're waiting, Mr. Spencer" over and over again until the sound of his nasal voice drove every coherent thought from your head. His name had been Doeden, Mr. Doeden—to his face. DoDo to his back.

Since then, the ultimate curse in J.J.'s book of four-letter invectives had been "DoDo."

"Digressing again," J.J. muttered. "Also talking to yourself." It was a habit he was marginally aware of most of the time, but it helped him think. He really had to watch out for it down at the newspaper office, though. They liked to get things on tape.

Scratching at the curly red hair that was at the moment the only thing covering his bare chest, he rocked sideways to peel his underthighs off the leather seat where the gym shorts had allowed them to stick. Wiggled his toes.

This really shouldn't be that hard to write. He had pages of notes jotted down, some supergreat titles for the stories, and a headful of ideas just hopping to get out. And what a premise: God has grown tired of The Job and decided to abdicate, come down to Earth, and become an adventurer. Truly great stuff. Even "Divinely Inspired," one might say; J.J. waggled his eyebrows in a Grouchoesque tribute to the pun.

If he could just get to work. *Was he having one of his doubting pangs again?*

Sometimes, in more conscience-ridden moments, J.J. worried about what his Methodist minister father might say about these stories. Most of the time he managed to avoid the thought, counting on the fact that his dad had a pretty good sense of humor. Still . . . maybe it might be wiser to submit them under a pseudonym when the time came.

The cursor kept blinking at him.

"DoDo."

Perhaps a break.

He saved what he had written to disk, got up and went into the kitchen for a Coke, saying hello to Buddy as he entered the sunny room. Buddy was a cockateel. Buddy could say "Hello, Buddy" and "Poot." Dal had taught him the latter; it wasn't in J.J.'s book of approved four-letter words.

At the moment Buddy wasn't talking—like J.J.'s muse.

He did whistle as J.J. opened the refrigerator door and leaned over to lift a can from the bottom shelf.

"Oh, you like that?" J.J. turned the other cheek. "Wish Charlotte Ramsey had your discriminating taste."

He'd been dying to date Charlotte Ramsey ever since he'd seen her walk into the courtroom beside that little pimple Willie Dee. She'd been representing Dee on a possession charge, misdemeanor stuff. She'd just come to work for Legal Aid.

He'd been covering the court scene.

That had been three months ago, and so far the closest he'd come to a date was lunch at the Downtown Deli. And they hadn't been sitting at the same table.

He'd talked to her, of course, was even planning to ask her out—he wasn't that big a wuss—and then he'd found out that she was already seeing someone on a semiserious basis. But he still had hopes. According to the courthouse grapevine, the relationship had recently moved onto shaky ground.

Now if he could just keep Dal from spotting her. Or vice versa, rather.

J.J. shook his head dismally at the thought of Detective Dallas Reid, his closest friend and staunchest competition. Dal was really more brother than friend; they'd grown up together and J.J. would walk across flaming coals for him if the need arose. But there were times when J.J. wished him to perdition. Women always noticed Dal first. Mainly because of his looks—a sort of Tom Cruise to J.J.'s Ronny Howard. But what was wrong with red hair and freckles, for pity's sake? Some people were just born to be Top Guns and some to be Opies. There was room for all sorts of taste.

Most of the time it didn't really matter, in fact he usually found it all pretty amusing—until he'd met Charlotte Ramsey, that is. Since then it had mattered a great deal.

The phone rang.

J.J. popped the tab on his caffeine-free Diet Coke and padded barefoot over to answer it, taking a big swallow as he went. "Hello?"

"Hello Buddy hello Buddy," the cockateel shrilled from behind.

"Cool it, Buddy," J.J. tossed at the bird, then repeated "Hello" into the receiver.

"Poot."

"I heard that," Mitch MacAlister, staff writer and J.J.'s backup for the Crime Watch column, remarked.

"Wasn't me."

"I've heard that too. Next you'll be blaming Buddy."

"What do you think I keep him around for?" J.J. downed another swallow. "This a social call, I hope?"

"*Nein.*"

J.J. groaned. "Can't I take a couple of days' vacation?"

"Shoulda gone out of town. Somebody offed another candy man last night and the boss wants you on it."

"I love it when you talk police slang." J.J. kept his tone light, but his expression clouded. This recent rash of drug-related violence was getting out of hand. "Anybody important?"

"*Nyet.* Low-level pusher named Coley Dean. Found him in an alley little while ago. Worked the State Street strip."

"Bet you can't say that three times straight."

"That that that. You owe me a beer, Spencer."

"Wait a minute," J.J. protested. "You didn't bet."

"Sure I did. Ask Buddy. And it coulda cost you a six-pack. Now haul your tail on down to the scene, Genna's already on her way. State, between Larson and Greer. Chop-chop."

The line went dead.

J.J. shook his head and replaced the receiver. When he'd turned off the police scanner he should have also unplugged the phone.

"Poot," shrilled Buddy.

"You can say that again," J.J. muttered, and went to get dressed.

Fifteen minutes later, he was turning his brand-new Ford Explorer off Glenwood and onto State. The four-wheel drive was a recent purchase, after months of comparison shopping, studying *Consumer Reports,* checking for the best interest rate. Dal had razzed him mercilessly about his attention to all these details—Dal made financial decisions by tossing a coin blindfolded, and usually ended up losing the coin. J.J. was more cautious with his money. Which is why he could afford to buy a new car while Dal had trouble scraping up change for a parking meter.

He could see the emergency lights flashing from two blocks

away. He slowed and pulled in behind a Channel 2 news van, returning the wave one of the camera crew shot him.

As crime reporter for the Phoenix City, North Carolina, *Review*, his was a familiar face around such scenes, and he knew most of the others whose jobs also drew them to local disasters like flies to an open wound.

The aftermath of violence was an open wound, J.J. thought, a gash on society that could be stitched up, but left its scar. Civilization was riddled with them.

This latest gash was beginning to spread infection. Three dead drug dealers in the past two weeks. Getting to be a regular epidemic out there.

Up until the past couple of years the drug trade in North Carolina had been mostly the white-collar variety: young professionals with ties to Miami doing a select volume business; high-level customers with standing orders of a key or so a week for their own recreational use.

Now it was becoming more indiscriminate, readily accessible to the guy on the street. Like fast food and take-out windows. User-friendly. Spreading its tentacles into the factories and schoolyards and public parks.

Lately it had taken an even nastier turn, moving boldly into the suburbs, out openly onto the downtown streets. Getting cheap, getting mean. Gangs had begun popping up, weapons were being regularly confiscated in the schools, even the elementary schools, and drive-by shootings were becoming almost routine.

Since the first of the year, there'd been seventeen homicides—a record high. Most of them were tied to drugs in some way. It seemed that what had already happened in several other North Carolina cities was now spreading into this one. Arrests were up, but the police department was having trouble keeping up with the swiftly rising crime rate. It took time to get additional funding so they could add to the force.

J.J. had chronicled the situation in a series of hard-hitting articles that had front-paged the local news section of the Sunday *Review* over the past few months, trying to raise public awareness. He'd tied a lot of the problem to a ring of Haitian drug traffickers who had been moving into the state, bringing their street violence with them.

Now there were these drug-dealer murders. Where might it be heading next?

He spent another moment scanning the activity up ahead. It was getting to where a pusher couldn't even be safe working the street corners anymore.

Maybe they should all just sit back and cheer on whoever was doing this, he thought cynically, though he knew that wasn't the answer. Anarchy came with that line of thought. Still, three dead drug dealers might mean a few less kids getting hooked.

Probably just wishful thinking. He got out of his car.

An ambulance, engine running, sat backed up to the alley where he assumed the coroner was still at work. Two attendants stood alongside it, one draped across the open front door, the other talking to a uniformed cop, both waiting for the official okay to load the body for its one-way trip to the morgue.

Two police cruisers had veed in on either side, blocking that section of the street. The lights on their light bars rotated briskly, sweeping the gray- and dun-colored area with chilly blue light, out of sync. Red and white flashers on the ambulance and other emergency vehicles added to the visual fray.

J.J. approached the police line where Genna Tosto, ace photographer for the *Review* and the best he'd ever worked with, stood eyeing the crowd. That was her specialty: sidebar shots. Anyone with a finger could snap the sensational subjects, according to Genna; but it took "eye" to see the rest. Often, her tie-in photos earned lead-story space, and he'd stopped counting the awards.

She didn't acknowledge him as he moved in beside her, too intent on scanning the crowd, but he didn't doubt for a minute that she knew he was there. He wondered how she managed to get a decent view, she was so tiny, barely up to his shoulder and he wasn't tall. Thick, curly black hair tumbled wildly across her shoulders and around her face. It almost obscured the delicate cheekbones and dark, liquid eyes that could turn hard and probing as a telephoto lens.

He knew she'd finished with the required shots since she was now focusing on the crowd. He took a moment to glance around with her, not wanting to break her train of thought.

A ragtag group had gathered: mostly street people and hookers; a few long-term residents and those just passing through; a smattering of workers from the various eateries and bars and discount shops that fed off the strip. He tried to see behind the booze, beneath the makeup and the dirt, down to the essence that Genna seemed able to reveal so elegantly on film.

But his mind's eye was less discerning than her camera lens.

"Have you been in yet?" She broke their silence, continuing to scan the area intently.

He shook his head. "Who's in charge?"

"Cutter. More's the pity. Wouldn't let me near the corpse." She lifted her camera to her eye, angling it first one way, then another. Took a couple of shots and lowered it again.

"I'm sure you managed." J.J. flashed her a knowing grin.

She matched it. "Snuck into that warehouse." She pointed toward the empty building on their left. "Got a great angle from a third-floor window. Telephoto lens, straight down. Took one of Cutter scratching his ass."

J.J. chuckled. "Which I'm sure will find its way to the newsroom bulletin board." Lampooning Cutter was a favorite hobby for some members of the press.

She flipped her hair back with a grin and raised her camera once more, stepping a pace to her right. "Dal's in there. If you can catch his eye."

The way she said it made J.J. suspect she'd tried and failed. He'd long believed she harbored a bit of a "thing" for his pal Dal.

Lord, didn't they all.

Leaving her to work, he tracked the yellow police line to a better vantage point, where he could observe the goings-on in the alley.

Spotted Dal right off. He was crouched beside the coroner, listening carefully as she pointed out something about the corpse's face and throat. J.J. craned his neck to see.

Trust Dal to be in the thick of this.

Dressed in faded jeans, black T-shirt, and an old gray zippered sweatshirt, Detective Dallas Reid looked totally out of place among the suits and uniforms surrounding him. It was a difference he wore with the kind of style that Cutter—for all his obeisance to the teachings of Hart Schaffner & Marx—would never equal.

"Yo, Dal," J.J. called as Dr. Grimes finished whatever she was saying and they both rose. J.J. wasn't about to just stand around trying to catch his friend's eye. With any luck, he could get this story filed and be back home at his computer by mid-afternoon.

Dal turned, acknowledged the hail with a little lift of his head, and said something to the doc, who nodded. He began walking over.

"You know him?" Queried a petite, pretty uniformed cop standing just inside the taped-off area.

J.J. glanced down at her and grinned. "Yep. Want me to introduce you?" This had happened before.

A slight blush crept onto the young woman's cheeks, but she nodded.

"What's your name," J.J. whispered as Dal approached.

"Mary Ann Lessing."

"Hi, Dal. Meet Mary Ann Lessing. Mary Ann, Dallas Reid." He stood back, watching his friend handle the moment with a polite, but slightly abstracted air. Then Dal was drawing him off toward one of the patrol units.

"I can't let you in, J.J.."

"Did I ask?" J.J. feigned a wounded grimace and pulled out his mini tape recorder. "So, what's the scoop?"

Dal gave him a disbelieving look. "You sound like Jimmy Olsen." He glanced caustically at the recorder, then spoke directly at it. "Cutter's an asshole. That's a-s-s—"

"I know how to spell it." J.J. flipped the off button, regarding his friend patiently. Cutter, with his rigid attitude and by-the-book approach, was a favorite target of his own department too. "Okay, let's get the hostilities out of the way, then maybe we can move on to something I can use."

Dal turned his restless gaze on the crowd, his expression sobering. "I wish it were that easy."

J.J. followed his look. "What do you mean?"

"Getting rid of the hostilities. There's something happening out there, J.J., something I can't get a line on. Nobody will talk to me."

Concern stirred in J.J. He frowned. "You mean something more than just the obvious—" He gestured toward the murder scene.

Dal took his time to answer, standing motionless, still scanning the crowd. He was rarely still for more than a minute at a stretch, and this must be some sort of record. "I'm not sure," he finally murmured. He seemed to be looking for something in the morass of heads, and seeing none of them at all.

J.J. restrained a sigh. "Care to speculate?" he prompted. His friend gave nothing away easily.

"Can't," Dal said.

"Can't, or won't?"

"Can't. It's just a feeling."

"What kind of feeling?"

Abruptly Dal turned back around, seeming to shed his somber mood like a dog shedding water. He tapped his gut.

J.J. eyed him sardonically. "Well, thank you for this startling scoop for the evening news, Detective Reid. And may I quote you on it?"

Dal grinned. "The part about Cutter being an asshole, by all means."

J.J. just shook his head. "Tough being an eagle in a world full of turkeys, is it?"

His friend laughed. "Can it, Harley. Meet me at the Bluelite around four? I'll try to give you something then." The restless energy that constantly fueled Dal now made him anxious to be on his way.

J.J. ignored it. "That's too late. Need something now for the evening edition."

"Then you'll have to settle for Cutter's Official Statement— that's spelled *b* period, *s* period. He'll probably call a press conference. Jerk gets off on holding press conferences. Sorry, but that's it."

"I'll see if I can spell his name wrong. What about a tie-in with these other two murders?" J.J. persisted. "Same MO? Think we've got some nut case—or vigilante, maybe—going around murdering drug dealers?"

"No comment."

"What about gang action or a rival drug ring hit?"

29

"Ditto." Dal was fidgeting to be off.

"Anything found at the scene?"

Dal just looked at him.

"Okay. I get the message." J.J. stuck the unused tape recorder back into his pocket. "By the way, what was that the ME was telling you?"

Dal eyed him smoothly. "Her phone number."

J.J. didn't bother probing further. Wouldn't do any good. Though he and Dal had been best friends since their moms had enrolled them in the same kindergarten back in 1965, the relationship took a back seat to the job. Always.

"Gotta go," Dal said. "Lunch date."

J.J. glanced toward the petite blonde who was still hovering in range, raising his brow. He'd missed that exchange.

"No, not her," Dal said irritably. "Christ, J.J. You think I hang around crime scenes to pick up women?"

"It just naturally evolves," J.J. remarked pleasantly to his friend's retreating back.

He watched Dal stride past the blonde, smile at her with that innate charm he had, then head over to where Dr. Grimes was waiting beside her car.

They spoke for a moment, then she got in and started up while Dal went to his death bike. He kick-started the motor, gunned it a few times, then roared off in her wake.

J.J. shook his head in amusement, and walked over to where the mobile crime lab techs were reloading the van. Maybe he could worm something out of them.

De Boneman hear you if you talk
Everybody hide when de Boneman walk

THREE

Clarence R. James, street name, Boogaloo, sauntered into the convenience store on Falkner and Eighth at about eleven-forty Tuesday night, and strolled over to the candy counter. He stood fingering the Baby Ruths, picked up a Milky Way then put it down again, and finally chose a Zero.

Mostly he was killing time while the store's single customer paid for her Marlboros and left; he wasn't here to buy candy. At least not the kind they kept out front.

The real candy store was in back.

"What' say, man." He ambled on over to the check-out counter where Billy Boy Webster was handing fat mama her change—which the bitch took, and her receipt—which she didn't. Billy Boy wadded the small slip and tossed it into the trash.

Clarence eyeballed the woman as she walked out, grinning at the ripples that shimmied across her big, stretch-pant-covered butt. "*Oooo*, mama. Is you fat," he hooted.

The woman snapped something over her shoulder that Clarence didn't fully catch, but that hadn't been complimentary, and exited the store. Chuckling, he watched her get in her ride and drive off.

Still chuckling, he turned back to Billy Boy. "Was she fat, or was she fat? Take a dick the size'a mine just to find that bitch's hole."

Clarence expected Billy Boy to laugh at his joke; Billy Boy always laughed at his jokes.

Billy Boy wasn't laughing.

"Somethin' wrong, man?" Clarence felt a little miffed.

Billy Boy shook his head. His eyes kinda shifted away.

If Clarence didn't know better, he'da thought Billy Boy looked scared. But that wasn't possible. Billy Boy Webster weren't scareda nothin'. Or nobody. Billy Boy Webster was one mean sonuvabitch that even the heat left the fuck alone.

Unless he'd been spooked by all this jive talk that was goin' round.

Clarence grinned. "Whazza matter, Billy Boy, 'fraid de Boneman's gonna gitcha?" He raised his eyebrows in mock terror. "Ooooo-*eeee*-ooooo."

Billy Boy blanched, and dropped the tube of pennies he'd just cracked open against the side of the cash register. Coins went everywhere. He stepped back, watching them fall.

Clarence's grin faded at the look on Billy Boy's face. Apparently the dude *was* spooked by all the talk. Whata dip.

Clarence decided he'd better just can the jokes, do his business, and be gone. Something about the way Billy Boy kept *not* lookin' at him made him kinda nervous. "Got my stuff, man?"

"Go 'way, Boogaloo," Billy Boy mumbled. "Just get outa here, man."

Th' fuck—Anger quick-flashed through Clarence. He didn't have time for this shit. He needed that stuff and he needed it now. He had orders to fill.

"I ain't got time for no bullshit games, bro. You wantta get scared outa business by that goddamn fuckin' Haitian bunch and their hoodoo jive talk, that's your problem. Now gimme my stuff and I'll be gone, man. And I won't be back neither, you hear what I'm sayin'? I'll take my business over to Bongo, I don't hafta put up with this shit."

Throughout this tirade, Billy Boy Webster's face had gotten paler and paler until now it looked like dingy chalk. He glanced nervously toward the rear of the store.

Clarence followed the look. A mirror he knew was one-way glass looked back at him.

He froze.

Was he under surveillance? Was that what Billy Boy's problem was? Had the man got to Billy after all? Cut a deal? Right now, was he bein' videotaped by the fuckin' pigs?

Shit!

"I'm outa here," he murmured and swung toward the front door.

Someone was standing there.

Clarence drew up, then saw who it was and relaxed: Big Manny Flint. "Yo, home. I heard you was—"

The word lay stillborn on his tongue. His mouth went dry. *Dead.* He'd heard Manny was *dead.* Killed in a grab-and-run by the pusher who hadn't been quite the pushover Juke and Manny had thought he'd be. Juke had seen it happen.

Mistake. Sure. Musta been some kinda mistake.

He searched Big Manny's face, looking for the joke that had to be there, waiting for the laugh to spew.

Big Manny's face was slack, expressionless. His glazed eyes stared at Clarence as if he didn't see him at all. Not at all. He didn't blink.

What was he on?

Clarence started backing up.

Big Manny stepped toward him.

"What's th' matter with you, asshole?" Clarence kept backing up, backing . . . "You dosed out, home?" He backed into the wall.

Big Manny grinned. Raised his hands.

Clarence ducked out from under them and darted away. "You crazy, man? You lost your fuckin' mind?"

He sprinted down the aisle between rows of canned goods and snack cakes, stumbling up against the shelves as he jerked quick looks back over his shoulder at the freak-out who was following. Potted meat and Beanie Weenees tumbled down around him. A can of Vienna Sausage whacked him on the knee.

"Ow!" he hollered, and tried to keep going.

His foot found a Little Debbie cake.

The package burst open. Icing squeezed out. He skidded and went down.

Breath left his lungs in an explosive gust. He sat there a moment trying to suck it back.

Then he was being lifted. By the throat. Hands. Circling his throat. Cutting off his air!

He felt his feet leave the floor, tried to kick Big Manny—and did!—kicked him in the legs again and again—*hard!*—but the guy wouldn't let go. Wouldn't turn loose and now Clarence was fighting for breath, clawing and gouging at the hands that were slowly crushing his throat.

Little sparkles of light danced across his eyes—he realized he was looking up at the ceiling fixture, staring into the fluorescent tube over his head that was going out, going . . .

Need a new bulb, Billy Boy was Clarence's final thought.

Big Manny Flint dropped Clarence's slack body among the shelf litter.

He turned and looked at the mirror glass.

The door to the left of the glass opened. A man stepped out.

The man was elegantly dressed. Handsome.

His skin was the color of café au lait—and at the same time, when the fluorescent light struck it just right, the color of bone, dry, old bone.

The man looked at Big Manny, then over at Billy Boy Webster.

Slowly, Big Manny turned and began walking toward Billy Boy Webster, who had flattened himself against the wall in back of the counter. His eyes were round and popping. He made little squeaking sounds.

Soon he made no sounds at all.

Once more, Big Manny turned to the well-dressed man, whose gaze had remained locked on him all the while. The man now flicked his glance away. Walked toward the door. Exited.

Big Manny followed.

During this entire time, no one had come near the convenience store.

FOUR

''I'm stepping down as God.''

''Say what?''

God looked at Saint Peter, who stood gaping back at him.

''You heard me, Pete. I'm abdicating as the Almighty, cashing in as the Creator. Tossing in the towel.'' God plucked at a drippy robe sleeve and frowned.

''But . . . but . . . You can't do that!''

The Almighty shoved up the errant sleeve and grinned. ''Of course I can. I'm God. I can do anything.''

''Lord in Heaven,'' Peter groaned.

''Not for long.'' God got up off his throne.

''But why?'' Peter shoved up his own drippy sleeves, hoisted his hem, and hurried to catch up with his Lord, who was striding purposefully toward the Pearly Gates.

God shrugged. ''Boredom, mostly. Itchy feet. I've got an urge to wander, check out a little action. See the real world for a change. Nothing much ever happens up here anymore.''

36

```
''But you can't just leave,'' Peter
protested. ''Who'll take care of
things up here?''
  ''How about you?''
  Peter stopped short. ''Me? Oh, no.
Not me. No way.''
  ''What about John, then?''
  ''The Baptist?''
  ''Don't hold that against him.''
  ''He loses his head in a crisis,''
Peter grumbled.
  ''Then let Junior do it. Time the kid
got some experience.'' God continued
his course toward the Pearlies.
''It'll be all right. You'll see.''
  ''Yeah. Sure,'' Peter mumbled at the
retreating back. ''But what if we need
you?'' he called out, hardly believing
it as he watched his Lord swing open one
side of the Pearly Gates and stride on
through.
  ''I'll be in touch.''
  And with a wave of his hand, the Lord
God Almighty disappeared into a
billowy cloud . . .
  And emerged—
```

where . . . ? J.J. tapped the tip of his index finger lightly against the spacer bar and thought a minute.

```
  —in a jazz joint on Bourbon Street
where Loose-lip Larry was blowing
his lean, mean trumpet mo-chine and
brother could he have showed old
Gabe a lick or two
```

"Nah. Not the image I want." He deleted the latter half of the sentence, thought some more.

```
—in a West Texas honky-tonk where
a bevy of babes were mud-wrestling
and two Saturday-night cowboys were
fighting each other with busted
beer bottles over who got to go
next on the mechanical bull
```

"No. Still not there." He deleted again, reread the first part of the sentence, thought some more.

"Wait a minute! Got it." He began typing furiously.

```
—on a street in downtown L.A.,
clad in jeans, T-shirt, and leather
bush jacket, bullwhip coiled at his
waist, wearing a felt fedora, and
calling himself Jehovah Jones—
```

Someone banged on the front door.

"Poot!" shrilled Buddy from the kitchen.

"Yeah," muttered J.J., and hit the "save text" keys with more force then necessary. Just when he was on a roll.

He glanced at his watch—two A.M.—now who the devil would be bothering him at two A.M.? *As if he didn't know.*

He got up to go see.

Sure enough. There stood Dal, leaning nonchalantly against the doorjamb, looking for the world as if there were no such thing as improper visiting hours and neighbors who might complain, and it was perfectly all right to interrupt your best friend when he was right in the middle of an important breakthrough in the story that had been giving him fits all day.

Dal was drunk. He also looked tired.

A cab hovered in the background.

"Pay the guy, would you, Harley?" Dal eased past J.J. and into the house, trailing beer fumes and a sheepish grin.

"You drink too much," J.J. snapped, casting a frown after his uninvited guest.

Dal just shrugged and headed for the couch.

At least he'd had the good sense not to ride his death bike. J.J. stepped out onto the porch to see about the cab.

"The things I do for you, pal," he muttered, not really rankled, but not about to let Dal off the hook too easily either. "This one's gonna cost you," he tossed over his shoulder, loud enough for Dal to hear. "Twenty-five percent interest should be about right."

"Yeah, yeah," Dal mumbled from behind.

The green and white taxi sat idling at the curb. Its burly driver had gotten out and was watching with an expression that clearly said *You bozos try an' stiff me you'll both be eatin' through straws for the next coupla months.*

J.J. started down the steps—stopped. He had on gym shorts, nothing else. No pocket. No billfold. Most of all, no money.

Decision: Dart back inside for some cash and risk mauling, maiming, and death. Try to explain first and risk mauling, maiming, and death.

"Why me?" he muttered, remembering the times, the too-frequent times when one of Dal's little escapades had run amok and turned into a major catastrophe for them both.

But that was past history. This was current events.

He began making hand gestures: beaming—blandishing—backing up.

"Uh . . . be right back . . . don't go away . . . get your money . . . Big tip . . . *B-i-i-i-g* tip . . ."

The doorframe tripped him. He whirled around, stubbing his toe on the metal edge. Yelping in pain and frustration, he remembered his pants were in the bedroom.

He glared at Dal in passing, already stretched out on the couch with his eyes serenely shut, and was back waving money at the cab driver by the time the burly ape had reached the front-porch steps.

The cab drove off. J.J. slammed the door, relocked the dead bolt, and put on the chain for good measure.

"Okay." He turned on his uninvited guest. "I know you're not asleep. And you're not that drunk either."

"Broke," Dal said. His eyes remained closed. Blue shadows rimmed them.

J.J. limped over to the couch, looked down. "So? What else is new? And do I look like a twenty-four-hour automatic teller machine?"

"More like Louie the Loan Shark," murmured Dal with a one-sided grin, still not opening his eyes. "Tell me, do you put 'usurer' on your résumé?"

"Not funny, pal, and you know what they say about beggars being choosers."

"Yeah, yeah, and a fool and his money." Dal nodded. "I know." He lifted a bleary eyelid. "What are you so bent out of shape for, anyway? Don't I always pay you back? With interest?" He shook his head and reclosed the eye.

"Yeah, if you can call bootleg Virginia lottery tickets and chances on whatever current raffle and sports pool you guys have going on down at the station 'interest,' " J.J. mumbled, regarding his friend critically. Dal really did look tired. Was there more to this late-night call than simple lack of funds, a chronic state of affairs with Dallas Reid? "Anything else wrong?"

Dal levered the bleary eyelid half-mast once more, met J.J.'s probing look with a "Who, me?" stare, then shut it again. He could be tight-lipped when he wanted to, which usually meant he'd been up to something rash.

In which case it was probably better not to know.

J.J. continued to study him a moment, seeing beyond the film-star good looks—rakish, now, with two A.M. stubble—to the little kid who'd never really grown up. There was something in Dal that fought the Time Bandit just as vigorously as he did the bad guys on the streets. Except now he was playing his serious adult games with his kid's-eye view to danger.

When J.J. thought about it—and he tried not to—it scared him. Scared him to death. Sometimes he wondered if his friend would ever see forty.

He stumped on over to an easy chair and sank down, examining his wounded toe. "Where were you, anyway, West Virginia? That ride cost me forty bucks."

"Chapel Hill." Dal settled himself more comfortably on the sofa. "Toss me a pillow, would you, Harley?"

J.J. leaned forward and pulled the throw pillow out from behind his back, tossed it over. The soft purr of the computer came from behind. He might as well get up and cut it off. There'd be no more writing tonight.

Sighing, he got up to do it. "Chapel Hill, huh." The state forensics lab was at Chapel Hill. "You at the crime lab?"

"No."

"What, then?"

"Dr. Grimes and I—"

"Oh, of course."

"It's not what you're thinking," Dal snapped, needled like clockwork whenever J.J. razzed him about women—which was mostly why he did it. "She did me a favor. I took her to lunch."

J.J. regarded him speculatively as he returned to the easy chair. "What sort of favor?"

Dal remained silent for a moment. "Don't you ever put that nosy reporter in you to bed?"

Now it was J.J.'s turn to shrug. "Oughta get something for my forty bucks."

"You will. Probably charge me *fifty*-percent interest, you goddamn bloodsucker." If Dal'd been looking, he'd have seen J.J.'s eyes light up. "Got anything to drink?"

"You know where it is." J.J. bit back the "Don't you think you've had enough?" he'd started to say. Sermonizing was not his style. But he was relieved when Dal made no move to get up.

Dal's drinking seemed to be taking a turn for the worse lately. And J.J. wasn't sure how to handle it. What used to be a few beers with the boys, or an occasional shot or two of the hard stuff at a party or after a particularly rough day, appeared to be escalating. At the ripe old age of thirty-two, was Dal on his way to the chronic alcoholism that plagued so many in his profession?

Don't carp, he told himself, watching the rise and fall of his friend's chest slowly smooth out. He'll work it out.

Maybe.

But ever since Dal had been reassigned—by request—to Phoenix City's fledgling drug task force, he'd been pushing it: working practically nonstop; manpower shortages and case overloads taking their toll.

Now this rash of drug killings.

It wasn't the extra work that concerned J.J., as much as the

41

obsessive attitude Dal took toward it. It was as though he, person-ally, was responsible for waging Phoenix City's war on drugs. Like some modern-day Elliot Ness.

But that was Dal. Never did anything halfway.

An admirable trait. Admirable but unrealistic. And a totally unobtainable goal. Drugs, unfortunately, weren't going to disap-pear down the drain like bathtub gin. Come to think of it, neither had the gin.

Negative thinking, J.J. admonished himself. *Gotta watch that.* But with the way the drug problem—and crime rate—had been es-calating over the past year or so, it was hard not to think nega-tively. The deeper J.J. had probed into the cause of this sudden surge in trafficking and violence, the more concerned he'd become. He loved his hometown. He hated what was happening here.

Today Dal had hinted at some new problem. J.J. hoped to God he was wrong.

"What was all that this morning about gut feelings and things that nobody will talk to you about?" he prodded cautiously. There was always the chance Dal might come across with some usable information while in his alcohol-weakened state. Not that J.J. would necessarily use it without Dal's permission—ethics were a stumbling block at times; but it would at least give him something to pin Dal down on when he sobered up.

"Ugmph," Dal grunted, not opening his eyes, and settled him-self more comfortably on the couch.

And with that, J.J. had to be content.

Silence stretched around them.

Carefully, he reached over and turned off the table lamp.

"Ever heard the term 'bone man?' " Dal murmured.

The question startled J.J. He'd thought Dal had gone to sleep. "Don't think so. Why? What's it mean?"

"Not sure. Something I overheard in a bar tonight."

"You spend too much time in bars." J.J. frowned.

"Part of the job."

Was that his excuse? "Sounds like a street name, Boneman. Maybe some pimp who thinks he's a superstud. Why? Is it impor-tant?"

"Everything's important, Harley." Dal's voice was fading. "Rule number one."

J.J. watched his friend's breathing smooth out. "And rule number two is: Never sleep on a friend's couch when a friend's bed is available. Why don't you go on in there and sack out on mine, I was going to work some more anyway; get yourself a decent night's sleep for a change—or what's left of it."

A soft snore rose from the couch.

J.J. sighed, got up quietly and went to fetch a blanket. Spread it over his sleeping friend.

In repose, Dal looked about fifteen, even with his unshaved chin. J.J. could almost remember what it was like for them to be that age, armed with youth and the bumper pad of parents. A frightening thing to be without.

J.J.'s parents had moved to Seattle a couple of years back, but they were still there for him, just took a little longer to get to.

Dal's parents were dead: his father of a heart attack when Dal was seventeen; his mother in an auto accident the year after that. That had been a bitter time. The punk who'd rammed his mother's car had been flying on LSD. Which accounted for a lot of Dal's attitude when it came to drugs.

J.J. sat back down in the chair, watching his friend sleep.

Sometimes he felt years older than Dal, when in truth it was Dal who was four months his senior. Maybe it was because he was more settled, had some stability in his life; he owned his own home, had some good investments, some money in the bank. He'd even been toying with the idea of marriage and having kids.

Maybe it was because his folks had sort of taken Dal in during that time, seen him through the anger, confusion, and pain of those last few teenage years. Dal had been drifting. They'd given him something to come home to.

Dal was still drifting. More than that, he was running. Running hard and on high. If he didn't watch it, he could burn himself out.

"Boneman." The word popped back into J.J.'s thoughts. It did sound kinda familiar, come to think of it. Maybe it *was* a street name; musician, maybe. Didn't they call a trombone a "bone"? Or maybe it was some guy who ran a floating crap game.

Could be anything.

43

Or nothing.
He'd think about it in the morning.
Maybe check it out.
Time to go to bed, now.
Get up, go turn off the lights . . .
. . . brush teeth . . .
. . . in a minute . . .

De Boneman dig
De Boneman take
Nobody make what de Boneman make

FIVE

Fog.

White, cotton-candy wisps.

Hovering about the tombstones like lost, tattered souls pulled from their final resting places and strewn on the wind.

Silence bracketed the graveyard. Dark and sullen. Chill, like the bottom of a pit.

Not even the fog had life.

Lit by the eerie glow of predawn, it hung pale and listless on the stagnant air.

Shadows moved among the stillness. Parting the fog, their steps kept an uneven gait.

Several shadows worked silently at an open gravesite. Digging down to the coffin.

They reached inside.

Old bones met grasping fingers. Cold bones. Being stuffed into sacks.

Eyes stared fixedly ahead as hands quickly worked. Empty eyes. Empty grins.

Soon it was done.

The shadows climbed from the opened grave. Passing single file into the night, they carried their sacks. Other shadows joined them, twining through the graveyard, some carrying shovels, some with hands empty and slack.

Fog swirled around them, parting at their coming, stirring sluggishly together in their wake.

Beside a gnarled old tree, another shadow stood, waiting for the line to pass. This shadow's eyes were not empty. But they were cold. Cold as bone.

And where this shadow walked, the fog lay still.

SIX

"In a minute" turned into several hours. J.J. woke up in the chair at dawn.

Pale gray light filtered through the mullioned windows. An early morning chill had invaded the air. For a moment the small stone house seemed as dank and cold as if he was inside a mausoleum.

He shivered, recalling the old adage about someone walking across your grave. Pleasant thought, first thing in the morning. He glanced at the raised window where cold air was bleeding into the room. Shouldn't have left it open.

Too late now.

Stretching to rid himself of the stiffness that had crept into his limbs during his unscheduled stint in the chair, he looked over at the couch and frowned, remembering his late-night visitor—the cause of his current discomfort. Why had he let himself fall asleep out here? Why hadn't he gotten up and gone to bed?

Dal slept blissfully on, a darker lump against the lighter couch. Wrapped snugly in the blanket J.J. had so thoughtfully provided, his six-feet-plus length stretched comfortably across the well-cushioned sofa, big feet dangling over the edge.

He'd shed his shoes. Which must account for the smell, J.J. thought as he rubbed his arms briskly to get the circulation going, still eyeing his slumbering friend. That was probably what had wakened him.

Sometime during the night, Dal had lost the throw pillow. His arm now lay wedged beneath his head. He'd have a cramp.

With a resigned sigh, J.J. retrieved the pillow and touched it lightly to his friend's arm. Like a whip, the arm uncrimped, hand snaked out and grabbed the pillow, stuffed it back under his head.

In seconds, Dal was snoring peacefully again, cheek pressed comfortably against the cushion.

J.J. shook his head and left sleeping beauty to his rest, heading for the bathroom where he emptied his bladder, brushed his teeth, and splashed his face, in that order. Then he donned his warm-up suit. Every morning he could, he went jogging.

Outside, the air was crisp and on the raw side for May. Temperature floating somewhere around the fortyish mark, he'd guess. He could see his breath.

Clouds hung low in the sky, but there'd been no rain yet, though the air was soggy with promise.

Mist covered the tiny, well-groomed front lawn, hugging the shrubbery that surrounded the small stone house and softening the building's exterior. Built in the 1920s, the house had a country-cottage look and a sort of gatehouse charm, nestled in among the larger, more formal brick and frame houses that lined the quiet street. Most of the others boasted fancy fix-ups and tone-on-tone paint jobs that their yuppie owners preferred.

J.J. supposed it was a yuppie neighborhood—a lot of college professors and young overachievers lived here—and maybe that made him a yuppie too; but the house had caught his eye the moment the real estate agent showed it to him. He'd loved the Art Deco touches inside. And the moderate asking price had made it a good investment. Besides, he could always rent it out when and if he and Charlotte Ramsey decided they needed more room.

Thoughts of Charlotte brought a smile to his face and an inner warmth that helped chase away the cold. He was going to have to do something in that quarter before much more time passed, or before some other guy—like the one on his couch, J.J. snapped a look over his shoulder, losing the smile—moved into the breach. Charlotte would not stay unattached for long, he'd bet. He resolved to do something positive about it this afternoon, tomorrow at the latest. No more waffling.

That decided, he began his warm-up routine, letting his heart rate gradually build before he ever got off the front porch. Most strokes and heart attacks occurred early in the morning, people jumping out of bed and hurrying about, not taking proper time to let the body come to terms with waking up. Put a lot of added stress on the heart.

He swung his arms across his chest, then out and back again, taking deep breaths as he counted slowly to ten.

The paper boy drove by, bypassing his house. J.J. didn't take a weekday morning paper since he could always pick one up at work for free. The past couple of mornings, he wouldn't have minded having one delivered, since he was on vacation.

He thought about stopping the kid, buying a paper; they usually carried a few extra around. But by the time the thought came and went, it was already too late. The kid had driven by.

He concentrated on his warm-up exercises, did a couple of deep knee bends, some side stretches, jogged up and down the steps a few times. Then he truly began to run, turning left at the first corner. Up Courtney two blocks, turn right onto Island Drive. Four blocks, then left on Turner. Straight stretch down to Archer Boulevard and the Methodist church.

He'd worked up a good sweat by the time he reached the church, but the air was still chill against his face and neck, cooling him off almost as quickly as the exercise heated him up.

Entering the drive on the east side of the steepled structure, he followed it as it circled around the building to where the shadows deepened perceptibly on the west side. The cobblestoned pathway was quaint, but rough beneath his running shoes. He slowed a bit to compensate for the uneven surface, the muddy dark. It'd be easy to stumble in the shadows, maybe sprain an ankle or worse.

Mist hovered about the stillness, congregating in handfuls and clinging to the ground like the chill that gripped the air. It seemed denser over here on the west side, more concentrated, as though banked against the oncoming dawn.

But, then, the atmosphere always seemed a little eerie on this side of the drive, near the cemetery.

The small graveyard sat to the left of the old stone church. It had been decades since the last burials, but the church maintained it as an historical landmark. Some tombstones dated back to the late seventeen hundreds.

He'd stopped once and checked it out, amused by some of the inscriptions, saddened by others. So many children. Many of the stones had crumbled away, markings obliterated by time and the elements. Lost messages, forgotten names.

A movement caught his eye.

J.J. slowed as the circular drive brought him around by the cemetery. Had there been someone standing near one of the graves?

A bit early for visitors, wasn't it?

He searched the area, slowing even more. Daybreak had yet to intrude on this somber place, due to the canopy of thick-leaved branches overhead. What would be a pleasantly cool arbor on a warm summer's day was eerily silent and chilly now, in the early morning hours, shrouded by gloom.

Wisps of fog lay scattered over the gravestones, a tattered coverlet of mist. Where the grass could be seen, it glinted dully with a patina of dew.

J.J. frowned at the hushed stillness, began jogging in place. *What had drawn his attention?* Something wasn't right, here. It was too quiet. Too still. *Where were the birds? Where was the breeze?* He shivered.

The movement came again. And along with it a muffled sound. He zeroed in on it.

A tall black man stood beside one of the graves, holding a shovel. The grave looked freshly dug.

The uncertainty gripping J.J. loosened its hold. Must be just the caretaker getting an early start on his work.

Seemed odd, though. Even if they were planning to use this old cemetery again, it was sure a strange time to be digging a grave.

Probably just wanted to avoid the heat of the day, J.J. thought as he continued his internal debate.

Still, it wasn't as though it were midsummer yet, when temperatures might soar into the mid-nineties before noon. And today was unseasonably cool.

So what gives?

Skirting the spiked wrought-iron fence around to the gate, he entered the enclosed area.

His reporter's nose was starting to twitch, egging him on when he really should be jogging home, minding his own business. What could possibly be wrong here? No doubt it was simply the church custodian getting an early start on his chores.

But digging graves? In the dark?

J.J. recalled the rash of cemetery vandalism that had plagued Phoenix City recently—another problem. Monuments had been desecrated, crypts broken into and the like, even some grave-robbing. The cops had found evidence of ritualism at a couple of the sites—some occult stuff, drug and voodoo paraphernalia—prompting J.J. to incorporate it into the series of articles he'd been doing at the time, making the appropriate tie-ins to cultism and the current drug situation in the state.

He'd cited those drug-cult killings down in Matamoros, Mexico, where a young premed student had been kidnapped and tortured to death. The police had uncovered a number of bodies there, along with evidence of bizarre and gruesome rituals using human remains. True believers could be a dangerous lot.

Could something like that be going on here?

Surely not.

Still . . .

Uncertainty gripped him again. Maybe he should just stop and think about this another moment before blindly rushing in.

Even as he debated the wisdom of what he was doing, his feet led him on.

"Lead him on, Devil, get him killed": one of his dad's favorite expressions when, as a kid, J.J. would goad him into a wrestling match. Perfect thought for right now. "Just great," muttered J.J., slowing from a trot to a walk.

Coldness seeped inside his warm-up suit as he moved forward, but this was a different sort of chill. It was like what one might expect to feel inside the basement of that church—if it had one; it probably did, didn't they all?—an old stone chill, stale and clammy, full of the hoary decrepitude of age. It was as though the tomb-stones here had soaked up centuries of cold and trapped it forever, like the bodies beneath the ground.

What would it feel like to lie here? he wondered. To be chambered in the earth? To be dead?

Why nothing, of course. You wouldn't feel anything. Wouldn't laugh, wouldn't cry.

He suddenly remembered part of an inscription from one of the tombstones that had caught his attention the day he'd visited here. It had held him for a long moment, the sun beaming down and the birds trilling in the background and the warmth of being alive smug within him: "All you who come this grave to see, / Just as I am so will you be . . ."

J.J. shivered, not from the temperature or aura of this place, but from a cold that had nothing to do with mist or dampness or age-worn stones. It was an age-old question that chilled him.

He shook the disturbing thoughts aside, catching the soft strands of what sounded like—*chanting*?

He took another few steps into the cemetery. Spotted the man.

The man did seem to be chanting something all right, J.J. decided, though he couldn't make out any words, only the rhythmic cadence of sound.

He moved closer.

The Lord's Prayer? Was that man reciting the Lord's Prayer?

What in the name of Jehovah Jones—

The man turned around.

For a moment J.J. froze, pinned by eyes that drove into him. Glittering black pools, stark in a face twisted by a savage grin.

Maybe he should ease out of here.

He backed up a step.

"Sacrilege."

J.J. stopped at the word offered in a trembly voice.

"Who would do such a thing?" The man held out his hand as though beseeching an answer.

J.J. stepped forward, realizing as he did so that this was an old man: hair mottled with gray, skin wrinkled, body thin. The fierce grin was due to outrage; the staring black eyes glittered with unshed tears.

"I don't—"

"Nothing's sacred anymore. Meanness everywhere. Such meanness." The old man dropped his hand, shook his head.

J.J. walked over to the desecrated grave.

The marker was an old one, sunk into the ground at an angle. Whatever words had been carved in the stone had become nothing more than vague outlines, indentations in the rough granite slab.

One corner was broken off, or had crumbled away. *Forgotten names.*

The unease of moments ago left him.

"Wonder who was buried here," J.J. murmured, looking down into the gashed-out hole. Fragments of the rotted coffin lay scattered about. Something white winked at him. *A splinter of bone?*

J.J. shivered, looked around at the surrounding area for any indication of who or why; any sort of evidence at all. There was nothing that he could see, and no reason to think that this was more than just random vandalism. But the police should be called.

"Probably kids, a lark, too much to drink," he said. It was getting to be that time of year—high school graduation parties, seniors on the rampage, that sort of thing. No reason to think it was anything else. Plus the downside that reporting these events sometimes brought an upswing in similar activity, copycat style.

That was one of the hardest parts of his job to rationalize, wondering every time he wrote about some negative event if he was providing fodder for another wacko to feed on.

"Meanness." The old man shook his head.

J.J. silently agreed. "Are you the custodian at the church here?"

The old man nodded solemnly.

"Then you'd better call the police. Notify the church officials, too. The city's had a problem with this sort of thing recently. It needs to be reported."

"Yessir, I'll surely do that. It's sacrilege, thought. It surely is."

J.J. nodded soberly, resolving to make the call himself, just to be on the safe side. It really should be reported.

He left the old man to his task, jogged home. Mitch could cover it if the city ed. wanted something for the evening edition. Probably not more than a line or two mention at the end of the regular column, if that. This looked like simple petty vandalism, no pagan blood rites, no occult rituals performed by the dark of the moon. Nothing that would be termed "good copy," and for that, J.J. was thankful.

Still, there might have been some similar occurrences elsewhere overnight. Whatever. Mitch could check it out.

When he got home, Dal was gone. So was J.J.'s new car.

The bum! Now that really made him mad.

J.J. stormed up the front steps and into the house. "This is gonna cost you, Dallas," he declared to the vacant sofa. "Big time!"

Fuming, he phoned in the vandalism report and, still irked, went into the pink and black tiled bath to take his shower, trying to remember if he'd mentioned to Dal that he was on vacation this week—or had the bum just taken his car regardless?

"And there'd better be some hot water left," he added, as the evidence of a wet floor and steamed-up medicine-cabinet mirror poured new fuel on the fire.

Well, at least it gave him a valid excuse not to go in to work today if they called him, he thought, beginning to calm down as hot water streamed from the shower massage and he stepped beneath it and let it drum against his neck—

Strike that. They'd just send someone to pick him up, or make him call a cab. And it'd take two months to get the fare reimbursed, as usual.

"Gonna cost you, pal," he murmured as he finished his shower and reached for the fluffy black towel he'd picked up from the laundry just yesterday and put out on the rack. The towel wasn't there. J.J. looked around and spotted it wadded in a damp ball atop the hamper. So the bum had struck there too.

Naked and dripping wet, J.J. stalked to the hall linen closet for another clean towel, adding "Laundry Costs" to Dal's growing debit sheet.

Sister, Sister, don't say a word
Somebody's listening . . .
Somebody heard

SEVEN

Cherry Pye tapped a long cherry-red fingernail against the black plastic tabletop of the booth where she sat and glanced at the clock over behind the bar. Nearly seven P.M. So far Mr. Dreamboat hadn't shown.

Her quick scan of the customers was more nervous than necessary. No one she knew ever came in here. In fact, the joint was nearly empty; this kind of place didn't get going till late. Which was why she'd picked it.

She glanced at the clean-up kid who'd been eyeing her for the past ten minutes or so while he swept and reswept the same section of floor. Another time she'd have offered him a five-dollar special. Right now she was afraid to risk the couple of minutes it would take to blow him off in the back room. Mr. Dreamboat might pick that moment to come.

Wouldn't do to have them both coming at the same time, she thought with a twist of her cherry-red mouth.

Much as she could use the quick five, she couldn't afford to miss the hunk. He could be worth a lot more to her than five lousy bucks.

Giving the kid a look that promised "Maybe later," she turned her back to him and resumed watching the door.

Maybe Mr. Dreamboat hadn't gotten her message.

It'd taken her a while yesterday to find out the name of the gorgeous cop in the black T-shirt. When she had, she'd called and left word for him to meet her at the Rainbow Bar between six-thirty and seven this evening, if he wanted some information on Coley Dean—*that cheap little bastard, he'd got what he deserved!*

But maybe she could still make some money out of the limp-dick little creep.

The fury that had contorted her face at the thought of the dead drug dealer smoothed into a smile. Then faded.

If only the damn cop would come.

Anxiously she panned the bar. Though her pimp didn't usually visit this dive—too low-class—and it was too early for him to be making his rounds on the street, there was always a chance. Jelly could be mean when he wanted to, and she hadn't been paying off so well lately.

But that was about to change.

If that damn cop would just get here!

She glanced back at the door. It opened. Mr. Dreamboat walked in.

God, he was good-looking! Thick black hair, kinda wavy, curling around his neck. He had what the romance novels she read called "chiseled features"—she just knew that's what they meant. She could see him as the hero in one of those books, with herself as heroine, of course. Skin smooth and lightly tanned. Broad shoulders. At least six feet two. But dreamiest of all were his eyes. Dark eyes. Bedroom eyes. Sexy as hell.

He strolled over and stood looking down at her—and God! She would have *killed* to have eyelashes that thick and long.

For a moment she just sat there staring up at him, pretending he had come for her—*for her, not information, like in that Richard Gere movie, come to take her away from all this, take her home with him and make love, real love, like in the books*—

"Are you the one who left a message for me?" He smiled.

It took her breath. She nodded.

He slid into the booth.

"How'd you—" She cleared her throat. "How'd you know I was the one?"

He shrugged. Made it seem an intimate gesture just between the two of them. "They told me a woman called. That she sounded like a looker."

Cherry was startled by the warm feeling that spread through her, though well aware that "they'd" probably said "babe" and not "woman", "*hooker*" rather than "looker." Plus, at the moment she was the only female in the bar. She smiled back.

"Message said you have some information?"

Lord, he should charge for that smile. He could make a fortune on the streets. Reluctantly, she pulled herself back from her rosy cloud, shaking off the almost mesmerizing effect he had. *A routine, Cherry. Cops got their routines just like everybody else. They use what they have to get what they want. Don't you forget it.*

No time for this bullshit, anyway. She had to get back out on the street.

"I got information." Her voice had hardened. "It'll cost you."

He nodded. "How much?"

"Ten big ones." She willed herself not to flinch when she said it. A thousand dollars was a lot to ask for, especially for a first-time deal. But it would keep her in rock for months—and no cut for Jellyroll off the top. She *needed* it. Needed it bad.

He remained silent. Looking at her.

The seconds ticked by.

Sweat tickled the insides of her palms. She rubbed them down her black spandex miniskirt.

"That's expensive information," he said at last, still watching her. His eyes didn't seem as sexy as before.

"It's a good buy," she hissed, leaning closer. "I know who clipped Coley Dean."

His expression didn't change. He leaned back in the booth. "I'll have to have a little more than that to do a deal for this kind of coin."

"Whaddya want?" she spat. "More than that'd be the fuckin' *name*, f'chrissake! I don't give nothin' more for free, Charlie." The warmth had fled.

So had the smiles. "Tell you what. You convince me what you've got is worth listening to, we'll see. I'll front you, say, a hundred now. If the name you give me checks out, I'll see that you get the rest."

"Not good enough." She glared across the table at him, wanting to run her hands through his hair, wanting to cry.

He stood. "Sorry. That's it."

She glanced nervously from him to the clock. Seven-twenty. She needed to get out on the street again, soon, before Jelly—"Okay, goddammit."

He slid back into the booth.

Suddenly it seemed as if the entire room had gone silent, every-one listening to what she had to say. She imagined ears grown to the size of grapefruits, *the better to hear you with, my dear,* eyes crawling up and down her spine. Freaky.

For a split second she was undecided. This thing could backfire. Get her in Dutch on the street.

Yet she knew a couple other girls who were paid informants. They made some good extra coin without buying any grief.

He was watching her. Waiting. Saying nothing. He had all the time in the world.

She was the one on the clock. She was the one who needed to get her ass back out on the pavement before that fat sonofabitch came around checking.

Sweat trickled down her underarms.

She leaned forward, voice a harsh whisper. "I saw him the night he got whacked."

"Who?"

"Who d'ya think, asshole? Coley Dean. Passed right by me on the street."

"And the guy who clipped him?"

"Coley was on his way to meet the dude—mad as crap, bastard wouldn't even gimme the time'a day." Her eyes glazed with the memory. "Bet he had that toothpick of his with him too. Always carried it, like an extra dick. Liked to fondle it when he screwed. Helped him get it up."

She'd clenched her hands until the knuckles had gone white. God, but she was glad that little creep was dead. "Probably plan-nin' to stick the dude and got wiped instead," she added with a smirk, relaxing her hands, flexing her fingers.

"What dude?"

Cherry's vision cleared. She shook her head. "Not so fast, gor-geous. Lemme see the color of your coin."

Mr. Dreamboat reached in his pocket and drew out a single hundred-dollar bill. Fingers pressing it to the tabletop, he slid it toward her.

She reached to take it— He pulled it back, fingers in place.

"Why the meet?"

"Real estate. Dude was moving in on Coley's space."

Her hand snaked toward the bill.

He kept his fingers on it.

"And this dude's name?"

"Poppy," she hissed. "That's all I know. Poppy. If you wanna know more, ask Willie Dee. He's the one told Coley 'bout the dude cruisin' in on him."

Mr. Dreamboat lifted his fingers from the hundred-dollar bill.

Cherry snatched it up, stuffed it in her purse for now. Later, when no one was watching, she'd tuck it into the slit she'd made in the hem of her skirt, where Jelly wouldn't find it.

She got up.

Mr. Dreamboat followed her with his eyes. They flickered in the dim light, as if a candle were lit deep down inside them, giving them a dark, intimate glow that brought warmth to her skin, fire to the pit of her stomach. Later tonight, when she was lying on the lumpy mattress in her rotten room, she'd put him in one of the fantasies she played to go to sleep by, imagine she was looking into those dark, dreamy eyes.

He caught her arm as she started to walk by.

"Your information better be good, Cherry."

She froze as he said her name. She hadn't told him that. How'd he known?

"I'll be back to see you if it's not."

"It is." She shook off his hand. "You'll see."

"Good." He smiled, and Cherry felt her anger evaporate.

"What about . . . I mean . . . I'm free now . . . how about you'n me . . . ?

"Another time." He met her gaze steadily.

But the warmth in her had died.

"Yeah. Sure."

She turned and walked out of the bar. Down the street.

She'd gone two blocks before the tears that threatened to ruin her mascara were under control.

Or maybe she'd just forgotten how to cry.

"Nothin' worth cryin' over, anyway," she muttered. "Nobody worth a shit." Much less a tear. "Bastards workin' their routines. No better'n me."

She crossed over Vance Street, down Morris Avenue, heading for State.

Darkness had crept into the early evening sky while she'd been inside the bar, making it closer to night than day. A feeble glow still hung in the west behind her, but the street ahead lay empty and deep with dusk. It was that twilight time before the streetlights came on, a time when righteous people were already home or headed there, and the not-so-righteous were just beginning to stir.

Somehow it made her feel lost and alone, caught in a no-man's-land between the buzzing, half-burned-out neon sign being gobbled up by darkness back there at the Rainbow and the glitter and faint traffic whine filtering out to her from the main strip still several blocks away.

The heels of her shiny black plastic boots struck the sidewalk with sharp clacks, marking every step she took. The sound echoed dully in the bloated silence, seemed to bounce off the darkened storefronts and hang on the still air.

She shivered. Remembered the money.

Spotting an alley just ahead of her, she hurried over to it, glancing around to make sure there was nobody around to see. Her heels did a little tap dance across the pavement, and she tried to silence them by walking on her toes; but it didn't work, the heels were too high. It didn't matter, though. The street was empty, everything closed for the night.

She stepped just inside the opening, fumbling in her purse for the hundred-dollar bill—

Something moved behind her.

Cherry froze, feeling her stomach clench as if someone had jerked her belt in about five notches. *Someone was in the alley with her.*

Jelly? Oh God, was it Jelly? Had he seen her in the bar with that cop and waited for her to come out?

She clenched her fists, wanting to scream her frustration—anger—pain! This was *her* C-note. She needed it. Had earned it! She wasn't gonna let him take it from her even if he beat her black and blue.

"Who is it? Who's there?" she demanded, backing out onto the sidewalk again. Wouldn't do to show fear. She couldn't see anyone, it was too dark, but the movement came again, a dry sort of brushing sound like clothes swishing faintly against skin.

Maybe it wasn't Jelly—he'd have been on her by now—but it still might be someone who'd tell him, someone who'd seen her and expect her to pay him off.

"Who's there, goddammit? Come on out and show yourself."

"You buy . . . ?" The words floated out like spider's webs, wrapping around her until her skin crawled as if she'd been touched.

She took another backward step.

"You buy . . . ?" The question came again, slightly closer now, voice scratchy, pitched low.

She peered into the dark interior, barely making out the lanky form, hand held out. *A pusher. It was a goddamn pusher.* Cherry felt the cramp that had seized her stomach relax somewhat.

Not Jelly.

"No, asshole. I don't buy," she clipped. "Not from you."

She walked hurriedly away, moving quick and confident (like you did on the street), tossing a couple of glances over her shoulder to make sure the dude wasn't following. This was not the time to be making purchases from a new source; might be a fuck-over, might be a cop—though she couldn't imagine why Mr. Dreamboat would want to set her up like this. Still, you never could tell.

She shivered again in the suddenly chill night, looking back one more time to make sure the dude wasn't following. No, no sign of him.

Good. The stomach cramp relaxed another notch.

But she still had that bill to take care of.

Spying another alley, she hurried on toward it and ducked inside, waiting just a moment to make sure she was alone this time.

Nothing moved.

She took a few more steps into the snug interior for safety's sake, pulled out the bill.

It was almost completely dark now, especially in here. Streetlights were making a feeble attempt to switch on, she could see their muted glow at the end of the alley, but the light barely reached in here.

Running her thumb along the inside of the hem, she located the slot, folded the C-note, poked it in.

She smoothed her skirt back down and started to walk forward—

"You buy . . . ?"

She jumped and whirled around, searching the dark interior of the alley. Where had that come from? How had that dude gotten down here so fast? Was there another way in?

"You buy . . . ?" This question floated toward her from the street.

Cherry spun back around and saw the tall, lanky form silhouetted at the mouth of the alley. *Christ, there were two of them!*

"You buy . . . ?"

"You buy . . . ?"

Their spidery voices and the soft sounds of movement came from both sides of her, hemming her in. There was something freaky about it. She wanted to jam her hands over her ears and run. But there was nowhere to go, they were blocking her path.

"Leave me alone," she shouted. "Get away from me!"

The movement halted.

Silence sank down on the alley.

Cherry held her breath, but the duo didn't seem to be interested in her now—hell, they didn't even seem to act like she was there anymore! What were they up to?

Slowly, she inched backward, feeling for the wall. She found it and started moving toward the street. If she could get to the end of the alley, she might slip past them, get away. A sudden break in the solid surface made her hesitate.

Apparently another alley bisected this one—*where had that come from? she hadn't noticed it before.* With luck, it'd be a safer way out.

She backed into the new passageway, then turned around and started to run, breathing a sigh of relief as she spotted the faint illumination that indicated the next street beyond.

She was nearly at the end when a figure stepped into her path.

With a gasp, Cherry drew up short, casting a quick glance behind her for the first pair of pushers. Was this some sort of gang setup?

The alley behind her was empty.

She turned back around, unprepared for the sight of the young, good-looking black man who had moved to within a few feet of her. Still expecting to hear sounds of the two weird pushers coming after her, she regarded the newcomer warily; but the only thing she heard was her own labored breathing.

She eyed the man—she could see him perfectly, though the alley was thick with shadows, the glow of the streetlights still dim. His skin seemed to have a soft radiance to it.

She'd never seen him before, she'd have remembered him, for sure. Like Mr. Dreamboat, this was the kind of man a girl didn't forget.

He had on a suit that had a sheen to it, not from being worn a lot but from what it was made out of, maybe silk. His collar was stark white against his rich milk-chocolate skin, and his eyes were the color of smoke, dark, sensuous smoke. They glistened, like bottomless pools reflecting the moon. Where Mr. Dreamboat's had held fire, these were cool; where Mr. Dreamboat's had burned darkly, these were smooth like polished stones.

The man smiled at her and shook his head, almost sadly she thought. "Cherry . . ."

The word was a caress. But it gave her goosebumps. Twice in one night, someone she didn't know had called her by name. *Who was this dude? What did he want? How did he know her name?*

Maybe Jelly had sent him, cut a deal for an all-nighter—

Which meant Jelly knew where she was.

Oh, God!

Ripping her gaze away from the stranger, she glanced over his shoulder, fully expecting to see her pimp. But fat Jelly wasn't standing there. The street beyond was empty.

She took a deep, ragged breath, trying to gather her frazzled wits.

No reason to be afraid of this man. Probably just a trick, f'cris-sake—some uptown john lookin' for a little downtown action—net her forty, fifty bucks if she were lucky. Hell, maybe even a hundred, judging from the suit. And since Jelly hadn't cut the deal, he wouldn't have to know about it, an' how's that for kicks.

"So, what can I do for you, hon? Got something special in mind?" Her voice sounded breathless, nervous as a first-timer as she moved into her routine.

She kept trying not to meet those strange eyes, but couldn't help herself. They seemed to pull her in.

For a moment she felt as if she were falling, spiraling down into an inky pit, floating through the void of space . . .

She shook her head, trying to rid herself of the dizzyness spreading through her, the pounding of her heart. What was the matter with her? Her ears were ringing. Little sparkly things seemed to be dancing in front of her eyes. She felt cold, so cold.

"Heard about me, have you, sugar?" She grinned, going on with her routine—but the words seemed to stretch out, somehow, echo down a long tunnel that muffled the sound. "Best on the block, an' you know it," she continued, hearing her voice as if from a long way off. "But, honey, I don't come cheap." She glanced nervously at the mouth of the alley—

and gasped. A tall, ugly black man had moved into the slit. She hadn't heard him coming. She hadn't heard anything at all.

She could see his face, and didn't know him either. He was grinning a stupid-ass grin.

She tried to focus her blurry thoughts.

Christ, a threesome. With Harry the half-wit. That dude gave her the creeps.

But she'd done more for less.

"Cost extra to include your friend, hon." She tried to sound coy, but her shallow breathing betrayed her. Her voice roared inside her head, and at the same time seemed to be coming from miles away. "Or does he just like to stand around and watch?" Most likely it was the other way around, and wasn't that the breaks. Two great-lookin' guys in the same night and she'd end up getting pumped by Ugly Harry.

She was having to fight to keep her mind on line.

She turned back to the first man—

it seemed to take a while

—just wanting to make the deal now, and get it over with.

"C'mon, honey . . . I haven't got all night."

But the man wasn't looking at her. He was looking beyond her. The eyes that had seemed to shimmer magically before had clouded, become remote. His skin seemed paler, too, as if the rich color had suddenly been leeched away. She shivered violently as a finger of ice traced up her spine—

She turned around.

The two pushers had moved into the alley. They stood motionless, blocking her way out.

Breath constricted her lungs, making it feel as if some giant invisible fist had gripped her insides and was squeezing her to death.

"Cherry . . ." The man spoke her name again, pulling her back to him with a word.

His voice . . . his eyes . . .

And suddenly she wanted to stay with him forever, be everything he wanted, do anything he said.

"Yes. *Yes,*" she breathed, and the man smiled. He smiled!

Oh, God! *She would do anything for that smile. Anything at all!*

He nodded once, gestured to the half-wit, stepped back. "Poppy . . ."

It took a moment for the name to register. Then Cherry felt her mouth go dry. Her heart jerked crazily, then seemed to plummet, like an elevator cage torn loose from its moorings plunging breakneck toward the ground.

She swung around—and almost died when she saw the first pair standing right at her back—*how had they done that? how had they gotten up so close? she hadn't heard them coming.*

What was going on here?

Big hands yanked her backward, sliding around her throat.

She twisted her head, trying to see—and did!—saw the half-wit grin—*oh God, this wasn't happening, please, this wasn't happening*—and opened her mouth to scream.

Hands—crushing in on her. Cutting off her air!

Please, God, don't let this happen, she cried in silent terror. *I don't want to die . . .*

EIGHT

Dal left the booth and went over to the bar, glad to get away from the cloying atmosphere created by the high-backed seats and the woman's heavy perfume. He took a couple of deep breaths to rid his lungs of the reeking scent—it'd taken all his willpower not to gag every time he'd breathed in. How did these hookers stand themselves? Or did they do it to mask the odors of their clientele? Pleasant thought.

He bought a can of beer and slid onto one of the rickety stools, resigned to giving Cherry enough time to clear the area before he followed her out. If her tip panned out, she might turn into a valuable informant. He wouldn't want to risk jeopardizing that possibility by advertising the association before it even got off the ground.

The bartender eyed him appraisingly. Dal shot him a look. The bartender moved away.

Pulling open the tab on the can of Bud, he watched foam bubble from the hole, trying not to fidget. In a minute he'd go track down Willie Dee. Right now . . . he took a long, thirsty pull.

The beer wasn't all that cold, but it filled the empty spot in his gut where supper should have been. And lunch, come to think of it; he hadn't eaten all day. Get something later.

It also helped wash away the residue of cheap perfume clinging to the back of his throat. God, that stuff had infested him.

A fly buzzed his hand. He impatiently brushed it aside, took another deep swallow of lukewarm beer, trying to stay still on the unsteady barstool. It squeaked every time he twisted it either way.

How he hated this time of day. There was something about

twilight that made him feel antsy; people going home to dinner and kids, getting ready for an evening in or out. It was an in-between time that left him feeling restless, as though he were waiting for something that never happened, someone who never came.

Oddly enough, dawn wasn't like that. He enjoyed watching the sun rise, and never minded being alone when night moved toward day.

But with dusk a sort of depression set in, chipping away at his mood like it did the sunshine.

He wondered what J.J. was doing right now. Probably calculating how much interest he could tack onto the mileage and rental fee he'd charge Dal for borrowing his car. God, the man was first cousin to a mob shark. Probably had money in Swiss banks by now, the way he funneled it in.

Dal grinned and shook his head at the thought.

In retrospect, he hoped J.J. really wouldn't be too pissed off about the car—it could end up costing him double, even triple, for what J.J. termed "nuisance value." J.J. was good at tack-on terms.

And then there was the nonmonetary payback, which could be even worse.

Thankfully, there hadn't been any irate messages when he'd stopped by the department earlier. But that didn't mean shit. J.J. was a great one for retaliating at a later date. He was devious, a schemer, at his best when plotting short-term investments and long-term revenge.

Dal remembered the time in junior high when they'd both been fingered for booby-trapping Chris Conklin's locker. Although J.J. had known about it, it'd been entirely Dal's idea, and Dal was the one who'd actually stuffed the falsies in Chris's locker. They'd come tumbling out during a break between classes, causing a riot and an improvised free-throw tournament in the hall. It'd been funny as hell, except to Chris, the dweeb, who'd lost no time pointing a finger at the duo. He hadn't been at all amused.

The principal hadn't been particularly amused either, Dal recalled. He and J.J.—who'd shared the blame by reason of association and out of some misguided sense of loyalty—had drawn a week's detention.

Dal had soon forgotten about the incident. J.J. had bided his time. One day, in the middle of prelunch dash, Chris had opened his locker and an inflatable woman had popped out—expanding fast—a naked inflatable woman with boobs the size of Texas.

It had been worth another week's detention.

Not that Dal expected to find an inflatable woman in his locker down at the station house. J.J. had matured out of that stage. That's what worried him.

He fidgeted uneasily on the squeaky stool.

Maybe he shouldn't have compounded the problem by sending the car back COD. But at the time he hadn't had ten bucks to give the kid from the police garage who'd agreed to return it during his lunch break. So what else could he do but promise that J.J. would pay him twenty at the other end?

That might have been a mistake.

Oh well, it was done now. He'd just have to keep his guard up.

He took another drag on the beer. Glanced at the clock. Decided he'd given Cherry enough time.

Polishing off the beer, he headed outside to where he'd parked the department loaner car: a tan, stripped-down, nineteen-eighty-something four-door that suited the streets—no chop value—but not him. *Where were the confiscated Ferraris when you needed them?*

Not that it particularly mattered. He didn't like cars all that much. Any cars. They made him nauseous. As a kid, family road trips had been a series of stops and starts interrupted by Dal's throwing up. Worst of all, he'd never been able to go on any amusement-park ride that went round and round. Must have been gross for those people on the Tilt-a-Whirl that time when he was six.

He'd mostly grown out of it, thank God. Getting car sick would have caused him no end of grief with the guys down at the station; they had no mercy. But it still made him queasy riding in the backseat, and he definitely preferred to drive.

With luck, he'd have the bike back in a couple of days. And no one the wiser about his wreck. He rolled his shoulder a couple of times. Still a little sore. But he'd beat that Mustang. The memory merited a quick grin.

Night had taken full hold while he'd been inside the bar.

He glanced up and down the near-empty street, then got into the car and cranked it to life. After a few twists and turns, he hung a left onto State, where the bright lights and glitter soon chased away the gloom.

Slowing the car to a near crawl, he trolled for Willie Dee, not really expecting to hook the little bastard right off, but you never could tell. Sometimes you got lucky.

He pulled to the curb a few times. Asked around.

Nobody'd seen him. Or at least they weren't owning to it, not even the ones Dal knew. Caution was the law of the land.

Did everyone seem just a little more paranoid tonight than usual?

Dal didn't know what was making him so edgy about the situation out on the street these days. Maybe it was just a natural reaction to the rising incidence of drug-related crime, a cop's gut response to the wave of killing and violence that had seized Phoenix City's underworld in the wake of the influx of Haitian traffickers. Maybe it was all in his head.

No. It wasn't all in his head.

People were scared. And by "people" he didn't mean the average John Q. Citizen out there. It was the subculture who were acting like Nervous Nellies.

Something was going on in the drug community. Some change in the wind. He could feel it—smell it—*taste* it. But he couldn't get a bead on exactly what it was.

And nobody was talking. Not really. Many of his regular sources were drying up, or fading into the woodwork like Willie Dee.

Something was going on.

He made the pass a couple more times, then decided to go back to the station house and check in, cruise some more later. Word would get out.

He left the car in a slot near the rim of the department parking lot, and went inside the four-story brick-and-cement-block complex that housed Phoenix City's law-enforcement body, the bowels of which was the city jail. Clacking teletypes, computer printers, typewriters, and voices spat a fusillade of sound at him as he walked through the door. Ringing phones followed him to the stairwell, met him again when he emerged on the third floor.

Here were the guts of the building: Homicide, Vice, Narcotics. And at the rear of the floor, a small office that used to be a storeroom but was now the Drug Task Force Division. Said so right on the door.

Greg Anderson was seated at his desk—positioned just outside the office because the room wouldn't hold but one—rummaging through some computer printout sheets that had rolled off the paper mountain like a white lava flow. Andy was a skinny little guy, studious-looking behind thick tortoiseshell framed glasses. He reminded Dal of Rick Moranis. Andy was also sharp as a tack and had a sweet tooth the size of Hershey, Pennsylvania.

Dal tossed him the Snickers bar he'd bought at a convenience store on the way in. One of Andy's favorites, it was snapped up midair.

"Hey, Hollywood," he hailed Dal, gripping the candy in his free hand as he jumped to his feet.

Dal had conditioned himself not to wince at the nickname. He wondered if there was anybody who'd believe it if he told them that good looks could sometimes be more of a curse than a blessing? He doubted it.

He went into the office, Andy and his printouts trailing behind.

"Got some more ID's on those pix." Andy rattled the yellow printout sheets and began peeling the wrapper from the candy bar with his teeth.

Dal sat down at the desk. The crowd pictures Genna Tosto had taken yesterday were spread on the desktop. Genna was a great photographer, a damn sight better than anyone the department had. He'd hooked up with her through J.J. during a major crack-house investigation last year. She'd been supplying him with crowd shots of crime scenes ever since.

He reminded himself to call her and say thanks.

Picking faces out of a crowd was tedious work. But it often netted unexpected rewards: information sources; eyewitnesses; even, on occassion, the perpetrator himself. People would be surprised at how often the cliché of "criminal returning to the scene of his crime" held true.

It was how he ID'd Cherry.

"Who've you got?"

Andy moved to the desk, laid the candy bar cigarette-style on the edge, licked chocolate off his fingers, and began fanning through the eight-by-ten black-and-white photos spread in front of him.

"This guy here." He pulled a sheet from the pile, laid it on top, pointed to a male Caucasian, about thirty-five, six feet, about two hundred ten to two hundred twenty pounds. Thumbed through his computer printouts. "Name's Ben E. Taylor. Call him Benny— how's that for originality. Lives over the Master's Touch Massage Parlor. Employed as a 'masseur' and general 'handyman,' if you get my drift." Andy waggled his eyebrows. Picked up the candy and took another bite.

Dal smiled absently, riffling through the pictures again, although he'd studied them pretty thoroughly already. Had something caught his eye?

"I'll check him out. Who else?"

"This one's a mite more interesting." Andy grabbed another photo from beneath Dal's rummaging fingers. Located the appropriate printout. "Eddie Green. Up from Miami. Rap sheet a mile long." He demonstrated by tearing off a three-foot length of the yellow paper, letting the rest slide to the floor. "Melrose over in Vice recognized him from a sting they had going couple of months back."

"Might be something . . ." Dal's voice faded out. For the past few moments he'd been staring at one of the photos he'd pulled from the pile, he wasn't sure why. Something about it seemed to draw his eye.

He reached over and flipped on the small desk light, sliding it toward him. Bending the neck, he focused the beam on the glossy print, studied it closely.

The crowd was sparser in this shot, mostly faces they'd already ID'd: there was Cherry, the trio that worked in the Oriental takeout, couple of street people.

His gaze traveled over them, moved on.

Beyond the crowd was a block of run-down warehouses, most of them empty, windows boarded up or gone. A small opening separated two of the buildings. It would be across the street and fifty yards or so farther south of the alley where the victim had been found. The opening was shaded, layers of gray thickening to black.

Something about the shading . . .

"Andy, look here." He pointed to the area, leaning back so Andy could get a closer look. "Make out anything in that alleyway?"

Andy studied it a moment, chocolate crumbs dripping onto the desk. He turned the photo one way, then another. "No."

"That shadow in the alleyway doesn't suggest anything to you? A shape, maybe?"

"What is this, Reid, some sort of Rorschach test?" Andy finished the Snickers, making little smacking sounds. Tossed the wrapper in the trash.

Dal shrugged. Kept looking at the spot. He couldn't be sure, maybe it was just a trick of the light. But he could almost see someone standing there, just the suggestion of a shape inside the darkness, a shadowy outline within the black. Perhaps a blow-up—

"Hey, Hollywood. You still with me?"

Dal shook crumbs from the photo and set it aside. Cut off the lamp. "Still here. Got anything else?"

"No, not yet. But I'm working on it. By the way, the chief wanted to see you if you happened by."

Dal glanced up at him. "Any idea why?" Though everyone liked and got along pretty well with Chief Davis Clifton, there was something about being called in to the head office that was reminiscent of command appearances before his high school principal.

"No idea. Sorry."

Dal stood. "Better go see." He picked up the single photo, stuck it in a manila envelope.

"Do something for me, will you?" he said to Andy as he followed him and his paper trail back to the outer desk.

"What?" Andy didn't look up from the printout he was refolding.

"See if you can pull up anything on the name Poppy. Street pusher. From outside the State Street district, I don't know how far, maybe even an import."

"Will do."

"And one more thing—check the files for any reference to the term 'boneman.' That's b-o-n-e-m-a-n. Don't know if it's one word or two. May be a street tag. May be something else. See what you can find."

"Gotcha."

"Thanks. I'll check back by on my way out. Oh, and hang on to this for me, will you, while I go upstairs?" He handed over the manila envelope.

He took the stairs two at a time up to the fourth floor.

Chief Clifton's office was to the left and down a long, narrow hall flanked by smaller offices, conference and interrogation rooms. It was quieter up here. And somehow intimidating.

And not only to the suspects who get brought up here, Dal thought, not for the first time.

Muffled voices filtered from behind the closed door, which bore the legend: Davis A. Clifton—Private.

Dal knocked.

"Come in." The chief's voice. Like Clifton, it was quiet and authoritative.

Dal entered the inner sanctum and immediately crossed glances with Lieutenant William Cutter of Homicide. They traded hostile nods.

Most people dealt with Cutter by ignoring him—like a well-dressed wart that you kept hoping would someday go away. Dal had never been too good at it.

Cutter was an asshole, plain and simple. They'd never gotten along. The animosity dated from the time Dal had done under-cover work for Homicide. His freewheeling approach had been a constant irritant to Cutter's textbook rigidity, and the fact that Dal had usually gotten results had simply added fuel to the flame.

Cutter was a jerk, and an idiot to boot. A perfect example of the Peter Principle in action. Unfortunately, he had the police commissioner's ear.

"Please come in, Reid." Chief Clifton gave him an economical nod of greeting. He sat behind his neatly organized desk—Dal had never seen it otherwise—shirtsleeves rolled up, favorite gray corduroy jacket draping the back of his chair. He gestured toward the third occupant of the room, a woman Dal had never seen before.

"Meet Special Agent Jackie Swann of the SBI. Agent Swann, Detective Dallas Reid. Heads up our Drug Task Force division."

The way Clifton said it made it sound important, though currently Dal, and Andy if you stretched a point, were the only two full-time members.

Dal acknowledged the introduction, wondering what a State Bureau of Investigation agent was doing here. The woman rose, and he made a quick assessment as she came to meet him, hand outstretched: late twenties, early thirties, maybe; attractive in a classy sort of way; wearing a dark silky dress and heels. Her heavy auburn hair was clasped demurely at the nape of her neck.

The demureness ended there. Her gaze collided with his, and Dal realized he was also being assessed. And not the kind of assessment he was used to either. Perversely, it rankled.

They shook hands. She had a firm grip.

Her measured gaze began to make him a bit uncomfortable. He got the feeling she could cause someone to squirm if they were guilty of something—hell, even if they weren't. An asset, no doubt, across an interrogation table.

He idly wondered what he might be giving away.

"Agent Swann is going to be with us for a while," Cutter inserted, oblivious to the protocol that said this was not his announcement to make. "She'll be working undercover."

Dal switched his glance to Cutter, then mentally cursed his lack of control. Cutter smiled and eyed him smugly, straightening his tie. The barb had hit home.

However much Dal might like to ignore it, the man seemed to have an uncanny knack sometimes of knowing what buttons to push. He did his best not to betray the twist of annoyance that came with the reminder that he could no longer effectively work local undercover.

At best, an undercover operative could work a specific area two to three years, max—and that was in a large metropolitan area. In a town the size of Phoenix City, maybe a year, year and a half.

Dal had worked it less than a year. Unfortunately, his was not just another face in the crowd, as J.J. had once so succinctly put it, no matter how he tried to scuz it up—and he'd gone so far as a beard worthy of Grizzly Adams, which was distinctive enough in its own way to defeat the purpose.

It still pissed him off.

The chief reassumed control of the proceedings, ignoring Cutter in his own quiet way. Chief Clifton was a pleasant, soft-spoken, diplomatic man, but with a core of steel. Nobody pushed him too far, not even the commissioner. "Have a seat, Reid."

Dal followed the chief's gesture to a chair while Agent Swann returned to her own. Cutter remained standing, propped against the desk like a shiny hood ornament.

"Agent Swann is here as part of an ongoing operation the SBI is currently fielding to investigate the efforts of certain Haitian and Jamaican drug cartels to move into the mid-Atlantic states." Clifton directed his remarks toward Dal. "You'll be providing her backup and whatever other assistance she might need while working undercover. At the same time, she'll be looking into this drug-dealer murder thing for us, so it's to our mutual advantage. Any questions?" He stared at Dal with a look that dared him to speak.

That was Clifton: make his decision, then let you in on it. He knew Dal didn't like working with a partner, would like taking a backseat role even less, so he'd presented him with a *fait accompli*. Dal avoided glancing toward Cutter.

He shook his head.

"Good," Clifton said. "With our budget cuts and staff shortages, I'm sure you'll agree that we can use all the help we can get."

A gentle warning not to make waves?

"I'll leave it to the pair of you to handle the setups and logistics on the street," Clifton said, then switched his gaze. "Agent Swann, anything to add?"

She straightened. "As I was about to mention when Detective Reid arrived, we think there might be some connection here to a Haitian drug ring that's been operating out of Charleston, South Carolina, more recently in the Manteo area and along the North Carolina coast. Headed by a man named Martineau—Maurice Martineau."

"I've gotten the bulletins on that," Dal told her, "and done some checking around. Can't seem to get a solid line on him, though," he remarked with a frown.

"Anyway, could be he's mixed up in your current drug killings," Swann added. "Where he goes, trouble follows."

"Got a profile on him?"

"I'll get you all we've got," she said, and turned back to the chief. "I believe that's about it."

"Thank you." Clifton made a couple more notes on the sheet of paper in front of him, then looked up at Dal once more. "Anything come from that meet you went to earlier?"

Dal shifted uncomfortably in his chair. "One of the State Street working girls. Says a guy named Poppy took out Coley Dean." As soon as he said it, he wished it unsaid. He didn't like going on record with the chief until he was sure—at least reasonably sure of the accuracy of his information. "May be nothing," he qualified. "Never worked with this informant before. Girl's a crack addict, might say anything for a hundred bucks. We're checking it out."

"Do that. On the plus side, she may be telling it straight. Ever hear of this Poppy before?"

Dal shook his head, trying not to fidget.

"You?" Clifton looked toward Cutter.

"Haven't had the pleasure," Cutter replied, adjusting a French cuff.

"One of our people may know the name," Agent Swann offered. "I'll ask around."

Clifton nodded, then swept them all with a glance. "You people stay sharp on this. Looks like we may have an ugly situation developing here and I want it stopped. Keep me informed." He pushed back his chair.

Meeting adjourned.

Cutter followed Dal out of the office as Agent Swann stayed back to exchange some final words with the chief.

"You heard him, Reid," Cutter said, tone brittle. "Chief Clifton wants to be kept informed—and so do I. Homicide's in charge of this case, so you'd better share whatever you get, as soon as you get it. None of your Lone Ranger bullshit."

Dal halted at the door to the stairwell, hand on the metal bar.

He turned and looked at Cutter. "Cutter, you're an asshole." He popped open the door.

"Now look here, Reid—"

"Detective Reid—?"

Dal had almost forgotten the woman. Immediately, he let the door swing shut again and glanced back down the hall.

"Agent Swann." Cutter stepped forward, switching on the charm. "Perhaps I could offer you a cup of coffee in my office. Or if you haven't had dinner yet . . . ?" He waited politely, straightening a cuff.

The man was a jerk.

Agent Swann smiled faintly. "Thank you, but no, Lieutenant. I try to get home to my husband and son at a reasonable hour whenever possible. I'll see you in the morning. Eight o'clock?"

Cutter gave a clipped nod.

Dal stifled the urge to grin, turning an appreciative eye on the woman. At the same time he felt a mild disappointment. *Married, huh.*

She met his look evenly. "Detective Reid, I'd like to get copies of your reports for the past several weeks, if I could, familiarize myself with what's been happening on the streets before we sit down to work out the details."

"No problem." Thanks to Andy and his nonaversion to paperwork. Dal reopened the stairway door and they walked down a floor. Cutter opted for the elevator.

"You and the lieutenant don't get along." It was obvious she'd overheard what he'd said to Cutter in the hallway.

"No." Might as well air the dirty laundry now as later. She was going to be working with them for a while.

"Is that going to be a problem?"

"Only if Cutter makes it one." Dal popped open the door to the third floor, turning to look at her. "The lieutenant fits the commissioner's standard for 'Proper Department Image,' Agent Swann. It's what he does best."

She made no further comment. Neither did he.

He led her through the maze of desks back to where Andy was spot-checking an eruption of new printouts.

"Agent Swann, Greg Anderson. Andy, Jackie Swann with the SBI. She'll be working undercover with us for a while."

"Glad to meet you." Andy transferred the Magic Marker he was holding to his mouth, stuck out his hand, shook with Swann, swapped back again. His left hand kept his place in the wad of printouts.

"Andy's our records expert and general researcher. Need anything statistical, he's your man. Be aware, he's also a chocoholic and works best when we keep him fed."

Swann laughed. For a moment Dal glimpsed a woman he thought he'd like to get to know—personally, not professionally. He wondered what she was doing in this business.

"I'm a doughnut freak myself," she said with a smile.

It only took a few minutes to get the records she'd need—Andy was more organized than it might appear. Agent Swann said her thank-yous and was gone.

"Nice lady," Andy observed. "Not bad lookin' either, eh, Hollywood?"

"She's married," Dal said dryly, and received a groan. "Got anything on those names yet?"

"Yep, and nope." Andy separated a sheet from the wad. Handed it to Dal. "Computer spit this out readily enough on your boy Poppy. Still working on the other."

Dal glanced at the sheet. "This is a coroner's preliminary report."

"Yep."

"The guy's dead?"

"Yep."

"Shit! When?" He located the date for himself: April 20—ten days before Coley Dean had been hit.

"Fuck. The little bitch." Cherry had lied. And now he'd gone on record to the chief. With Cutter as witness. "Sonofabitch!"

He tossed down the report, then grabbed it up again. "You got that envelope I gave you?"

Andy wordlessly handed him the manila envelope that had been sitting in plain sight on the edge of the desk.

Dal stormed out.

Brother, Brother, watch what you say
Somebody come an' take you away

NINE

Willie Dee sat on a board slung across two vegetable crates in the basement of Mel's Diner and hungrily tore hunks of sausage and bread from the sandwich Merrita had fixed for him. Grease ran down between his fingers. He used the ends of the thick bun and his tongue to mop it up.

When Merrita had come down a few minutes ago with the sandwich, she'd said some cop was looking for him, had been asking around.

Willie didn't know if that was good or bad. Right now he couldn't consider it. Right now he had other troubles to worry about.

He was teetering on the edge with this thing. Had gotten caught up in it before he'd known what was going on. Now people were turning up dead. He could be next.

Willie wanted to avoid that.

Something made a noise over in the corner.

His gaze darted toward the sound, breath hitching, stomach doing a little kick jump.

The soft rustle continued for a few seconds—while Willie's heart rate skyrocketed—then scurried away.

Rats. That's all it was. Rats.

Willie returned to his supper, stomach and heart settling back down. Rats didn't concern him. Not that kind, anyway.

He finished the food, licked his fingers and wiped them down the front of his coat. Shivered. It was cold down here. And it smelled like moldy cardboard and vegetable rot.

But it was off the streets. At the moment that was the safest place for him to be. There was food, and Merrita, and right now he was afraid to go back to his own crib. Somebody might be watching.

He glanced around, noticing how the shadows seemed to crowd the light. But they were just shadows, empty shadows. Nobody hiding in them. Nobody watching him from the dark.

Just the rats.

He turned back around.

Soon, he was going to have to come up with a plan for getting out of here—not just out of *here*, but out of this whole damn town. Bad shit was going down. *Bad* shit. He didn't want to be caught in it.

Being scared was nothing new to him. Fear was something you learned to live with on the streets, and it didn't bother Willie all that much anymore. But this was a different kind of scared. Something he'd never felt before. Freaky stuff. Out-of-this-world stuff.

He wanted away from it. As far away as he could get.

From the darkness came the scurry of more tiny feet. He hugged his old coat tighter, nicking little glances all around, searching the shadows as if they were beasts crawling closer and closer to the light. Every time he looked away, they seemed to inch a little nearer. Gobble up a little more room. Gave him the creeps.

It was like what was happening out on the streets. What had started out over on the south side was now spreading its poison tentacles over here—Maurice Martineau and his Haitians, shadowy forms in the alleys whispering *You buy? You buy?* Willie shivered at the thought of dealing with one of those creeps. He knew too much about them.

Of course, that Martineau dude was bad news, Willie had always known that. But he wasn't the worst of it, not by a long shot. No, sir.

He had to get out of here, quick as he could. Things were going crazy out there, and he wished he'd never said a word to Coley Dean—nothin' at all!

He glanced up at the metal fixture dangling above him. It held a single bulb. The pool of light it shed was meager comfort at best— *Did it suddenly seem dimmer than before?*

His breath hitched again as he thought he saw it flicker.

What if the light went out? What if he had to sit here by himself in the dark?

With the rats.

But the light didn't go out. And it didn't flicker again, so it must have just been his imagination.

Shadows creepin' up on him.

Shadows all around.

He closed his eyes, trying not to think about the shadows, thinking back instead to the night he'd visited Coley Dean, told him about the pavement pusher movin' into his territory. He'd heard the rumors even then, but he hadn't believed them. He still didn't know it all. But he knew all he wanted to. He knew enough.

Enough to get him killed.

Despite the chill in the air he began to sweat.

Sounds from the street. Sounds from above.

He glanced toward the one small window on the wall to his right, high above him. The narrow slit opened onto the back alley, too small for anyone to climb through. Yet it was like a peephole into his space.

It made him nervous.

He got up and moved around on the other side of the concrete support column to be out of the line of sight.

The glass was busted. Sometimes Cannibal Bob pissed through the hole. Willie had no desire to get too near anywhere Cannibal Bob had pissed. Cannibal Bob would eat anything.

The old building popped and creaked. People walking upstairs.

Hollow footsteps. Hollow talk.

Down here . . . shadows.

He turned up the collar on his coat and hunkered down, feeling the cold stone floor hard beneath his butt.

He wondered what that cop wanted.

He didn't care what that cop wanted.

He wished he was out of here.

Out of this stinking rat hole. This city. This state!

Somethin' was coming, that's what they'd said. He shoulda listened to 'em. Kept his mouth shut.

Now that somethin' was here.

TEN

"Stuff's here." Marcus Valentine, who'd been pacing at the door to the warehouse, nervously smoking a cigarette, watched the dark blue panel truck ease up to the loading dock and flash the prearranged signal. He dropped his cigarette among the dozen or so others peppering the cement floor and straightened, glad the truck was here at last.

"Right. Let's get crackin'." Once, Jimmie Rodriguez might have intended the word as a joke.

Once, Marcus Valentine might have responded to it.

Tonight it didn't register.

Night was thick outside the isolated warehouse where they waited. But inside the dark, cavernous building it was thicker still. Not even the MAC-10's they carried were enough to dispel the heavy gloom—and the sense of unease that had been growing in them ever since the goons had begun to trickle in, walking singly, in pairs, coming silently to stand at the rear of the warehouse like huge, hulking slabs of stone.

And the smell; it was like someone had dug up a septic tank, cracked it open and let the gasses spill out onto the air.

The two men moved quickly toward the truck, just wanting to get this over with and be gone, trying not to hear the sound of stirring behind them, the rustle of clothing, the shuffle of restless feet. Goons coming to life.

Freaky, how those dudes had stood so still, not even talking among themselves while they waited. They just filed in, stood back there in the darkness, filed out again. Made Marcus think of a

84

funeral procession, pallbearers waiting for the casket to arrive. Gave him the creeps.

Maybe they didn't speak English. Lot of these people were just off the boat. But didn't people in Haiti speak English too? And besides, that was no reason for them not to talk at all. They shoulda been millin' around back there, mutterin' among themselves, maybe passin' around a joint—

And that was another weird thing. None of them smoked, not even cigarettes; he hadn't seen a single one of them light up. It was unnatural. Like they were totally spaced out. And those grins.

Marcus shivered.

Freaky.

As fast as possible, Jimmie and Marcus took the small brown-paper-wrapped packages passed to them from inside the truck, checking each one thoroughly, counting them twice. All was in order.

The truck drove off.

Darkness settled around them again, making Marcus feel more nervous by the second. They were alone, him and Jimmie, alone with those goons in the back. At least before, the truck had been coming.

Behind them, the stirring grew louder, closer, like wind in dry leaves. Footsteps moved slowly across the cement floor.

Freaky sound, coming toward you like that. Freaky as shit.

The two men stood by the door where they'd hovered all night, Jimmie nervously gripping his MAC-10 at ready, Marcus quickly handing out packages as the silent line filed by.

But no one gave them any trouble. No one even looked them in the eye. Just those grins.

Marcus shivered.

Not a word was said as each shadowy form shuffled up, took a package, shuffled by. Marcus was careful not to touch the hands that reached for the packages.

For a minute he thought he recognized one of the bunch, looked a little like a dude named—Boogaloo, was it? Yeah, Boogaloo, that was it. Dealt through Billy Boy Webster up around Avondale Park and the high school. But what would a brother be doing down here with these creeps? And besides, hadn't he heard somewhere that Boogaloo was dead? Nah, maybe not. And what did it matter anyway? He just wanted to be done with this shit and get outa here.

One by one, the pushers disappeared into the night, taking their packages and weird silence with them.

Marcus breathed a sigh of relief. "Those goons give me the creeps."

"Yeah, me too," Jimmie agreed, then glanced nervously around as though someone might still be lingering in the shadows, listening. "Whaddya think they're on?" he whispered.

"I dunno, man, some sort of goon dust—jungle junk." Marcus shivered again. "I just know I don't want any of it. That's some bad shit."

"Yeah." Jimmie nodded. "It's like those guys are totally zoned out—I mean, *past* zoned out, they've moved into the O-zone. And those grins." He shuddered.

"Yeah," Marcus agreed. "Let's get outa here."

"I'm on you, man."

The pair slid the double doors closed, looped the thick chain around the dual handles and fastened the heavy padlock to it. Walked briskly to their parked car.

It was getting weirder all the time, doing business with these Haitians. They had some real freak-outs working the streets now—more of them coming in all the time. Cutting in on a lot of the established trade.

But that wasn't Marcus's or Jimmie's concern. They just did what their people told them: met the trucks, distributed the goods. They didn't even collect the money, all that was done by higher-ups.

Neither ever questioned their role in the scheme of things.

Wouldn't be wise.

Rich man, poor man,
Low man, high
One day you live
Next day you die

ELEVEN

Richard Davenport, D.D.S., woke from a deep sleep about two A.M. He'd been dreaming. He couldn't quite remember what, but it had been something about that handsome young black man who'd visited his office this afternoon. A pleasant dream.

Smiling, he got up without waking his wife, Paula. Went out into the hall.

The small Tiffany lamp on the antique table at the end of the wide hallway cast a muted glow on thick, pale gray carpeting, soft mauve walls. It was an elegant hall in an elegant house in one of Phoenix City's wealthier "west side" developments.

It was a good life, dealing drugs and drilling teeth. He planned to retire, with his wife and two young sons, to a house in the Bahamas before he was thirty-five.

But right now there was something he had to do.

He went downstairs, got the stainless steel carving knife from the expensive set Paula kept in the dining room sideboard, climbed the stairs back up to the elegant hall.

Richie's room was first on the right. He went in, slit the boy's throat, came out again.

Next he visited Jason.

Then it was his wife's turn as she lay sleeping on her back, mouth slightly ajar. He tried to close it afterward, she didn't look her best that way, but it wouldn't stay shut.

Grinning, he lay back down beside her, thinking again of the wonderful life they were going to have as he drew the saw-edged blade across his own throat.

He didn't even bother to wipe the others' blood from it first.

TWELVE

Maurice Martineau wiped the sweat from his brow with a massive handkerchief he kept near at hand for just that purpose. A big man with coal-black skin and thick features, Maurice used his size to advantage—to intimidate and subdue—often letting it do the talking for him. Body language, he liked to call it.

Maurice enjoyed his size. It served him well as the head of a drug cartel. He dwarfed most people he came in contact with, a visible sign of power, control. But there were negative aspects of it, too, profuse sweating being one of them.

Right now, his size was not the only thing making him sweat.

He glanced toward the suave young black man who sat facing him across the desk, but far enough back that the lamplight somehow managed to cast shadows on his handsome face instead of illuminating it. *Why did this man make him so edgy?* Fucker was crazy, that's why. But he'd been useful to Maurice—instrumental, in fact, in securing close to half of Phoenix City for the cartel, and the rest would soon follow.

The man had come to Maurice's attention through channels, channels that led all the way back to Haiti. It was said he had special talents, possessed certain knowledge that went beyond what others might use. He could do things for people, it was said, make things happen. Or not happen. For a price.

Fine. Maurice was willing to pay what it took to get the job done. And it was working, too, local street vendors disappearing, being replaced with his own men; some of the upper-crust traffickers meeting tragic ends. And all without Maurice having to lift a hand. Another few weeks, Maurice would have the whole city in his pocket.

So why was he liking this less and less? What did being crazy matter, as long as the fucker did his job?

Maurice mopped away sweat.

"Everything still on track?"

The man nodded. Once. The merest dip of his head. Yet it seemed to mock Maurice somehow, as though he'd asked a stupid question, and the man had only answered out of amused tolerance.

Bastard. He didn't like dealing with this smooth-as-silk fucker, Maurice thought, didn't like it at all. He toyed with the idea of killing him when the takeover was complete, decided he'd enjoy that; but not yet. Things were going too well just now, and the man still had his uses, no doubt about it.

But Maurice didn't like him, not one bit.

"There's this reporter guy." Maurice opened an envelope, slid out a picture and several data sheets. "Name's Spencer, J. J. Spencer. Works for the local newspaper. Been gettin' kinda nosy lately, writin' some things I don't like." He shoved the material back into the envelope, passed it across the desk. "Get rid of him."

The man picked up the envelope, withdrew the picture, studied it in silence.

Maurice felt his lip curl as he eyed the man opposite him. Who did he think he was, sitting there in polished perfection with his legs elegantly crossed, wearing an expensive silk suit, Italian leather shoes. Very nice. But hardly in keeping with the image he'd chosen for himself.

Boneman. That's what he liked to call himself. After that old Haitian legend about a voodoo sorcerer, a sort of ultimate witch doctor who could take control of the living and the dead—Maurice had heard the tales. He even thought he could remember some of those old rhymes, remember chanting them in a singsong voice when he was a kid. Must have been kinda scary back then.

But Maurice wasn't a kid anymore. He was a businessman. And he didn't believe in all that crap.

Boneman, shit. Who did this dude think he was kidding? Something to scare the kids with, the dopers on the street. What a scam. Made Maurice want to laugh. He'd half expected the dude to show up here with a bone stuck through his nose. Or dressed like Baron Samedi or something.

But he hadn't. He'd looked much as he looked now—like he'd just come from a tailor on Savile Row.

Boneman, what a joke. But . . . whatever worked.

And it *was* working, no doubt about that. Maurice had to hand it to him, he knew how to play this scam to the hilt.

But it only worked on the ones who believed.

Fools on the street wanted to believe, let 'em. They might be intimidated by this fucker's game, but not Maurice. Oh, no. He was too smart for that. All a scam, done with drugs and stage-show mysticism. Island hocus-pocus. He knew the tricks. He'd even used a few himself from time to time.

Crazy bastard. Maurice mopped his brow.

The man slid the photograph back into the envelope, met Maurice's gaze. Again, that little almost-smile of amused tolerance.

Maurice's hand tightened on the handkerchief, wadding it into his fist. Be damned if he'd wipe his face again, not with this fucker staring at him.

"And what about that nosy cop?" Maurice clipped.

Now the man did smile, the corners of his mouth etching dimples into his smooth milk-chocolate skin. "It's being taken care of," he said softly.

THIRTEEN

Two-twenty A.M.

Dal stumbled up the stairs and across the threshold of his garage apartment, kicking the door shut behind him. Fumbling his way across the room, he managed to locate the end table and flick on the lamp without knocking anything over in the process.

He was tired as hell, and more than a little drunk—shouldn't have stayed so long in that last bar.

Tossing the manila envelope onto the table, he sank down on the sofa bed that he never bothered to refold anymore, and sprawled back against the tumbled pillows and wrinkled sheets.

Home.

The word had no particular claim on him. It was merely a four-letter word for living space/domicile/place of residence. It provided him with somewhere to sleep, take a shower; an address to put on his personnel files.

What else did he need it for?

The efficiency apartment had come furnished with early-attic junk, which suited Dal's lifestyle, and a minimum of kitchen implements, most of which he'd never used. He rarely ate in, used the fridge mainly to keep his beer cold. In fact, there were very few items in the place that even belonged to him. Sometimes he wondered where his money went.

J.J. was always after him to budget his income, plan ahead, get some stability in his life. But that was J.J.'s way, not Dal's. Besides, he was pretty stable. He'd lived here seven years now. He did okay. Drove a BMW, didn't he? Even if it was a bike.

Thunder rumbled in the distance. The occasional flicker of lightning. A storm was brewing; he could feel the pressure in the air.

Working his feet out of his shoes, Dal unfastened his jeans then lay there deciding whether it was really worth the extra effort to take them all the way off. He wasn't sure he had any clean ones, so he decided he'd better not sleep in these.

He raised his hips and shoved the jeans partway down, cursing when his underwear rolled with them. Using one hand to yank up his briefs, he sat up and pulled the jeans the rest of the way off then left them lying in a crumpled heap on the floor—just for now, he'd pick them up in a minute. He sank back down across the bed.

Tonight had been a total bust. He'd cruised for several hours, hit a few bars, some topless clubs, even gotten out and walked the streets looking for Willie Dee. No luck. Nobody would even admit to seeing the little bastard recently, though some of them were obviously lying, he could read it in their eyes.

Something else he could read: fear. What were they all afraid of? What the hell was going on out there? Dal had never known the atmosphere on the streets to be so skittish. Nobody was talking. He couldn't get a line on anything, not just the whereabouts of Willie Dee.

But right now he was too tired to think about it anymore. His mind had gone to mush. He just wanted some sleep.

Lightning streaked across the cloud-choked sky. Closer. It flashed through the dimly lit room like strobe lighting. Thunder rumbled along behind it.

He shut his eyes as the lightning spiked again, counted *one one thousand, two one thousand*—thunder boomed.

Softly, the rain began to fall . . .

Dal jerked awake to the sound of rain slamming into the windowpane. Gusts of wind howled by, driving water against the glass in short, staccato bursts. For a moment it had sounded like rapid gunfire.

He lay back against the pillows again, taking a few long, deep breaths to still his racing pulse. He felt a sense of unease. Not *threat* exactly, but something tickling the nerves at the back of his neck.

He continued to lie there motionless, eyes shut, attempting to separate the storm sounds from other noises that might signal some intrusion into his night.

Nothing.

Slowly, he opened his eyes and glanced around. He'd left the lamp on. Its muted glow fell on the usual messy room, nothing out of place, no one poised in the shadows waiting to strike—a cop always tended to consider that possibility first.

He lifted his wrist to squint at his watch: 3:44 A.M. *Damn.* He'd barely slept an hour.

Outside, the rain hammered down.

Inside, its muffled drone echoed throughout the room, making it feel close and tight, setting up an answering roar in Dal's head.

Something seemed out of kilter.

He levered himself upright, paused a minute for everything to stop spinning, and looked around the room, mind still leaden with tiredness, too much booze, and the desperate need for sleep. But sleep seemed to have abandoned him for the moment.

His stared into the silent shadows, wincing slightly each time a bolt of lightning flashed and the thunder boomed. His vision seemed to click from color to black-and-white every time it hit, like a photograph negative randomly spliced into a piece of Technicolor film. *God, he hated hangovers.*

Dampness had seeped into the room, the air was heavy with it. The sheets felt clammy and cold.

He still felt as if something were wrong.

Maybe "wrong" wasn't quite the word he was looking for; the feeling was more an awareness that there was something in the room he wasn't seeing, just sensing. A cop's paranoia? The storm? Both of the above? Maybe even a dream already lost down the well of awakening, but leaving an afterimage lingering in his mind.

He ran a hand through his hair, wanting to go back to sleep but feeling restless enough to know he was going to have trouble doing it.

The manila envelope caught his eye. It had fallen to the floor.

He reached over and picked it up, deciding to have another look at the photograph.

The paper felt cold to his touch. Like the sheets. Dal repressed a shiver.

For a moment he sat there, holding the envelope unopened in his hands. Why had he even brought it in? He should have left it in the car so he wouldn't take the chance of forgetting it in the morning. Should have left it lying right there on the front seat.

So why hadn't he?

He'd been planning to drop it by Genna's earlier tonight so she could do a blowup on it, but somehow he'd never gotten around to doing that. Now he'd have to take care of it first thing in the morning, before he went to work.

So. Why bring it inside?

He shrugged. Turning the envelope over, he reached for the flap.

The coldness seemed to transmit itself to his hands. He peeled back the folded edge and pulled out the photograph, carefully placing the envelope back on the table. His fingers felt thick and kind of numb. He flexed first one set and then the other to get the blood flowing down them, the feeling back. Tilting the picture, he held it toward the light.

Nothing about it had changed. Holding it at the edges, he worked his eyes methodically left to right, bottom to top.

Dal frowned, focusing on the narrow alley that ran between the two buildings, where the pattern of shadows played hide-and-seek with his brain. It was as if he could almost see an image there.

He studied it more thoroughly, trying to come up with a template that would fit. It was like one of those goddamn hidden picture puzzles that your brain refuses to delineate, but if you stare at it long enough, all of a sudden, *presto,* the mind shifts gear and the picture pops out and you wonder why you hadn't seen it in the first place.

He stared at the spot until the darkness at its center seemed to swirl slightly, sucking at his gaze like a magnet pulling iron. Light became little wormlike creatures, crawling around the edges of the pitch-black hole. He kept his focus directly on the alleyway, shoving everything else aside.

Coming . . . it was coming . . .

Suddenly he felt dizzy. Vision blurred.

He swayed forward, gaze still locked on the narrow slit—

The buildings on either side of him shot outward, zooming past him left and right and it was if he had actually entered the alley . . .

Sound receded, rushing away from him as though escaping

down a long corridor into the night. Far behind him, the storm raged. Here in the alley, everything was hushed.

He leaned closer—the shadows seemed to ooze and separate, opening a pathway for him through the dark—

Someone was in here with him. Someone standing just beyond him out of sight.

The atmosphere was charged with static electricity; it crawled across his skin. Little sparkles danced before his eyes.

He could just make out the form, the outline of a body standing among the shadows—a man, waiting for him in the dark—

The man stepped forward.

Dal recoiled, dropping the photo as a double flash of lightning shuddered across the sky, followed by a bolt of thunder. It was as if the floodgates opened and the storm came crashing down on top of him, a huge tidal wave of sound and sensation and blinding light. He sucked in a breath, heart pounding, mouth gone dry.

What the fuck—?

Bending down, he scooped up the photograph and flipped it over with hands that felt as if they had been asleep and were now being stabbed awake by fiery needles from inside.

What was the matter with him? Had he actually thought a shadow figure had stepped toward him? Out of a photograph?

He looked at the picture again. Nobody standing there. No sinister forms playing hide-and-seek in the dark.

God, he must have gone to sleep sitting up.

He lifted an arm to swipe sweat from his brow—jumped as the contact shocked him. The air *was* charged with static electricity. The hairs on his arms prickled as if they were alive.

Taking some more deep breaths, he blew them out slowly, studying the picture while his pulse rate eased back to normal. He must be more tired than he thought. Eyes playing tricks. Sleeping sitting up. Must have had some sort of fatigue-induced hallucination.

Or one too many Kentucky blends.

His breathing began to return to normal. He regarded the photograph with narrowed eyes.

The faint outline did look somewhat like a person standing in the shadows—

Did it seem just a little clearer now than it had before?
Dal frowned.
No, of course not.
And it certainly wasn't moving.
What was the matter with him?
He slipped the photograph back into its envelope and laid it on the floor with his jeans and shoes where he'd be sure to pick it up in the morning.
Sinking back onto the bed again, he drifted almost immediately into an exhausted sleep.

Seven forty-two A.M.
Dal woke to the steady drone of rain pummeling the roof. He glanced at his watch.
"Oh, shit."
Jerking upright, he ran his hands through his hair and searched frantically for his jeans—*Christ, there they were, balled up on the floor*—*what had he done that for?* He grabbed them and pulled them on.
His gaze fell on the manila envelope. For a moment he froze, remembering the previous night.
Had that really happened? Or had it all been some sort of crazy dream?
He reached down and seized the envelope, started to rip it open, stopped. Christ, he didn't have time for this now. He'd had a dream, that's all. Nothing but a combination of a dream, the storm, and too much to drink. He'd been hallucinating. He tossed the envelope toward the door, where he could grab it on his way out.
No time to stop by Genna's. That meant he'd have to take care of it later in the day. Try to remember.
A quick trip to the head; he splashed cold water on his face and upper body, brushed his teeth, cursed at not having enough time to take a proper shower. The shave could wait. Rummaging around in his drawer for a clean T-shirt and socks, he yanked them on, stepped into his shoes, and was out the door, grabbing his waterproof bike jacket and the envelope on the way out.
He saw the car and cursed some more as he remembered that

he didn't have his bike and God only knew what it was going to cost him to get it out of hock. Muttering to himself, he jumped in the car and started it up.

Traffic was snarled due to the weather. Dal avoided the expressway, taking the back roads into town.

He got to the station in record time, but the main lot was already full, so he had to use the alternate parking lot two blocks away. He ran the two extra blocks, cursing the rain all the way back to the station house.

At least he had on his rain jacket. Now to deal with Cutter and the SBI.

Entering the building by a side door, he shook the water off and ran a hand through his dripping hair, then took the back stairs two at a time up to Three.

Andy sat at his desk, scribbling something with one hand, holding a double-dipped chocolate doughnut in the other. A bag from the local doughnut shop sat open at his elbow. He spotted Dal and quickly looped an arm around it.

"Mine."

Dal just shook his head and sloshed some coffee from the pot Andy kept brewed and ready on a table against the wall into a Styrofoam cup. Headed into the office.

Agent Swann was already there, seated at the desk with the files Andy had given her the night before spread out in front of her. She was dressed more casually this morning: slacks, shirt, khaki blazer; made her look younger. She still looked all business. An almost-dry raincoat hung by its hood from the corner of the door.

She glanced up. "Detective Reid."

"Dal, please."

She nodded and smiled. "And I'm Jackie."

He set his coffee cup on the edge of the desk and began shrugging out of his jacket. "Sorry I'm late."

"No problem." She closed the file she'd been looking through and began restacking the pile, preparing to get up.

Tossing his jacket atop a nearby file cabinet, he gestured for her to keep her seat, and she settled down again.

Retrieving his coffee, he took a careful sip, badly in need of an adrenaline boost. It was as hot as usual. She wasn't having any, he noticed, and figured she probably didn't touch the stuff—or smoke, or drink, or any of the other things that made life tolerable. No doubt drank caffeine-free herbal teas and diet Cokes; these state people were always so clean-cut. If she'd been single, he would have introduced her to J.J. Well, maybe.

"Lieutenant Cutter won't be joining us," she said as Dal took the only other seat available: a straight-backed wooden chair they'd scrounged from one of the interrogation rooms. It was hard as cement. "He's at the scene of a multiple out in Westridge—have you heard about that?"

"Yeah. Caught it on the radio on the way in." Guy had killed his wife and two kids, then himself. *What made people do such things?* At least Cutter would be kept occupied and out of their hair for a while. "So"—he nodded toward the files—"anything there you want to talk about?" Gingerly, he took another sip of coffee. Still hot.

She looked at the files again as though channeling her thoughts. "They're very thorough and concise."

Like maybe she'd expected otherwise?

"You can thank Andy for that," he said.

"I did." There was the hint of a grin in her voice, on her face, and Dal grinned back, then studied her a moment, wondering how this was going to work out. Some of these state people could be a little intense.

Face it, Dallas, you just don't like someone else getting to do the job you'd like to do.

He speculated on how long she'd been married. Long enough to have a kid. He shook off a little twitch of condemnation. Cops didn't have any business being married, particularly undercover cops.

"Any suggestions on how you might like to work this thing?" He turned his mind back to the business at hand.

She sat back in the chair, regarding him with that direct gaze of hers. He tried not to squirm. "Pretty routine, actually. Simplest is usually best, as I'm sure you'll agree."

He nodded.

"I thought maybe one of your informants could introduce me," she went on, "friend of a friend, that sort of thing. We might use the college angle, say I know some frat guys looking for a steady source. Just enough to establish credibility. Start off with some small buys, maybe work up to the bigger stuff. Try to build confidence, make contacts, listen to the talk. Mostly listen to the talk. I'm not particularly interested in making even a mid-level drug bust here, though you can act on whatever information we manage to obtain. I mainly want to find out what the word is out on the street."

Dal refrained from wishing her a rather sarcastic "Good luck." He'd been attempting to do just that for several weeks now. But in all fairness, she'd have an advantage he no longer had—they wouldn't know she was a cop.

"I've got an informant that might fit the bill," he told her. "College dropout with a habit. Alternates between rehab and the gutter. Should be able to intro you in."

"Good. When can I meet him?"

"Today, maybe. I'll see if I can set it up."

She nodded. "By the way, any update on that hooker's lead you were telling us about last night?"

Dal felt his annoyance rekindle at the reminder of that little fiasco. "Dead end. Literally. Andy came up with a preliminary coroner's report on that Poppy guy last night. Been dead for over a week when Coley Dean got it. So apparently that's down the tube." Along with a hundred of the department's bucks—*the lying whore, and mark that one down for further attention.*

"Too bad," she remarked, sounding genuinely sorry. "Would have made the job a bit easier."

Dal shrugged. "Is it ever?"

The phone rang outside. Andy picked it up, talked a minute, then got up and stuck his head in the door. "That Davenport multiple over in Westridge—they found drugs at the scene. Lots of them. Want you out there now. One twenty-two Willow View Drive."

Dal glanced at Jackie. "Want to come?"

"Sure." She got up and retrieved her coat.

He grabbed his jacket and they were out the door.

"Thanks again for the doughnuts," Andy hollered as they raced by. She waved a "You're welcome."

It was still raining when they exited the building. Jackie pulled up her hood, then glanced over at Dal as he hesitated. "My car's right here if you want to take it." She pointed out a blue Mercedes station wagon parked just two slots from the door.

God, Dal wondered, did she do undercover work in that? Maybe he should be working for the SBI.

He shook his head. "We'll take mine." Gritting his teeth, he sprinted off toward the far lot, ignoring the look she shot him, turning up the collar of his jacket as he went. If she wanted to think he was a male chauvinist pig, then fine. He had no great wish for another jog in the rain, but it was infinitely preferable to letting her drive. His stomach might not take it this morning.

They dashed to his car and jumped in. Dal started up, and pulled out into the flow of traffic, deciding to chance the beltline. Traffic should be thinned by now.

Rain pelted the windshield and streaked by the car like a gray ticker-tape parade. Although the state law requiring "Wipers on—Headlights on" was more than a year old, there were still violators.

They drove in silence for several minutes, he concentrating on the road, she—who knew what she was concentrating on. He risked a quick glance her way. She was staring straight ahead, a slight frown marring the smoothness of her forehead. *What is she thinking about?* he wondered.

Despite the hood, her hair had gotten damp and began curling around her face. It softened her profile, made her look kinda like a kid. Fresh, like she'd just stepped out of the shower. By comparison, he felt downright grungy.

Since it looked as though they were going to be working together for a while he might as well come to terms with it, Dal decided. Reluctant as he was to have an unknown "partner" connected to his hip, he could sure use the help. He just wasn't too comfortable with it, that's all. But give it time.

He slowed for the Westridge exit, made the turn.

"Mind if I ask you something?" She still wasn't looking at him, he could tell by the sound of her voice.

"Shoot."

"I read the reports. Got all the background data. Have my own notions to draw from. But you know this city, how it feels. Any off-the-record opinions that might be helpful?"

He remained silent for a moment, wondering just how much he should tell her. He had no concrete evidence—he'd opened his mouth prematurely last night and look where it'd gotten him. He wasn't too keen on doing it again.

On the flip side, she was working in the dark. He knew how he'd feel in her place. Working undercover was a specialized job. Anything that might help the agent handle it safely and successfully was a plus to stack against a whole lot of minuses.

"There's something going on out there," he told her. "I don't know what, exactly. A mood shift. A tenseness. Nobody's talking about it—and that's what bothers me. People seem genuinely scared." He paused, added soberly, "It takes a lot to scare some of these people."

She made no comment, but he could sense that she was weighing what he had said.

"Now I've got a question for you." He glanced at her profile. She had a beautiful profile. "Ever heard the term 'boneman' before?"

She thought a minute, shook her head. "No, I don't think so. What's it mean?"

He shrugged. "Just something I heard a guy in a bar say the other night. Kinda stuck with me." He let it go at that.

So did she.

They drove along in silence once again, Dal's thoughts still lingering in that bar. The guy had been drunk. Talking kind of crazy. He'd kept mumbling something that sounded like a child's rhyme, something like "the boneman will get you if you don't watch out." It'd been weird as shit. The man had giggled every time he said it; but from nervousness, Dal remembered, not good humor. Just thinking about it gave him an odd sense of wrongness.

He peered through the rain, seeing it all clearly, as if he were right there, sitting on that barstool in that dive next to that old drunk. He could smell the stale smoke fumes, taste his last shot of Kentucky blend. He licked his lips, surprised to find them dry.

What had it been that made it stick with him so? The way the bartender dropped a glass at one point? Or the black dudes who'd walked up, *then moved away quickly when they'd heard the old man's rummy chant? One of them had been wearing sunglasses, but Dal had seen fear spring up in the other one's eyes—*

"Is that your turn?"

Dal snapped back to the present, mashing down the brake. "Yeah."

The elaborate stone columns flanking the road bore bronze plaques that stated: Westridge Valley Estates. He turned the car, headed toward the clutch of vehicles and flashing lights that marred the otherwise pristine landscape of the exclusive residential section.

Dal flashed his badge at the uniforms who approached the car, got flagged through, drove along the circular driveway, pulled in beside the meat wagon, and parked. He cut the engine off and turned to face Jackie.

"Whatever's going on out there"—he hesitated to make sure she understood he was talking about the streets, not what was happening beyond the car—"it's got me worried. Bad worried. The mood isn't normal. It's like a ripple under the skin. Something's crawling around down there, and I don't know what it is. Makes me nervous."

She didn't say anything.

"When I was a kid," Dal said softly, "there was this story going around about a girl who was supposed to be crazy, kept insisting there were *things* crawling under her skin. She kept trying to claw her skin apart. So they put her in a straitjacket until finally she stopped screaming and got still. Then they took it off. Her fingernails had grown—it'd been a long time. The minute they pulled the sleeves off, she reached up with both hands and clawed open her face. Ants poured out. Thousands of them."

He regarded her in silence.

She met his look blandly. "I heard that story too."

He grinned. "Like I said, it made the rounds." He reached for the door handle. The grin faded. "But that's how it feels out there on the streets; like there's a straitjacket on that's fixing to come off. Then watch out."

He swung around, popped open the door.

She followed him out into the rain.

De Boneman catch you if he can
Everybody run from de ol' Boneman

FOURTEEN

Curled against some burlap potato sacks in a corner of Mel's basement, Willie Dee spiked a loud snore and woke himself up.

His little ferret face jerked this way and that, eyes probing, ears pricked for any signs of imminent danger. Nothing seemed to be amiss.

He hacked a couple of times and spit. Wiped his nose on his sleeve. Sat up and looked around.

It was murky in the basement. Murky light. Murky air.

Upstairs, the rattle of dishes and clatter of feet signaled breakfast customers; the traffic noise outside, delivery trucks and people going to work. He heard the steady drumbeat of rain.

Those sounds didn't bother him. He'd got used to them a long time ago, all part of life on the streets.

He stretched, lifting himself off the lumpy makeshift mattress. His body felt stiff, sore. He had to pee.

Looking around, he spied some empty lard buckets tumbled against the back wall, popped the lid off one and relieved himself into it. It wouldn't have bothered him much to just urinate in a corner—Cannibal Bob pissed through that hole in the window, didn't he? But, then, Cannibal Bob was a totally no-class dude.

Willie scratched his head and yawned, rubbed at his right shoulder. It pained him some when the chill got in, and this basement was downright cold. And damp. Even his jacket felt weighted down by it. He shivered, drawing the old Salvation Army issue coat more closely around him, wrinkled his nose. Cloth smelled like mold.

A whiff of bacon frying drifted by and caught his attention. Smelled kinda rancid, minglin' in with the musty air. Still, it set his

105

mouth to watering. And coffee—he breathed deeper. The thick, heady aroma of coffee.

Wondering if Merrita was meaning to bring him some breakfast down without his having to go up and ask for it, he stalked over to the stairs and stared up, wondering what he should do. He didn't want to risk being seen. But he was hungry.

Light from the metal fixture overhead got lost about midway up the steps, making the rest of the wooden staircase ascend into shadows. Something about that bothered him.

Mel should keep his basement better lighted, Willie thought. A person could fall.

He decided maybe he'd just wait a little while longer for Merrita to bring him his breakfast down.

Rubbing his shoulder some more, he wandered back over to the bench where he'd sat the night before, eating his sausage sandwich. He remembered the feeling of unease that had come over him while he'd been sitting there, the idea that someone might be peering in through the window. Somehow it didn't seem so menacing today.

But things always seem better in the daytime.

A comforting lie. The kind you had to look out for. A lie like that could make you careless. Make you dead.

He shivered again, and this time it wasn't from the cold.

The shadows at the top of the staircase reclaimed his gaze. They looked as if they were moving.

"Merrita?" he whispered, searching the dark.

The door hadn't opened, at least he didn't think it had.

"Merrita, that you?"

There was no sound.

Again, that sense of movement. Like the darkness was swirling, kinda, shifting this way and that.

Willie drew himself backward, toward one of the cement columns that supported the floor above. He crammed his small, wiry body against the far side, still watching the staircase, waiting for the movement to come again.

Nothing happened. Musta been the light—yeah, that's all it was, the metal light, musta got nudged by a drift of wind, set to swinging. He glanced at the metal fixture. It wasn't moving now, but it had been; sure, that's all it was.

Willie began to feel like a fool. Here he was, staring at shadows. Hiding from—

A little tingle of fear sped through him. Jolting his insides like a mild electric shock.

Ghosts. Is that what he was doing down here? Hiding out from a ghost? Was that what he was scared of?

"No such thing as ghosts," he muttered, feeling no better at having voiced the words. In fact, he wished he'd stayed quiet. He'd given his position away.

But could you really hide from a ghost?

Despite the cold, Willie began to sweat.

Goddamn Haitians. Moving in. Takin' over the streets. Wasn't that enough? Did they hafta bring their island mumbo jumbo with 'em too?

But didn't you have to believe in all that shit? Wasn't that how they got to you? Used your own fears against you? A simple trick of the mind?

"I don't believe in ghosts, I don't believe in ghosts," Willie murmured, repeating the words like a magic chant, imagining them spinning around and around him, forming a protective barrier that nothing could get through, no evil could touch.

Behind him, the scamper of little rat feet flew across the cement floor. Willie whirled around, heart jumping, slamming into overdrive, a fist against his chest.

He stood there for a long moment as the adrenaline ran its course, waiting for the panic to subside.

"I gotta get outa here. Gotta get outa this town." He swung around—

A man stood in front of him.

Willie yelped, jumping back in surprise and fright. *Where'd he come from? How the fuck'd he get so close?* Willie hadn't heard a thing—not a goddamn thing!

"Who're you? Whaddya want?" His voice sounded foreign to his own ears, shrill and stretched like piano wire. Or a garrote. He swallowed convulsively.

The man was standing in the pool of light shed by the metal

fixture. Light fell around him, striking his head and spilling off in all directions. It didn't touch his face.

Willie stared hard, but couldn't see his face at all. Just shadows.

For a moment, he felt the strongest urge to step closer, get a better look. He needed to see this man's face—*needed to.* He actually felt his right foot move forward—

Fear grabbed hold. *Who was this dude? What was he doing here?* Something about this wasn't right.

The man wore a suit. He looked as if he'd just come out of a bank or stepped away from some important business meeting where people dressed like they do in those glossy men's magazines and all the clothes have those funny designer names.

He had no place in the basement of Mel's Diner.

This wasn't normal.

The man hadn't said anything. He still hadn't moved. It was as if he were standing in the center of a stage, standing in a spotlight with the audience all hushed and waiting around him, waiting for *what?*

Willie could have heard a pin drop, it was so silent in the basement.

and where were the traffic sounds? where was the noise from above?

He held his breath, unable to move, unable to talk, frozen to the spot.

The man simply stood there, bathed in light.

And suddenly Willie felt as if he were getting sleepy, felt his thoughts starting to spin . . .

was this a dream? was he having a dream?

Little sparkles danced before his eyes, droplets of light spatter-ing off the man and misting his face. He closed his eyelids, feeling the soft, cool darkness pour in on him.

"Willie?"

"*Hmmm?*" Willie felt himself sway forward.

"Look at me, Willie."

Willie opened his eyes. The light fixture must be moving again. A soft glow touched the man's face briefly . . . again . . . *Light . . . dark . . .* He was a black man—young, handsome—with smooth, flawless skin the color of chocolate cream—

and for an instant stark white and hard like the glitter of bone. Willie was gazing into the eyeless, grinning face of a skull—

He blinked, the light shifted, the skull was gone.

The man smiled.

It was a beautiful smile. Soft. Inviting. Willie took a step forward.

He could see the man's eyes now. They were beautiful eyes. Wonderful eyes. He was numbed by the gift they offered him.

Fear was gone, curiosity in its place. And a deep sense of belonging. He stepped closer, his initial caution beginning to fade. He was hungry to see the man's face, avid to know what he looked like, who he was, why he was here.

Another step . . .

Light dazzled his eyes. Willie reached up and stirred it with his hand, felt it coat his skin like fine, soft rain.

step . . .

He gazed into the brilliant eyes. Gazed deep into their liquid depths.

And in them saw what he must do . . .

FIFTEEN

Water dripped from the brim of J.J.'s rain hat and felt as if it were soaking through the shoulders of his all-weather coat as he dashed back across the soggy lawn to his car. He was cold, he was wet. This was no way to spend a vacation.

Scrambling into the four-wheel drive, he tossed his hat to the passenger's seat and quickly slammed the door. Instantly the cacophony retreated, dulling to a muted background roar.

Water trickled down his neck as he fished for his keys, finally dragging them from his pants pocket. He started the car and let it idle for a moment, rubbing his hands together as an involuntary shiver traveled the length of him, pimpling his skin.

His feet were soaked: socks and sneakers squished and squeaked every time he placed them against the vinyl floor mats, rubber soles wanting to slip off the brake and accelerator pedals. He'd have to be extra careful driving.

He peered out the blurry window.

The scene at the Davenport murder/suicide was a maelstrom of police, news media, related service personnel, made doubly manic by the pouring rain. And he'd given up a dry house, a freshly brewed pot of coffee, and a quiet morning at his computer for *this*?

Was this really how he wanted to spend the rest of his life? Sometimes he felt like an ambulance chaser.

A TV-2 news van had pulled in behind him and was now blocking his way.

He sat there for a moment waiting impatiently, staring out at the blurry scene made almost surreal by water cascading in sheets across the glass.

Motion and color were blunted and fused, scattered by the runnels in the glass. Rain drummed against the roof, a solid, steady sound . . . the soft thrum of the engine . . . The sounds had an almost hypnotic effect. He felt himself beginning to relax, locked in his own snug world, separate from the storm outside and the violence that had been inflicted within that elegant house.

For a moment, J.J. felt encapsulated, in a space all by himself, where there was order, not chaos, and people didn't do to other people the sort of things that had been done inside that house.

He stared out at the shifting landscape, vividly imagining the scene inside the Davenport home . . . the bodies of the man, his wife . . . their children.

It was inconceivable that such horror lay only a few hundred feet away, separated from him by a couple of walls, a lawn. The rain.

He hadn't been allowed inside, but his mind could readily construct it all: the blood, the violence. The obscenity of death.

How could people—even *insane* people—commit such atrocities?

Mrs. Davenport and the two little boys had been killed while they slept. Apparently Mr. Davenport had then lain down on the bed and drawn the knife across his own throat. The word was they had died "almost" instantly.

But wouldn't even seconds be an eternity with your lifesblood pumping out?

According to one of the two patrolmen who were first on the scene, Mrs. Davenport and both children had lived long enough to "thrash about some" before they died. Mr. Davenport, on the other hand, had been lying serenely on his side of the bed, covers tucked neatly around him, blood soaking through pillow and mattress, pooling on the floor. "Damndest thing I ever saw," the patrolman had told him.

J.J. had wanted to question the man further, but Lieutenant Cutter had vetoed that, along with the possibility of getting anything more from anyone else at the scene, by clamping down the lid on talking to the press. An "official statement" would be issued by the department later in the day.

Some kind of coverup? J.J. wondered. Or just Cutter being Cutter.

Whichever the case, it looked as if he'd have to be content with what he had for the moment. Which was enough for the evening edition and should make front-page news. Now all he had to do was go down to the office and write it up.

The thought gave him little pleasure. It would be hard to write about the children.

Suddenly impatient, he revved the engine and honked his horn, miffed that the TV-2 van still hadn't backed out of the way. Did they think everybody could do remotes?

He flicked on the heater. Warm air flooded the interior of the car, chasing away the dampness and chill. It felt more like March today than May.

J.J. had seen Dal drive up earlier, accompanied by a woman J.J. didn't think he recognized, though it was hard to tell with her raincoat hood pulled up around her face. She must have been official; they'd let her go in.

At least he didn't think Dal could get away with squiring a date around a crime scene.

Scratch that. Dal wouldn't act so irresponsibly.

Maybe she was a new, much-needed addition to the task force. He sure hoped so. Dal could use the extra manpower.

More to the point—what was the drug task force doing on the scene? Was Dal's visit impromptu or official?

J.J. frowned. Not much chance of finding out with Cutter in the way.

Oh, well. He'd run that angle down later. Right now he needed to be outa here. He'd have to get this story written up soon if it was going to make the evening edition. And there was some additional background research that'd have to be done on the victims.

He craned his neck to see if the van had backed up enough for him to get by—

The door on the passenger's side jerked open.

J.J. swung around.

A man was climbing into the car. Small, wiry—he wore a soiled stadium coat, an old toboggan pulled down over his ears. The smell was rank.

J.J. recoiled from the first whiff, so it was a moment before he uttered an indignant "Hey—"

By then, the intruder had gotten fully into the car and slammed the door shut. Turning around, he plunged his hands into the pockets of his coat.

J.J. drew in a sharp breath, following the man's actions with his eyes. What was about to happen here? What was going down?

But the hands stayed where they were. The man looked at J.J. and grinned.

Willie Dee.

J.J. released his breath. He recognized the little slimeball now, though he looked as if he'd aged a couple of decades since J.J. had seen him last. What in blazes was he doing out here?

"Something I can do for you, Willie?"

"Yeah." Willie regarded him smugly. "You can listen. Got a message for ya. Real important. Tol' me to tell ya."

"Who? Tell me what?"

Willie giggled. It sounded strange. J.J. searched the grinning face, trying to fathom just what it was about the little man that suddenly made him edgy.

"Oh, you'll find out soon enough. When he wants ya to, you'll know." Willie giggled again. "Right now he just said to tell ya that he's comin'. Comin' for you all."

He shot J.J. a look that made goosebumps break out on J.J.'s skin.

"Who's coming? What in blazes are you talking about?"

J.J. tried to make his voice sound harsh, and succeeded. Barely. Had Willie flipped his lid? Was he sitting in the front seat of his car with a certifiable crazy?

Maybe he should open the door, flag down a couple of uniforms . . . He reached for the door handle.

But before he could grip it, Willie had whipped around and shoved his own door open.

The little man bolted from the car, slamming the door behind him.

"Whew." J.J. released the breath he'd been holding, and felt his stomach muscles start to unknot. "Now *that* was truly weird."

Tension began to subside. He turned back around, saw he was grasping the steering wheel with what amounted to a death grip. The knuckles on his right hand were white and stiff.

He relaxed his hand, peeled his fingers off one by one, flexing them a few times.

"Totally weird," he murmured again, hardly crediting the scene that had just transpired. Willie Dee was obviously operating on half a tank these days.

But why in the name of Jehovah Jones had the little street urchin been all the way out here?

Could he have something to do with what had happened inside that house?

Behind him, the driver of the van honked to let J.J. know he'd moved enough for him to get by.

J.J. waved an acknowledgment and backed the Ford out, executing a three-point turn at the end of the driveway. It would take him the longer, but faster, way around the block—and the traffic snarl that always marked a disaster scene. He needed to get down to his office and write this story up as soon as possible.

He'd think about Crazy Willie later. Get in touch with Dal; it was something the police should probably know.

All the way downtown he put pieces of the story together in his mind, so that by the time he reached his desk it was practically written. He set the research department to work getting background information on the victims, and started keying it in. By lunchtime he was through and hungry from no breakfast.

He put a call in to Dal, who wasn't back yet, decided to take a run by the courthouse, maybe see if Charlotte Ramsey was free for lunch. He needed a change of scenery.

She was in court.

J.J. slid into a bench beside Mitch MacAlister, who was wearing a red power tie with his jeans and checked shirt, and a pained expression, no doubt from having to sit overly long on these wooden benches. He should take a cue from the Court Watchers, they brought cushions.

J.J. glanced around, but didn't spot any of his particular favorites from the citizen's group. Pity. The elderly members, who called themselves the Gray Blades, could add shine to even the dullest session of criminal court.

He remembered the time they'd brought score cards to a sentencing—it had been during the Olympics—and given Judge Harrolds a 2.0. It was a wonder they hadn't drawn contempt citations. As it was, the elderly scorekeepers had been escorted from the courtroom and barred from ever monitoring one of Judge Harrolds's sessions again.

"What are you doing here?" Mitch hissed.

J.J. shook his head, zeroing in on the reason for his impromptu visit: Charlotte Ramsey, poised beside the witness stand, looking wonderful in a pale gray suit and crisp white blouse.

Whatever else Mitch was murmuring faded into oblivion.

Her short blond hair swung softly toward her face, framing delicate features made outstanding by a creamy complexion and dynamite blue eyes. She seemed to literally glow with health, vitality, perfection. She was questioning the witness in a voice warm and full of sympathy for something that had been done sometime or another by somebody other than her client. How could the jury not agree?

Too bad he wasn't on it. He sighed.

"Yeah, me too," Mitch interjected, prompting a sharp glance from J.J. He'd considered Dal as possible competition. But Mitch . . . ?

"She's not your type," he growled softly.

Mitch looked at him as if he'd spoken in tongues. "Huh?"

J.J. realized Mitch's comment hadn't referred to Charlotte Ramsey at all. He relaxed and shook his head. "Never mind."

"Anyway, how *do* you stand it?" Mitch continued. "There's been no action since I got here, none at all. Where's the fiery prosecution? Where's the impassioned defense? I've been sitting here for nearly an hour and there's been *no* drama—*no* witty dialogue—most of all *no* break for lunch. When do they eat around here?"

"Patience." J.J. grinned. "They'll break soon. See the judge checking his watch?" You learned to read the signs after a while. "As for the rest of it, you gotta remember this isn't *L.A. Law.*"

"Ain't that the truth." Mitch retreated into silence.

J.J. smiled, returning his attention to the front of the courtroom where the attorney for the defense was winding up her questioning. Apparently she'd also picked up on the judge's fidgets.

Actually, J.J. rather enjoyed his stints in the courtroom, and was a more frequent visitor than the job required. Mitch was wrong. There was drama here, and passion too, and wit. Maybe not as flamboyant or jam-packed as an hour of *L.A. Law,* but it was here. You just had to look for it, sometimes on the slant—more *Twin Peaks* style.

He liked to people-watch, and all types passed through a courtroom. The cases were like temporary windows into their worlds, sometimes funny, often sad. Helped him with his writing. And it wasn't just the witnesses who drew his attention.

He remembered the time he'd noticed several jurors looking as if they were trying hard not to laugh. The case wasn't particularly funny, so J.J. had caught up with a couple of them afterward to see if he could find out what was.

It seemed that during lunch break one of the jurors had purchased a goldfish to replace the one her small daughter had found dead that morning. She'd brought it back into court with her, safely packed—she thought—in a water-tight plastic bag, never thinking about the limited amount of oxygen in the water. Several hours into the afternoon session, the goldfish had begun to asphyxiate and thrash about, causing all these horrible sounds.

Luckily, final arguments were by then being presented, and the jury was soon dismissed to the deliberation room just in the nick of time. The goldfish lived.

The story didn't. J.J. had written it up, but the city editor had vetoed it. Said it didn't belong in the Crime Report section and hadn't enough substance for a feature article. *Bet Lewis Grizzard wouldn't have had a problem,* J.J. had thought sourly at the time. But even snappy headline suggestions such as JURY JOKES WHILE GOLD-FISH CROAKS or VERDICT IN: NOT KILT HE could sway the boss's decision.

The piece resided now, along with similar rejects, at the bottom of J.J.'s dead drawer at home. Maybe one of these days he'd gather them all together into a book. *Hmmm . . .*

He shifted in his seat—these benches *were* a little hard on the rump. But it shouldn't be much longer now.

Basking in the rosy glow of anticipation, he began mentally plotting his course up the aisle, around the wooden railing, over to the defense table—where Charlotte would be gathering up her papers, putting them into her briefcase. He'd walk up to her and smile, say something simple and direct like "Have lunch with me?" She'd flash him a look of pure joy, reply "I'd love to." End of plot. Beginning of a beautiful relationship.

"Wake up, man. I said, do you wanta go grab a sandwich or not?"

J.J. blinked, stared up at Mitch who was standing there towering over him.

Oh, no! Frantically jumping to his feet, he scanned the thinning crowd for Charlotte Ramsey.

Gone.

Great.

He plopped back down. Incredible. Utterly incredible. He'd sat here daydreaming like a goof while she'd—

"Yo, J.J. You gonna sit here all day or go eat?"

"Yes. No. I mean— You go on ahead. There's something else I've got to do."

Mitch shrugged. "Suit yourself." He turned and sauntered out.

J.J. exited the courtroom by the side door closest to the rest rooms. Maybe she'd stopped by to powder her nose.

He hung around for a while, checked the courthouse cafeteria a few times until the cashier began eyeing him suspiciously, and finally decided she'd left the building and was probably having lunch with someone else, somewhere else. Oh, well.

"Bet this wouldn't happen to Jehovah Jones," he muttered as he donned his rain gear and dashed across the waterlogged street to his car.

On second thought, he ducked into the Downtown Deli on the off chance Charlotte Ramsey might be lunching there. No such luck. He was beginning to feel a bit like Charlie Brown in pursuit of the little red-haired girl.

He settled for chicken salad on an oat-bran sub roll, with a dill pickle and a glass of milk on the side, then headed across town to the police station where he hoped to catch Dal.

He struck out there too. Dal was still out. No idea when he'd be back in.

Frustrated with the world at large, J.J. decided he might as well wait. The day was half shot anyway.

They were supposed to make that "official statement" on the Davenport killings sometime this afternoon, so he needed to hang around for that. And Dal might drift back in at any time, the bum. J.J. owed him a big one for taking his car, and he'd have to spend some quality time later thinking about that.

Meanwhile he could make some notes for the next Jehovah Jones story, since the first one had sort of petered to a standstill at the moment—no pun intended. Well, maybe. Anyway, it wouldn't hurt to get a jump start on number two.

Locating a chair in a relatively quiet corner of the downstairs lobby—near the press room where he could keep an ear peeled for the announcement to be made—he sat down and pulled out his notebook and pen.

This one was going to be "Jehovah Jones and the Ten Amendments." He grinned smugly as he flipped open the small fine-lined pad, thoroughly pleased with the titles he had for these stories. Good titles were very important.

He thumbed past a few pages that already had notes jotted down on them, searching for an unused part—

Something caught his eye.

He flipped back a page, puzzled at a notation written sideways in heavy red marker. He didn't remember making that.

He turned the pad around and stared at the large block letters that made up some sort of a silly three-line verse—they looked like something a child had done. Not his handwriting at all.

Where the heck had this come from?

Scraping a fingernail over one of the letters, he discovered that the writing was in crayon, not Magic Marker as he'd thought at first. *What gives?* Was this some sort of joke?

Frowning, he reread the rhyme:

> *DE BONEMAN WATCH*
> *DE BONEMAN SEE*
> *DE BONEMAN COMIN FOR YOU AN ME*

De Boneman he can raise the dead
Everybody do what de Boneman said

SIXTEEN

Cherry woke up in the dark. She couldn't see anything, couldn't feel anything. Fear gripped her insides like the sudden, agonizing need for crack.

Where was she?

She tried to move, and couldn't. Tried to cry out, but nothing seemed to work.

Oh, God. What had happened to her? What was going on?

Panic swept through her. For a moment she was caught up in a frenzy of mindless horror—trying to remember, terrified at what might have been done to her, even more afraid of what would come next. *She couldn't remember. She couldn't remember!*

But after a moment—or an eternity—in which nothing happened, the wave of panic began to subside.

She could think. But her thoughts were muddled, fuzzy, swimming beneath the heavy darkness like slippery fish—when she tried to grab one, it wriggled away.

Thick darkness pressed against her body, her face, smothering and solid, squeezing down on her like—

hands!

She remembered those! Hands around her neck—choking off her air!

Then what? What had happened next?

Was she dead?

No. No, of course not. She couldn't be dead.

Could she?

She lay there trying desperately to remember, find parts to the puzzle and fit them together so that she could understand what was going on. But terror kept getting in the way.

Pieces of thoughts swam by, fragmented memories drifting

through her head. She tried to reach out and grab one—another. The effort made her dizzy. She felt as if she were going to be sick.

Surprisingly enough, that reassured her a bit. At least she could feel *something,* nausea being better than nothing at all.

But she didn't want to throw up, so she fought it. She'd always hated throwing up—the way it burned her throat and nose, filled her mouth like lumpy oatmeal, the horrible taste afterward.

Even when she was a child, she'd fought throwing up whenever she got sick. When her sister would set the old slop jar by their bed—"so you won't puke all over the floor"—she'd fought it because her sister would never come and get the jar and rinse it out afterward and the smell would keep making her throw up all over again. But sometimes she just couldn't make it to the outside privy.

She couldn't remember.

She lay as still as she could, trying not to vomit, trying to listen, to hear anything that might tell her where she was, what was going on—*why couldn't she move? why couldn't she see!*—but she'd think about that later, when she was out of here, not now. Another surge of nausea filled her. She battled it back down.

Experimentally, she tried to move her hand, only her hand, one finger of one hand. Concentrated on it hard.

Nothing. She felt nothing. Not even what she was lying on— *the floor? a bed? she should be able to tell.* But it was as if she were floating on air, or the water, like one of those isolation tanks she'd read about sometime, somewhere.

Who had done this to her? Why were they doing this to her? She'd never hurt anybody. Never done anything so very wrong, not enough to deserve this.

I'm sorry! her mind shouted to whatever God or devil might be listening. *Please, I'm sorry. I'm sorry! Just get me out of this and I'll be good, I promise.*

She felt swollen with the darkness. Drowning in it.

Buried alive—

Oh, God, could that be it?

Was she shut up in a satin-lined coffin, buried by mistake inside a cement vault under six feet of earth?

She almost went crazy then, mind recoiling from the impact of that image and sending shock waves of terror exploding through her like the screams she couldn't force out.

Where was she? What had happened to her? WHAT?

She wanted to pound her hands against the darkness, claw her way through and out but she couldn't move—*she couldn't move!*

And suddenly an infinitely more horrible thought struck her:

What if she really were dead? What if this was what it was like to be dead and she could lie here forever feeling nothing, doing nothing, *being* nothing at all?

No. Oh please, God, no. I didn't mean to be bad. I just had to get away from Daddy and that dirty tobacco farm, had to try and make it on my own. I didn't mean to turn out like this.

Tears gathered in her eyes. She couldn't even blink them away.

Think, Cherry, think.

She couldn't be dead. When you're dead, you're dead, that's all. She wasn't dead. She just wasn't!

A face floated through her terror—*faces.* In the alley. Those strange men.

Or course! That was it. They had done this to her. They must have given her something, brought her here. She wasn't dead. Wasn't buried alive. This was just a trick gone bad, that's all.

She remembered the handsome man, the others—that big ugly brute with the stupid grin and huge hands. She shuddered inwardly.

Bastard must have choked her unconscious. Shot her up with some weird drug and brought her back here—*wherever here was*—so they could take their time getting their kicks. Nothing more than a bad trick, that's all it was.

Cherry had been involved with bad tricks before—been beaten up a few times, even cut a couple. There'd been more than one pass-around surprise party.

But she'd never known this kind of helplessness before, not even the time that freak had cuffed her to the bathtub and she'd thought for sure he was going to kill her—it could happen that way sometimes, some wacko'd stiff a girl in the bathtub so the blood would go down the drain. And he'd hurt her pretty bad. But somebody'd heard her screaming and called the cops and she'd survived.

She'd survive this too.

Only it was scarier this time, scarier not to see, not to know.

A little whimper tried to escape. It sounded muffled, trapped there inside her head, spinning round and round.

Was she breathing?

Must be.

She just couldn't tell.

She concentrated on opening her mouth, expanding her nostrils and sucking in air, but she didn't know if it worked, though it must be working, even if she couldn't feel her chest moving or the air coming in and out, it must be there.

Maybe they had a gag over her mouth—*sure, that was it*—a mask over her whole face, maybe, and that's what was making it so hard to breathe, to see.

She tried to feel the gag, tried to trace the edges of it, locate where the knot was tied beneath her head.

Nothing.

But she *was* breathing—she *was.*

Wasn't she?

She couldn't feel her chest at all. Couldn't tell if it was moving up and down, in and out, *breathe,* dammit! *Breathe!*

A sob was aching to get out; she couldn't make it come.

Someone was coming . . .

Movement. The faint rustle of clothing. The dry, spidery sound—*those goons from the alley?*

She lay there faint with dread that at any moment a knife would plunge down, carve through her skin. She'd heard about that happening, knew there were people out there who did all kinds of crazy stuff. Devil worshipers, or cultists, that might be who they were. Drugheads who tortured their victims, cut them up in pieces, drank their blood. She'd even heard sometimes they ate their victims' hearts.

Oh, God! Don't let that happen to me—please, please! Don't let that happen.

Movement again, closer now.

Don't hurt me, she silently begged. *Please don't hurt me, I'll do anything you say, just don't hurt me.* If only she could tell them that.

A hand brushed her cheek.

123

She recoiled—physically? mentally?—feeling a shock wave spread outward from the spot like ripples on a pond.

Who was it? Who was in here with her? Was it those goons?

What were they about to do?

Who's there? she wanted to say and couldn't.

The sob swelled in her chest like an inflating water balloon.

Again, a touch, fingers stroking her breast. They crawled like bugs across her skin. She felt her nipple pucker. Realized she was naked.

And something else: she'd felt those fingers caressing her skin. Felt them!

For just a moment, the panic in her subsided and reason took hold: *A trick, that's all it was, just a john, and the drug they'd given her was beginning to wear off, and they weren't going to kill her, just some wacko who got off on fear, but it was just another trick and Jelly'd probably set it all up, the bastard, get paid a bundle, he would, sure as shit, and she'd never see a penny of it, but she'd be all right, she'd be all right—*

She braced herself for what would happen next, trying to get ready for the pain, prepare for the hurt that was about to come—but nothing happened. No sound. Nothing.

All part of the setup, Cherry, supposed to make you more afraid.

And she was afraid—she *was*—she WAS—oh, why didn't they come on and get it over with? Why didn't they just do it and be done?

She strained to hear the sound of breathing, but everything had gone silent.

Were they still here? Standing over her, looking down at her naked body, getting off on her fear?

She could have screamed with the helplessness of it—if she could scream. *Why couldn't she scream?*

Please, God! Let me live through this and I'll be good, I promise. I'll quit the streets, I really will.

Minutes trickled by. Hours. *Days*—

"Cherry . . . ?"

Her mind jerked to attention at the sound of her name. It came again—

"Cherry?"

—real? Imagined?

Yes? she wanted to shout, stabbing blindly at the dark. *Yes, I hear you. What do you want?*

"You will do something for me."

The voice was cultured. Soft as snowflakes lighting on her skin. She'd heard it before. In the alley—the handsome black man.

She was cold.

Anything, she sobbed. *I'll do anything you say, only let me out of here. Let me out of the dark—*

She was a child again, crouched in the tangle of weeds and bushes at the side of the porch beyond where the light fell, feeling the night things crawling around her and begging her daddy to let her come in, come in from the dark and she'd do whatever he asked . . .

She waited in torment as the silence loomed.

Where was he? Where had he gone? Had the whole thing been a dream?

No, don't leave me. Come back. Come back!

Suddenly the darkness seemed to shift a little, growing pale in one spot. Gradually the space lightened, grew wider, deeper, a corridor stretching from the endless night. It shimmered brilliantly, like heat waves above white desert sand.

She watched it hungrily, fear of what she'd been through surpassing her fear of what might come. She felt as if she'd been drowning in a sea of night and this would be her only chance, this would be her only way out of the darkness if she could just manage to reach it—walk through.

A man stepped into the light, his shadow eclipsing the sun. Slowly, his face took shape.

It was the man from the alley. The handsome man.

He'd come to save her. Take her from the darkness. Bring her into the light.

He stepped nearer.

His eyes . . .

She was drifting . . . drifting . . . into the warmth of his gaze.

Gently he pulled her toward him, slowly lifting her from the terrible cold black sea.

She began to cry, huge, hiccuping gulps, so thankful he'd come to rescue her, wanting only to hold him, love him, do anything he said.

"Anything," she gasped as he drew her in. "Just tell me what you want me to do. I'll do anything you say . . ."

He smiled. And the world was full of light.

SEVENTEEN

Jackie Swann climbed behind the wheel of the battered old Ford LTD, closed the door, then sat there a moment before inserting the key into the ignition and starting the engine. Behind her the brightly lit house stood elegant and slightly aloof, as though it, like her husband, Philip, were giving her the cold shoulder for not staying home tonight.

Home. The house had never truly felt like home to her. She wished they still lived in that quaint little carriage house they'd moved into when they first got married, before the law-firm partnership, before the money and position and Philip's "image" had intruded into their lives.

But eventually they'd outgrown the cottage—because of her pregnancy as well as Philip's rising career—and moving had seemed the only logical choice.

Sometimes she wondered if they could ever truly be happy again, even back in that small cottage.

She started the car and drove off, not looking back, feeling as if the house watched her with satisfaction as she drove away. Or disdain—for the battered old car she used when working under-cover.

Philip hated it when she drove this car, particularly when she left it outside where the neighbors could see. She supposed he had a right to feel that way, it did scuz up the neighborhood. She'd have to remember to pull into the garage when she got back.

She imagined what the neighbors might think if they knew some of the places this car took her, and grinned ironically at the thought.

Philip lived in constant dread that someone who knew them might run into her on one of her jaunts—while she was dressed as a prostitute, in the company of drug addicts, or worse. She'd tried to convince him this was highly unlikely, and that even if it should occur, the person would probably be too busy trying to keep from being recognized to bother identifying her. The humor had escaped Philip. In fact, humor and Philip seemed to have parted company back around the time Bush had become President.

Their acquaintances and neighbors, and Philip's business associates, knew she worked for the State Bureau of Investigation, but most had automatically assumed she was clerical or technical, a charade Philip carefully nurtured and Jackie didn't dispute. Why bother? It was something he could live with, they both could live with; and if she occasionally had to bite the bullet while some oaf made cracks about bored housewives and fluff jobs, it was a necessary grief.

Night swelled as she passed from the stately, well-manicured and lighted streets to the darker two-lane road that led to the interstate.

It was a weird feeling, this sense of not belonging in her own home, with her own family. She loved her husband and son dearly, she honestly did; but too often she felt apart from them, from the life they were living, the plans Philip had so meticulously mapped out.

Philip and his plans. It annoyed him that Jackie didn't automatically fall in with his plan for their lives.

Putting herself in Philip's place, she could see why he would feel annoyed. It wasn't just his plan, after all, it was *their* plan. She'd had a say in everything.

So what was the matter with her?

Philip could give her total financial security, a beautiful home and lifestyle, love. What more did she want?—which was his closing remark to most of their arguments. And she honestly didn't understand her attitude herself sometimes. This was what they'd talked about in that little carriage house. This was what they'd planned for, worked toward, dreamed of. Why did she so stubbornly continue to hold down a job that took her out at nights, drained her mentally and physically, even risked her life?

Certainly not for the pay, Jackie thought ironically.

So what was she arguing for? The right to dress up like a junkie or a hooker? To leave her husband and son, her home, in the middle of the night to go into some of the roughest parts of town? To involve herself with drug dealers and psychopaths and school kids who would murder you over a pair of gym shoes? Was that what she was fighting to hold on to?

Yes.

But why? She could be home, spending her time with the two people she loved most in the world. She could be going to bed at a reasonable hour, making love with her husband, spending afternoons with her son. And what about those art courses she'd always wanted to take? And the stack of books she'd been wanting to read?

She could join the spa. Buy season tickets to the theater without worrying about having to miss most of the performances. Get a part-time job, if she really wanted to work.

So what was the problem?

Hers was a job that needed doing, she kept telling herself. And that was true. But the real truth was that she was afraid to give up her job, afraid that if she did she'd gradually be absorbed into Philip's world and lose her own identity. She didn't want to just be somebody's wife, somebody's mother. She had a right to her own career, she'd worked hard enough for it, by God—and she was good at her job. Why should she give it up? Wasn't that what women had fought for?

So far, she'd managed to maintain, though at times the house seemed like an armed camp waiting for the first shot to be fired. Thank God for their treasure of a housekeeper, who allowed her to keep the kind of hours her job often required. If it weren't for Mrs. Brady . . .

Jackie picked up speed as she merged from the entrance ramp into the steady stream of traffic on Interstate 40. The old car looked like a wimp but it was fine-tuned and reliable, fast enough to give her options, heavy enough to afford some protection should the need arise.

It would take her about twenty minutes to reach Phoenix City. Another fifteen to meet up with Detective Reid and his contact, then move into position. That would put it about ten o'clock.

She was okay for time.

They'd arranged to meet in the parking lot at the Friendly Road K Mart. The contact—a man named Lonnie Talbert—would get into her car, and they'd drive down to State Street and start "making the scene." Reid would follow, working surveillance.

She continued to think of him as Reid, though she called him Dal easily enough. It was always wise to maintain some emotional distance when working with a member of the opposite sex, keep it cool. Physical proximity over an extended period of time could bring on complications. Whether sexual bias or just plain sex, potential problems often lurked in the wings.

She had encountered both situations in the past, plus a couple more, and felt prepared to handle anything. But Jackie knew she was a little emotionally vulnerable just now, and Lieutenant Reid was a very attractive man. She wasn't immune to a good body and great pair of eyes. But what she didn't need—or want—was a very attractive man complicating her already way too complicated life.

She'd sensed Reid's spark of interest the night they'd met, and had immediately put up her guard. She'd already heard about his reputation.

Fine. It wasn't a problem, she told herself. And if it became one, she could handle it.

Nothing would be allowed to interfere with their work. They were professionals. They would act like professionals. And if Reid chose otherwise, he'd be making a big mistake.

To be fair, he'd said or done nothing so far to suggest they be anything more than partners in crime-fighting. And she'd made her wife-and-mother status completely clear that first night. Maybe

129

she was too quick, anticipating a situation that would never materialize. Reputations could be undeserved.

In fact, Jackie had sensed a certain antagonism on his part toward working with her—controlled, but present. Of course, that could be male bias, like his insisting that they drive his car rather than hers; some men couldn't relinquish even symbolic control to a woman.

Whichever the case, she meant to keep their relationship strictly textbook, and hoped he did too.

Jackie didn't want to become a statistic in somebody's computer file. The divorce rate was high among law-enforcement personnel. She didn't want to fall victim to the odds. She'd fight to keep her marriage intact.

Even if it meant giving up her job?

She frowned at that thought, switching back to her earlier contemplation. For a while now she'd lived with the possibility that Philip would suddenly decide to issue an ultimatum, force her into making a choice. If it came to that, she'd make one. But she didn't need an indiscretion clouding the issue—though God knew she could use some good sex, she thought with a twinge. Lately that area of her life had been cursory at best. Philip used sex as a weapon.

She exited the interstate, turning her mind back to Dallas Reid and the job at hand. She felt a pang of unease, but anxiety at this stage of the game was not uncommon, and had a way of keeping you sharp. At best, it took a while to become comfortable with your cover. And your backup. And sometimes the latter could be the most hazardous of all.

On the downside, Reid appeared to be something of a hotshot, a wild card, not keen on teamwork, unhappy taking a backseat role. On the plus, he was obviously good at his job, with a high arrest—and conviction—record, and well liked and respected within department ranks. Except for Cutter, apparently, though she tended to disregard that; she'd met his type before. She put more credence in Chief Clifton's assessment that Reid was one of his best men, though a bit unorthodox at times.

She didn't question Reid's ability to respond to any situation, which was a big plus to an undercover agent. But if he did have to act, would he act responsibly? She hoped so. Her life might depend on it.

Working undercover was a high-risk job, a balancing act that put you at risk from both sides of the fence: the bad guys if they made you; your own people if they fucked things up.

Jackie grimaced as her mind began automatically shifting to the gutter language of the street. A bit disconcerting, how easy it came sometimes. Often harder switching back again, but then she'd always known it was easier being bad than good. It took work to be civilized.

She and Reid had spent a good deal of time together yesterday and today, setting up her cover, getting a feel for each other's patterns, each other's quirks, talking to the contact. If she'd had serious misgivings, she could have begged off the assignment at any time.

The K Mart loomed on her right. She slowed, pulled into the lot, spotted Reid's car right away. Sometimes she wondered if their undercover cars didn't mark them as much as wearing a uniform would. These days it seemed even the lowest-level drug dealers drove high-dollar Mercedeses and BMW's.

Jackie pulled up beside Reid's car. Reid got out, as did the man on the passenger side: Reid's informer and her intro into the State Street scene—Lonnie Talbert.

The man emitted a long, low whistle as he closed the gap between them, which she ignored.

"Shirley." Reid greeted her using the name she'd assumed for this case, the name of a favorite instructor at the academy. She never used her real name on the street. She nodded in return, then switched her gaze to the informant, doing a quick spot evaluation of the man.

Reid had expressed confidence that Lonnie could handle this, and they'd briefed him thoroughly; but this was performance night, not a run-through, and Jackie relied heavily on her own instincts. After all, she was the one going on-line here.

The man had been good-looking, once. Drugs and the street had taken care of that. He was still young; his file said twenty-six, though he looked forty. An old forty. A football player's husky build had shrunk to a husk, clothes hanging on him like a scarecrow's. High, aristocratic cheekbones only emphasized the hollows above and beneath. His eyes were bloodshot and a little spacey—probably just had a hit. But he seemed reasonably steady, and full of his standard bravado.

He saw her inspecting him and grinned, gave her another good once-over in return, running a jaunty hand through lank, thinning hair that Jackie guessed had once been thick and wavy blond. The gesture was ludicrous, pathetic.

She smiled faintly, wondering if her expression betrayed the disgust and pity she felt, and switched her gaze back to Reid. "Everything a go?"

"Let's do it." The words, and tone, were casual, but Reid's eyes flickered briefly with anticipation.

Jackie felt a sliver of apprehension, like a cold breath of wind on the back of her neck. She didn't trust that kind of look. She'd seen it before—in the eyes of glory hounds, the ones who liked to take it to the edge, play in the danger zone because only there did they feel truly alive.

Though Reid's case files didn't brand him a health hazard—at least he'd never put any of the people he worked with in the hospital big-time or got them killed—there was a strong thread of evidence running through the reports, and his own dossier, that he brought a certain high-risk profile to the job.

It was not an unheard-of attitude.

She clamped down on her nagging doubts and glanced at Lonnie again. "Get in."

He came around and climbed cockily into the LTD, grinning at her suggestively and immediately sliding an arm along the back of her seat. She'd expected something like this, and ignored it. Reid got back into his car, and they drove off.

At the edge of the parking lot, their cars veered in different directions, hers north, his west—he'd circle back around to come onto State Street from the opposite side. It was simply an added precaution that they not be seen driving up close together.

"Let's get something straight right now, Lonnie," she said, keeping her voice neutral and her eyes on the road. "You put your hands on me when it's necessary for the cover, that's fine, no problem. But you better be careful where you put them—and until then, keep your fucking hands to yourself."

She felt the fingers that had crept onto her shoulder move away again.

Night spread its arms once more as they left the day-bright lights of the K Mart behind. She followed the route Reid had mapped out for her, keeping a sharp eye to speed and turnoffs. Wouldn't do to get pulled over by a traffic cop, or wander too far off the designated path, though she'd always had a pretty good sense of direction, and he'd set her a fairly easy course. Keep It Simple—the number-one rule of the game.

After the put-down, Lonnie had kept quiet. Jackie was glad. Making small talk with a drughead informer was about as attractive to her as concocting social chitchat at one of Philip's business gatherings.

Streetlights became heavy again. Traffic picked up as they turned onto Glenwood, came up on State.

She swung a right.

"There it is." Lonnie pointed to a glitzy sign on their left: Godiva's. It looked like what it was—a topless bar. She spotted a parking place half a block down and pulled into the curb.

They got out.

It wasn't unusual for a woman to be seen chauffering her guy around down here, especially a guy like Lonnie who'd probably lost his license before he'd lost his virginity and wouldn't be able to afford a car anyway. Drugs took their toll on one's budget.

She also fit into the scene with her choice of dress: a crotch-length skirt and tank top—no bra—lots of cheap jewelry and a denim jacket with fringe. Black tights, and her one concession to comfort and efficiency: low-heeled shoes. Her makeup was flashy, her hair was a frizzy cloud. Philip had taken one look at her tonight and walked from the room without a word.

She couldn't understand it. Lonnie certainly seemed to approve.

The street was alive with people and music. Loud talk, boisterous laughter cut back and forth through the air. She smelled onions cooking, and old sweat, and the occasional sweet whiff of a joint.

She didn't look around for Reid. He'd be somewhere nearby—

she had to rely on that. It was his job to keep tabs on her. Not vice versa.

Letting Lonnie throw his arm around her, they walked into the bar.

The place was dark and stuffy. Bump-and-grind music pumped from giant speakers mounted along the walls, the heavy bass line thudding like a huge, lumbering heart. It made her body vibrate, set her teeth on edge.

Meeting a drug seller in a public place was out of the norm. Most of the time it was in an apartment or motel room, on a street corner, or even in their car. Lonnie had explained that the guy was uneasy right now about making initial contact with a new buyer in an isolated spot and had insisted on meeting them here. But was Lonnie playing them straight? She damn sure hoped so.

Sweat began seeping from her pores in the overheated, smoke-filled atmosphere.

She made a quick assessment of the general layout, located all the exits. It was second nature for her to do that—even when she was out with friends or Philip—doubly so when she was working with an unknown team. You relied on yourself most of all in the field.

Lonnie steered them to a table.

He pulled his rickety wooden chair up close to hers and, when the waitress came over, bought them both a drink—with the money Reid had given him. His body began moving in time with the music, gaze roaming from one near-nude dancer to the next. Every few beats he'd just happen to bump up against her, rub a shoulder or the side of his arm against her breast.

Jackie allowed it, sitting there breathing in smoke, her companion's musky scent, her own sweat. Suddenly Philip's plan for their lives was looking more attractive by the moment.

She saw Reid stroll through the door. He sauntered up to the bar and straddled a stool. Ordered a beer. The bartender brought him a frothy glass.

Jackie switched her gaze back to Lonnie, laughing as though at something he'd said. She let her head rest momentarily on his shoulder, and he used the opportunity to scoot a little nearer with his chair, draping his arm around the back of hers. He looked as if, despite her warning, he might attempt to kiss her. She playfully ducked away, pretending to take a sip of her drink, some of which she sloshed on the table in a calculated move.

Time passed in an endless barrage of music, babble, heat. Her nose became inured to the smells. Her heavily made-up face felt as if it might crack from all the smiling and inane chitchat, melt from sweat. No one but the waitress came near them.

"So, what's the deal here, Lonnie?" Jackie asked, as the waitress left a third Scotch/rocks on the table in front of him.

"Don't worry, Crick'll show." Lonnie nervously gripped the drink, took a gulp. "I told you he's been kinda jittery lately; it's these drug dealers getting killed—his own supplier right down the street from here just a few nights ago. Crick's probably watching us now, checking you out. He'll be around."

But Jackie didn't like the feel of things. It didn't look good when a new customer kept hanging around a place waiting for a meet, even if that was the deal. Made them look too conspicuous, overly anxious, maybe, which in turn could arouse the suspicion of the supplier.

They were all ultraparanoid anyway, these drug scums, the least little thing could set them off. And it was a guessing game which little thing might do it. Stay too long; go too soon. You practically had to be psychic to know.

She made a decision. "Let's go."

She stood, waiting for Lonnie to slug down the rest of his drink, then join her, reluctantly, as they threaded the gantlet of tables, chairs, and people. He cast a long, leering glance at the redheaded dancer he'd been eyeing most of the night, until Jackie nudged him sharply, as though jealous, and pulled him away.

"If you'll pardon me a moment," he said, sounding snide rather than polite, "I need to take a piss."

Jackie accompanied him down the narrow hall and entered the door on her left while he went right. Might as well take advantage.

Light bombarded her from the naked bulb in the fixture above the sink. It took a moment for her eyes to readjust.

The two-stall toilet appeared empty. As a precaution, she opened both doors before entering the second. Not that she really expected to be accosted in here, but there was always the chance, and it was safer to stay wary at all times, even when off duty.

It annoyed Philip that she always insisted on taking the seat facing the door whenever they ate out at a restaurant or went to a bar, any public place. Like locating all the exits, she did it almost by rote. If she ever once broke the habit, even when it didn't count, it might cause her to break it when it did.

The noise level had receded as the door to the hallway swung shut. Now the music vibrated a dull rumble in the walls, sounding like the rush of tiny feet.

She had the sudden, revolting thought that the walls were teeming with cockroaches, and it was their scuttling about that she heard, and that any moment now their sheer weight of numbers would cause the plaster to crack and break and they'd all come swarming out—thousands of them—pouring over the sink and stalls and floor.

Good God, what a thought.

There was just something about the bathrooms in these places.

She relieved herself, squatting over the toilet seat rather than sitting on it—her mother had always warned her never to sit on a strange toilet seat, and this was stranger than most. Wiping herself with tissues from her purse—these bathrooms never had any toilet paper—she went out to the sink and turned the water on to wash her hands, glancing in the mirror as she finished.

A woman stood behind her.

Jackie managed to keep from spinning around, but she couldn't help the startled jump. She hadn't heard the woman come in. She hadn't heard anything at all.

Except the pounding rock beat, which of course could have drowned out everything else.

The woman's face was heavily made up, not surprising, but her skin looked pasty-white and artificial beneath the bleached-blond hair. It was as though she'd used a thick pancake foundation that was several shades too light for her skin tone and ladled it on. Her pallor made her bright red lips look garish, like overripe cherries. They glistened in the mirror, as if she'd just applied lip gloss or finished licking them.

She grinned at Jackie, staring back at her in the glass—*how long* had they been standing here, staring at one another? Jackie smiled faintly in response and turned around.

The woman was disappearing into one of the stalls—was actually already inside it, the door was nearly through closing by the time Jackie looked around.

Had it taken her that long to turn around?

Jackie felt slightly off kilter, as though she had a slight buzz on. It couldn't be from the drinks, she'd only taken a sip or two. Maybe it was all the smoke.

She took a moment to wet a tissue and run it around her neck, pat her face. She couldn't do much more without stripping off her makeup. Splashing her face with ice-cold water, which was what she wanted to do, was entirely out of the question.

She kept hoping the woman would reappear so she could get another look at her; she wanted to see her one more time, there was something so odd about the way she'd stared at Jackie. But there was no sound or movement in the toilet stall, and Jackie couldn't stay in the bathroom forever. She left.

Lonnie stood waiting for her outside the door.

"Took you long enough," he said huffily, striding away from her toward the exit. The hit must be wearing off.

She followed silently, breathing deeply when they got outside to clear her head and lungs.

Dal chugged down the rest of his third beer and slid off the stool as soon as he saw Jackie and Lonnie make their way toward the door of the club.

At last. It felt as though he'd been sitting here all night.

Stuffing a couple of bills beneath his empty mug, he began pushing through the crowd that stood bunched around the bar. He hated doing this. Hated playing backup, sitting here twiddling his thumbs while someone else took the lead.

But there wasn't a damn thing he could do about it but follow along like a good little doggie.

Shit.

He didn't know what had happened to Lonnie's contact man. Could be any number of things, all of them innocent.

He just hoped to shit Jackie had a handle on the situation.

She'd seemed pretty savvy during their conversations and the preliminary meet with Talbert, and her record showed high marks for field performance—top notch, according to the chief, who'd also given him some background information. She'd been an agent for nine years, working undercover most of that time. So she ought to know what the hell she was doing.

A woman stepped into his path. She was one of a group of singles who were occupying a table to his right, up near the dance floor. He'd noticed them when they came in.

"Hi. My name is Sheila. I was wondering if you might like to—"

"Some other time." He smiled automatically and brushed on past.

"When?" he thought he heard her shout after him, and some female laughter, but he continued his trek through the crowd.

His nose and eyes burned from the cigarette smoke that clotted the air. At least one person nearby was smoking a joint. They had to be pretty drunk or spaced to burn one so openly, he thought, even in here.

It'd be good to get back out on the street. It already felt better to be moving again, though only as far as the next dive. Maybe that's where this thing would get going. Dal wasn't sure how well he could handle an entire night of sitting idle at a bar. The reality was a damn sight worse than the expectation had been. Now he knew for sure: time definitely passed more slowly when you weren't having fun.

At the edge of the throng he turned toward the door leading to the outside world. As he reached for the handle Dal just happened to glance down the narrow strip where the rest rooms were located.

Cherry Pye was emerging from one of the doors.

He checked his forward motion, hesitating only a moment before starting toward her, unwilling to let this opportunity pass. Nothing was going to go down outside in the next few minutes, and besides, he knew where Jackie and Lonnie were headed next.

Cherry spotted him before he'd taken more than a couple of steps her way. She stopped short. Whirled around. Disappeared through the door just beyond the one she'd exited.

Dammit. "Hey!" Dal quickened his pace.

The door she'd gone through led into a hallway lined with storage rooms, unused offices, and the dressing area, a communal room where a couple of the dancers were taking a break. One didn't bother covering her nude torso, eyeing him speculatively, but the other grabbed up a flimsy garment and clutched it to her bare chest—a gesture symbolic rather than effective. The garment merely hung down in the ample valley between her large, pendulous breasts.

"Hey! Get outa here!" She glared at him as he stopped in the doorway. A long mirror behind her was framed by small round light bulbs. Half the bulbs were burned out.

"Did a woman just go past?"

"What's it to ya?" She nailed him with a look that said it all. The other woman just shrugged and grinned, giving him a thorough once-over.

Dal wasted no more time. He sprinted down the hallway, pausing a couple of times to check out a closed room.

At the end of the corridor he stopped, glancing back the way he'd come.

Nothing. Where the hell had she gone?

A breeze tickled his neck.

He turned around again to see the door at his back standing slightly ajar. Had it been that way before?

No matter. This was the end of the line and there were only two possibilities. One: he'd missed her. Two: she'd exited through this door.

He chose the second option.

The door opened into an alley, dark as pitch and narrow as a bigot's thought. Another building faced him. Solid brick, where the light struck it, but old and crumbly, with a patch of slimy green mold gleaming wetly in the refracted light. The dirt out here was pockmarked with puddles of greasy water that looked and smelled like sewer runoff.

Maybe they drained their toilets out here.

He stepped into the alley, trying not to put a foot in the muck. Leaving the door open as a reference point—and for the light it shed—he glanced left, then right, unsure which way to go. He couldn't see very far in either direction.

Footsteps. Off to his right. Moving away.

With a grin, he took off after her, savoring the wind as it knocked the sweat from his face. There was something heady about being in the flow of things. He hated surveillance, hated pulling backup. Even chasing a third-rate hooker down a deserted alley was better than just sitting.

Why was Cherry so bent on running, anyway? Did she think he meant to arrest her? Do her bodily harm?

Yeah, probably. He'd come on a bit strong the other night, and there was precedent, though not with him. But she was a product of the streets, she knew the language.

Maybe she had something to hide. Something worth knowing that she didn't want to tell him and he'd really like to know about.

He hoped that was it. It would sure be good to get a little more out of this than just the chase.

He rounded a corner and nearly knocked himself for a loop when his shoulder impacted with a wall because he didn't swerve fast enough. But he was beginning to get his night eyes.

"Cherry? I'm not going to hurt you, babe. I won't even run you in, just talk, promise."

Yeah, right. He could almost hear her saying it.

Where was this alley taking him? It seemed to be going on forever. Shouldn't he have reached the street by now?

"Hey, Cherry. C'mon, now, hon, I'm getting tired of this."

He stopped running, stood listening again.

No sound. Nothing. Not even the traffic noise out on State.

He looked back over his shoulder for the light from the open door. But he'd come too far. Everything was black. Or dusky gray—moon must be out, though he couldn't find it in the narrow slit above his head.

The silence seemed somehow menacing.

"Fuck that." He'd been watching too many episodes of *Tales from the Crypt.*

He moved forward once more, heard footsteps behind him, echoing his own.

He stopped. Listened.

Nothing.

All around him, the silent walls. Even the breeze had gone.

He reached beneath his jacket and pulled the big Sig Sauer 9mm automatic from its shoulder holster, feeling it slip into his palm with the familiarity and comfort of a cold can of beer. Wherever this alley might be leading him, it didn't hurt to go prepared.

Pumping a round into the chamber, he began walking forward again.

Shadows hovered thickly on either side of him. Darkness in front, at his back. It felt as though the space on either side of him was getting smaller, as though the walls were squeezing in. A silver sliver of moonlight guided his steps.

Someone was in here with him.

Cherry—

Not Cherry. Someone else.

He stopped. Held his breath.

Listened.

The gun in his hand felt heavy as sin. He had to take a piss.

But the sweat had popped back out on his brow, and something was causing the hair on his neck to stand up.

Soundlessly, he blended into the shadows on his left.

Who was in here with him? Why did he suddenly have this feeling of déjà vu—

The photograph. It was like the alley in the photograph.

But that had been a dream.

Hadn't it?

Sweat rolling off him, Dal peered into the shadows, trying to make out a shape, *just like in the photograph . . .*

Buildings loomed on either side.

The wind sprang up again, teasing the sweat on his neck and back, sounding like whispering voices, whispering, whispering . . .

EIGHTEEN

The street was sour with humanity: sour faces, sour smells. Even the gaiety seemed painted on, like a clown face on a corpse.

Jackie shivered as a cool breath of wind brushed her bare skin. Did the atmosphere out here seem suddenly forced? The laughter artificial? The music tinny and coarse?

Maybe it was just the sleaze of Godiva's still clinging to her, like the smoke fumes polluting her lungs. But for a moment Jackie felt as though she'd blundered onto a cheap movie set, complete with third-rate actors rehearsing their parts, reciting their lines by rote.

At least the throbbing rock beat was gone. For the moment.

They crossed the street and headed down the block, Lonnie leading the way. He'd cut the cockiness in favor of a morose silence; could be a drug low or alcohol-induced depression. Great.

She checked a couple of times for Reid, but didn't spot him—not that she expected to every time she looked. Wouldn't be much of a surveillance if he made himself too obvious. Still, she was working with an unknown partner, and she'd like it better if she could see him from time to time.

"In here." Lonnie opened the door of another juke joint and ushered her through.

Music blared, at least as loud as in Godiva's. Trouble was, the place was considerably smaller, so the noise had nowhere to go. Jackie wondered if one day she'd claim a disability for job-related hearing loss.

They sat at the bar this time, Lonnie knocking back a double Scotch before she'd even made a pretense of sipping at her beer. He'd ordered it minus the ice.

"Slow up on the sauce, eh, Lonnie," she murmured in warning, getting an exaggerated grin in response that was more like his old cocksureness. But he made the next one a beer and let it stretch through a couple more bone-jarring cover tunes. He'd taken to biting his nails.

Must be a habit of long standing. She'd noticed his cuticles and the ends of his fingers were raw in places, nails bitten down to the quick. Looked as if they'd been repeatedly and systematically gnawed.

She glanced around, keeping her eye out for Reid—he hadn't come in, or at least she hadn't seen him.

The place was a den of forty-year-old juveniles and failed beauty queens, kids on their way up to losers, losers desperate to delay their slide back down. Mostly overflow from the street, cruisers skimming for whatever action might present itself.

Talk was loud. Beer was cheap. A group of leather-clad lowlifes standing downwind of them began making obscene cracks and tossing propositions at her. There'd been no suggestion of a possible contact.

"You see Crick anywhere?" she murmured, and Lonnie shook his head.

"Let's move on." She touched his arm and saw he was as ready to quit this place as she was.

Back out on the street, he steered them right, swaying a little as he walked. His cockiness had ebbed again, and he looked as though he might be feeling sick, though in his permanently ravaged state it was hard to tell.

"You okay, Lonnie?"

He clipped her a nod, not looking at her, glancing back and forth at the people lining the street ahead. She sensed a certain urgency in him.

"Something wrong?"

"Thought I saw Crick," he murmured.

"Where?"

"Up ahead. Looked like him crossin' down at the far intersection there."

"Coming this way?

"No. Heading the other."

Before she could question him further, Lonnie took off down the block. Cursing softly, she glanced around once more for Reid, then headed after Lonnie; he was setting a quick pace. She kept him in sight, trusting Reid was somewhere close behind. She hadn't seen him come into the last place, though that didn't mean he wasn't there. Just that she hadn't seen him.

He'd better be around.

"Hold up, Lonnie, honey. Wait for me," she called when she saw he was not going to stop, putting a whine in her voice that was worthy of her bimbo outfit. She didn't like this. They'd already gone two—no, three—blocks and were halfway down the fourth. What's more, they'd left the thickest part of the milling crowd and most of the street action behind.

She glanced back the way they'd come, surprised and a bit nonplussed at how far away from the main strip they now seemed to be.

It was like a small, glittery island back there behind them, an oasis of light and life in an otherwise murky sea. Most of the steady stream of traffic was veering right at the last big intersection they'd crossed.

The block around them was devoid of people.

The single streetlight at the next corner shed the only light.

"I know I saw him." Lonnie had stopped and turned to face her as she caught up. "He was walkin' with Willie Dee."

"Who?"

"Willie— Never mind. Just a street dude. Nobody you need to worry about."

Right.

Did Lonnie seem a little too anxious?

"Maybe not." Jackie kept her voice low. "But this is as far as we go."

"Shit! What's the matter with you? Don't you think that maybe he *wants* us to follow him? Maybe that's the deal," he hissed.

"Maybe. But I'm not willing to bet on it."

"Fine. You stay here while I go find out."

He started to stalk off.

Jackie grabbed his arm.

144

"Look, goddammit," he said, whirling around angrily, "do you wanta connect with Crick or not?"

"Wasn't he supposed to connect with us?"

"Yeah, well, maybe it didn't work out that way. Maybe he missed us or something. Maybe he decided he didn't like the lay of the land back there."

"That's a lot of maybes," Jackie remarked dryly, aware that Lonnie's argument might spring from his growing need for a hit. He probably hadn't wanted to risk bringing anything along—or, more likely, had depleted his stash—and by now was beginning to hurt.

She held his gaze a minute longer and watched his anger back off. She released his arm.

He swiped the back of his hand across his nose, giving her a disgusted sniff. "Yeah, well, I told ya he was twitchy," he muttered, shifting his stance and glancing again down the darkened section of street.

Jackie was getting a bit twitchy herself. Might be time to call it a night. She didn't like the path this thing was taking. It was looking rockier by the minute.

For the first time tonight, she regretted not wearing a wire. They'd chosen not to take unnecessary chances since they weren't working a bust and had decided that a few simple signals would do instead. Plus they'd plotted out the course she was to follow. Now Lonnie had altered it.

She peered up the lighted street, wondering where Reid was, if he was even back there. Maybe. Probably. But could she depend on it?

"Look. You wanta do this thing or not?" Lonnie demanded impatiently.

Jackie made her decision. "Not. Let's go." She started to walk back the way they'd come.

"Hey, Lonnie—"

The hail came from behind them, from the darker end of the block. They both turned around, Jackie tensing. She let her hand glide down toward the open mouth of her pouch-type shoulder bag. Her gun was nestled inside.

"It's just Willie," Lonnie murmured as a little man materialized out of the shadows.

The newcomer sauntered up to them, looking grizzled and smelling of dead meat. Jackie couldn't help wrinkling her nose.

Willie grinned as though aware of her instant aversion, giving her a glimpse of rotted teeth and a gap where two should have been. His hands were stuffed into the pockets of his filthy coat, a position Jackie was always leery of. He might be carrying. She would have felt better with his hands in plain sight.

"How's it goin', Lonnie?" After his initial scan, the newcomer treated Jackie as if she weren't there—it was fairly common to be dismissed as somebody's bimbo along for the ride, and Jackie managed to relax slightly.

Sometimes being ignored worked to her advantage. Sometimes it didn't.

"Great, everything's great," Lonnie said, retrieving some of his earlier bravado. In an unexpected and unwelcome move, he slung an arm around Jackie's shoulders, pulling her toward him with a possessive squeeze. The gesture compromised the use of her gun hand, and she gritted her teeth against the strong urge to jerk away, shifting their bodies so that her purse was behind them and she could reach into it without being seen.

"Wasn't that Crick I saw you with a couple minutes ago?" Lonnie asked, oblivious to the problem he'd caused.

"Mebby." The little man eyed him snidely. "How come ya wanta know?"

"None of your fuckin' business, man. Is he down there or not?"

Careful, Lonnie, Jackie thought. *That's not exactly the way to win friends and induce answers.*

But to Jackie's surprise the little man replied, "Yeah, he's down there. In an alley. Tol' me t' tell ya. He's waitin' for ya. Waitin' for ya both."

Willie spread his look to include her as he said it, giggling in a high-pitched, wheezy sort of way. It grated against her eardrums like the squeak of chalk on slate. Almost as quickly as the laughter started, it stopped.

Lonnie slid his arm from Jackie's shoulders and grabbed her arm, steering her past the strange little man who continued to stand there, grinning.

"See? I told you," he whispered as they moved away. "No problem." He tightened his grip on her arm.

Jackie let herself be propelled about half a block before drawing up sharply. *What was she doing? She didn't want to go down here.* She felt slightly dizzy. "That's it. We're not going any farther."

"What's the matter now?" Lonnie balked.

"We're getting out of here." Jackie swung around. This didn't feel right. Something about it was screaming "setup" loud and strong.

"Now just a fuckin' minute——" Lonnie hissed.

"You buy?" The raspy voice came floating out of the alley just in front of them, an opening so crammed with shadows that she hadn't even seen it until now. Something about it made her skin crawl.

But Lonnie seemed unconcerned. He swerved around.

"Come on, Lonnie." She reached out to pull him back.

He shook off her hand. "Crick? That you?" he called toward the alley.

A muffled reply. Could have been a "yes."

Lonnie rounded on her with a grin. "See, like I told you, babe, no problem. He's waiting for us in there. C'mon, what's the matter? Isn't this what we came for? Don't tell me you're scared." It was a taunt.

And it was right on target. She *was* scared. Scared as hell. Warning bells were going off in her head. Danger gongs. Where was Reid? Was he waiting out there, ready to back her up? Or was she on her own? She had to behave as if it were the latter.

Slipping her hand down inside her purse, she found the small Beretta .25 automatic in the side pocket. Released the safety catch.

She could be walking into a trap with nobody the wiser. Especially her. What she wanted to do now was get them out of here without blowing her cover. *Don't let this go too far,* a little voice in her mind belatedly whispered.

Right.

She glanced around. Not that she expected to see Reid, he

wouldn't be that obvious, but she did hope to see someone: a few people walking the street; that Willie person.

The block behind them was empty. Totally empty. No people. No traffic. Most of all no obvious device she could use to get them out. The apprehension knotting her stomach pulled tighter.

She had been a fool to let herself get drawn off down here. *Why had she done that? It wasn't like her to behave so amateurishly.*

"Come on, Lonnie—" She turned back but he was gone. Into that alley?

Shit. She wanted nothing more than to just get the hell out of here. But she couldn't leave Talbert—*damn the bastard.* And where the *fuck* was Reid?

Cursing her absent partner, she gripped the Beretta. Her stomach tightened another notch.

Giving it her best bimbo whine, she stepped into the alley. "Lonnie, honey, it's dark in here. Where'ja go?"

The stillness of the alley mocked him. Dal stood in the eerie silence, waiting for someone to come forward, waiting for a shape to materialize out of the shadows and step toward him, like in the dream.

But nothing occurred.

The weird dusting of moonlight colored everything with shades of black and gray—as if he'd stepped into an old movie frame alongside Bogie doing Sam Spade.

What gives, schweetheart?

He even felt a little two-toned.

Tomorrow this might all seem funny. Right now it felt like shit.

Nothing was happening. Yet every nerve in his body was pulled tight as piano wire. He had the weird sense of being watched, yet there was no real feeling of another presence here, and after a few more seconds Dal decided that his imagination was working overtime, like the other night, and at the moment, at least, he was alone.

Shapes in the shadows—*shit.*

Where had Cherry gone? What kind of game was she playing here?

He couldn't figure it. Why drop him that dummy line about Coley Dean, then bait him again tonight?

Okay, for a hundred bucks the first time. But that didn't explain now. Had she simply been running away from him and not leading him into some kind of trap at all?

Maybe. Because it was certain nothing was happening here.

Dal started to relax, though he wasn't ready to discount the possibility of a setup just yet. Not till he was back out on the street.

And which way was that?

He peered left, then right, searching the darkness for some indication of which way he should go. He'd become totally disoriented by the twists and turns he'd made—he hadn't been paying that much attention to direction while intent on the chase. Bad mistake. Apparently these alleys were like some sort of labyrinth, branching off in oddball directions and bisecting each other at unexpected turns. He had no idea where the hell he was.

But he couldn't be too far away from where he'd been, or the street.

So why couldn't he hear the traffic noise?

Probably a wind shift, enclosed area. Sometimes conditions had to be just right to hear—or not hear—sounds even a few yards away.

As if in response, the breeze again brushed his face; silently, though, this time; not whispering to him as it had before. It brought a whiff of rotten meat.

Whew. Dal scrubbed at his nose. That smell had been nearly strong enough to make his eyes water. Apparently more than one establishment was dumping its refuse in violation of city ordinances.

He couldn't remain static any longer. Arbitrarily deciding to head left—better to go forward than back—he got moving again.

Rounding yet another turn, he was brought up short at the sight of a shadowy form. He jerked sideways and down into a crouch, gun leveled.

The figure didn't move. It was too dark to tell who it was, but it wasn't Cherry. It was a man.

At that precise moment, the moon shifted a bit. Pale light drifted into the alley, revealing the grinning face of Willie Dee.

The little man was looking straight at Dal—as though he had no trouble at all seeing through the darkness.

Dal rose from his crouch and began walking toward Willie, calling, "Hey, Willie, I'd like to talk to you, man," as he went. The moon shifted again, dropping the shadows back into place. By the time Dal got to where Willie had been standing, the little man was gone.

What in hell?

For the first time since this whole thing started, Dal got the distinct impression that he was being toyed with. First Cherry. Now Willie.

But why? What would make them want to do such a thing? It didn't make sense.

He didn't like feeling like a pawn on somebody's gameboard. Not at all.

"Willie, you got some stake in this, you'd better rethink your position." He spoke loudly enough for anybody standing nearby to hear and kept threading his way forward, every instinct finely tuned to the slightest wrong move. If something was going to happen, bring it on.

Jackie stopped walking, unnerved by the heavy silence. She'd come about twenty feet into the alley and it was as if she had stepped away from the edge of the world. Streetlight from the corner back behind her did nothing to alleviate the total darkness here. Not even a little bit.

Where was the moon?

There'd been one earlier. She recalled the pale, silvery ghost-light casting its frost-white sheen on the countryside as she'd driven into town. It had looked like snow.

She remembered when she was a kid her mother calling it ghost-snow. The way the moonlight would sometimes shine eerily white on the landscape.

Where was it now?

She looked up and there might as well have been a roof over her head. There was no suggestion of sky. It produced a confused, slightly disorienting effect on her equilibrium, and she quickly glanced back over her shoulder to find the gap where the street was, afraid for an instant that it wouldn't be there.

But it was; a beacon at the edge of the world.

Solid darkness on the opposite end, all around. Except for that one pale reference point, she might as well be blind.

And alone. She felt totally alone. Like she was the last person on earth—

not alone . . .

The thought crawled up her spine and settled on her shoulders, like the silence and the darkness, a deadweight blanket pressing her down.

She felt she was being watched. Eerie. Unsettling. This must be how a blind person feels when he walks into a silent room, not knowing if anybody is actually there or not and equally certain that the room is full of people all standing around quietly staring at him.

What had happened to Lonnie? Why hadn't he answered her?

She started to call out again, but something stopped her. Some inner caution, some paranoid notion that all was not right.

How had she let herself get into this position?

Not good, Jackie.

Holding the gun ready in her purse, she reached into her pocket with the other hand and drew out the butane lighter she carried as part of her standard equipment. Too bad it wasn't the big, sturdy flashlight from her car.

She flicked the flame control on the lighter to maximum. Held it up. Thumbed it on.

Flame shot up—

—right into the grinning face of a huge black man standing not two feet in front of her.

With a reflexive gasp, she stepped backward, allowing the flame to wink out. Quickly shifting her position, hand taut on the gun, she thumbed the lighter back on.

The nightmare face was still there, features shifting madly in the flickering light—

or was it her hand that was shaking?

She eyed the man warily, trying to keep the lighter steady and slow her breathing, ignoring her heart beating rapid-fire in her chest.

Get a grip, Jackie. Christ.

It didn't look real, that face; nose gouged from clay, eyes glassy and sunken, mouth painted on. He hadn't moved, not an inch, even when the flame had shot on.

And surely it had burned him, he'd been standing that close— *how had he gotten so close without her knowing?*—but he hadn't jumped back, hadn't yelped in pain. He didn't even seem to breathe as the light danced over him, casting weird shadows across his dark, waxen skin.

She shivered. One moment it looked like a man's face, the next a cadaver's, as though flesh and bone had merged and the features had been plastered on. It was like one of those weird double-image pictures that keep changing shape at a flick of the hand.

Just a trick of the light, Jackie, that's all it is, that's all.

She took another backward step from the man towering over her, relieved when he remained where he was. It was obvious he was stoned out of his mind; there was no telling what he was on. The more distance she could put between herself and this dude, the better.

Behind him, another shadow moved—then another—shifting backward and forward in the moving light.

Wait a minute, here. Wait a minute.

She felt her teeth clench as a sudden jolt of adrenaline burst over her. Were there more of these grinning gargoyles back there? Had they killed Lonnie? Was she next?

Her heartbeat pounded in her ears. She pulled the gun from her purse.

But no one else moved toward her, it was just his shadow darting back and forth in the stillness, playing hide-and-seek with the flame.

Wasn't it?

Still fully expecting to see another weird form or two material-ize from the darkness like something out of Michael Jackson's *Thriller*, she took another backward step, hand gripping the gun. But none did. No army of ghouls pressed forward to block her path. Yet she had the feeling that this man was not alone.

Time to get out of here.

She began systematically backing away from the cadaverous face, which hadn't changed expression, even when she'd pulled out her gun. If this was Crick, she didn't want any part of him. Not here. Not now. Possibly not ever.

"Lonnie?" she called again, but got no answer. Kept backing up.

Where was Reid? Was he monitoring this?

He could step in any time he wanted—

"You buy . . . ?" Jackie jumped at the unexpected question from the big black man. He still didn't move, just stood there grinning at her as she inched away. His dark eyes reflected the dancing light, twin flames on glass. His scratchy voice sent renewed shivers sprinting up her spine, down her arms, across the back of her scalp.

"Yeah pal, I buy. Just lemme go get my . . ." *What?* What was she trying to say? Her mind had gone blank. The voice she was hearing was barely recognizable as her own. She didn't know when she'd been as frightened as she was at this very moment. It was taking all her will power not to turn around and run.

Somewhere deep within the logic center of her brain a little voice was cooing, *You're a professional, you've been in scary situations before, worse situations, more obviously dangerous situations.*

At the moment she couldn't remember a single time.

Right now that didn't seem to matter. Coming up with a good excuse to withdraw didn't matter. Only the withdrawal counted.

What had happened to Lonnie was a problem to be put temporarily on hold. She just wanted to get the hell out of Dodge, secure some backup, come back *en masse* and check this alley out.

The grinning gargoyle wasn't following her, thank God. He remained standing where he was as she continued to back away. His face had lost some of its luminosity as the flame of the cigarette lighter got dimmer and farther away. Only those eyes continued to glitter across the darkness, as though reflecting the flame.

She shuddered again, uncontrollably.

The lighter was beginning to get hot. She stood it as long as she could, then let her thumb slip off the switch, scooting it and her fingers back from the heated tip. Shivered again. The last glimpse she'd had of Crick—or whoever the hell it was—had been the crazy illusion that his face had begun to melt and run down onto the darkness, sagging flesh dropping away from the bone.

Christ.

She turned toward the mouth of the alley, surprised and not a bit pleased to see that it was still ten or twelve feet away—

A figure was standing there.

For a moment it didn't register, she'd been so focused on making her retreat.

Reid? Was it Reid?

Even as her mind posed the question, she knew it wasn't him— too short, too heavy. A second, then a third figure stepped up to join the first.

Shit. What was going on here?

Had this whole thing been a setup, then? But why?

"Hey, babe," one of the trio catcalled. "Seen ya go in there. Now how about spreadin' a little a' that action around, dude who was with ya sure looked like about a half a fuck t' me."

Laughter. Leather jackets. The lowlifes from the bar.

This was too much. Too damn much. It was also something she could deal with.

Still unnerved—but beginning to get a bead on some good, healthy anger—Jackie swung the gun forward and veered to the edge of the building where she'd have a wall at her back instead of the alley and its freaky occupant.

Were they all in this together, including Lonnie? She doubted it.

"You jerkoffs better know I've got a gun. Back off now or I'll use it."

Shoving the cigarette lighter into her pocket, she gripped the Beretta in both hands. She only hoped her voice sounded hard and convincing enough, and that the unaccustomed edge of panic running through it was the sort that made believers out of skeptics.

Leading with the gun, she began moving toward the trio of would-be assailants, careful to keep the wall at her back. Her palms were hot and sticky; her back was alive with sweat.

Anytime, Reid. Come out, come out, wherever you are. What the hell was he waiting for?

Part of her attention remained tuned toward the alley for any advance from that quarter. But the big black man did not appear.

"Keep going." She pointed the gun directly at the front guy's gut.

"Sure babe, sure. Just take it easy now." The leader of the pack put up his hands in a placating gesture and began nervously edging toward the street. The others edged with him. They all eyed the gun warily.

Okay. They knew she meant business. She didn't want to shoot this creep—she'd only shot one person in her career, and hadn't killed him, thank God—but it proved that she could do it if she had to. Then. And now.

"That's right. Keep it moving." The three stooges had come to the curb. They stepped off it into the gutter where they belonged.

"Okay, now turn around and get the fuck out of here. You've got ten seconds—nine—eight—"

The trio swung around on "nine" and were off and running by "eight."

Jackie breathed a deep sigh of relief, though she didn't relax her vigil on the alley just yet. She was half expecting the ghoul to burst out of there at any moment.

Maintaining watch—and her grip on the gun—she began inching toward the sidewalk again, stumbling slightly as her left foot encountered the edge, *welcome back into the real world.*

Hurriedly, she crossed over the still-deserted street, keeping the gun ready, glancing from the dark alley up the street to where the lowlifes had already disappeared, then back at the alley again.

Nobody came after her. Nothing disturbed the utter stillness of the night.

She kept walking, quickening her pace. She could still feel the darkness at her back. She suspected she'd be having nightmares about this night's work.

What she needed to do now was get back to her car, radio in, try to find Reid—

Reid, the bastard! Where was he? What had he been doing while she was being lured off—terrorized—set upon by thugs? Just wait until she caught up with Detective Dallas Reid.

*   *   *

Dal raced down the narrow passageway, throwing caution to the wind. Anger swam through his veins. He'd caught another glimpse of Cherry—like she wanted him to see her, the bitch. Then she'd darted away again.

Just wait till he caught up with her.

Another part of his brain was beginning to slow down a bit, back off and rationally consider events: Were Cherry and Willie in this together? Had he been drawn off for a purpose? Did that purpose have anything to do with Agent Swann?

Agent Swann. He felt a twinge of real concern at the belated thought of her. He was supposed to be tailing her right now. Watching her back. If she were in real trouble . . .

Dumb-ass. He'd been a real dumb-ass to get suckered into this, involve himself in a stupid, useless chase. He didn't need to run Cherry down. He could have her picked up anytime he wanted to. Should have kept to the plan, done his job. Right now Swann could be in trouble.

He felt his jaw tighten, teeth clenched from the exertion of running, the strain of knowing he'd made a stupid move.

He'd been gone too long. Too long.

Should have kept to the plan.

The alley T-boned to an abrupt end, still narrower paths branching left and right.

Which way, which way?

Left—no, right.

He sprinted in this new direction, toward the smear of light he saw at the far end, hoping, counting on it being the right way out. He was determined to catch Cherry now, committed to it. The goddamn bitch had led him a merry chase and there'd be dues to pay. Oh, yes.

There she was.

He glimpsed her for a moment, standing near the end of the narrow slit, silhouetted against the meager strip of light. Must be an opening to the street. Just a little faster, he'd have her.

He burst from the opening in mid-swerve, turning the way he'd seen her veer—and crashed right into her.

She whirled. Something hard jammed his gut. He felt his balls contract. *Jesus!* she had a gun. He loosened his hold on his own piece, raised his hands.

"Whoa now, Cherry, take it easy here, hon."

"Back off, buster, or I'll blow a hole right through you. It's been a rough night."

The voice. The hair— "Christ, Swann, it's me. Don't shoot!"

"Reid?" She looked at him a moment and the savagery fled her face, leaving good, solid fury. "Goddammit, where the hell have you been?"

She pulled the gun away, and he felt his gonads drop back into place. Furiously he shoved his own gun into its holster.

"What do you mean, where have *I* been. What the hell are you doing off down here when you're supposed to be up there?" He stabbed a thumb in the direction of the strip while his glance strafed the more immediate area. "And where the fuck's Lonnie?"

"In an alley with his head probably bashed in by the King of the Ghouls. We've got to get back there right now."

"Let's go." He started to move that way.

"Wait." She grabbed his arm. "We need light, maybe some backup. Where's your car?"

He glared at her, ready to clip a curse about her dispensing orders, then realized she was right.

"Up there a couple of blocks."

She was off at a run, assuming, no doubt, that he'd follow.

He followed. "We'll talk some more about this later," he tossed angrily, trying to keep up with her and not pant for breath.

"Bet on it," she replied, not even bothering to glance at him over her shoulder.

They dashed to his car. Jumped in. He gunned it to life.

She reached for the radio as he sped away from the curb and he said: "Hold up on the call. Better check this out first."

She didn't argue.

They approached the alley, slowed down. He recognized the place immediately. It was where Coley Dean had gotten his the other night. He could even see a tag-end piece of yellow police-line tape still clinging to the edge of an adjacent building.

"This is the alley where that drug dealer got killed Monday night," he told her, and felt her sharp glance cut his way.

He spun the car in an arc that had it nose-in toward the dark slit, popped the headlights on high beam.

"Shit."

A body lay crumpled against the side of the right-hand building about two thirds of the way down. Other than that, the alley looked empty.

"How many were there?" he clipped.

"One in the alley—that I saw. Three in the street, though I doubt those three are still lingering, seems that was some separate action. Dude in the alley was big, crazy-looking. Strung out on dope, maybe. Watch out for him."

Dal slammed the gearshift into park, stomped the emergency brake, and thrust open his door. She did the same.

"No," he told her. "You stay here while I check it out. Anything happens, make that call."

Again, she didn't argue, for which he was grateful.

He got out, unholstering his gun and using the opened door in front of him as a temporary shield. Out of the corner of his eye, he saw her doing the same. He glanced over and saw that she'd pulled out her small automatic—looked like a .25—and taken up a similar stance behind her own door barricade.

"There's a 12 gauge pump under the dash, fully loaded," he murmured, saw her nod, added "Watch your back," and heard a soft "Yeah, you too."

He glanced back down the alley. Nothing had changed. The body still lay crumpled like a bundle of cast-off clothing.

Swinging his door halfway closed, he edged around it and the front fender and entered the alley.

The powerful headlights shone their double beams out in front of him, illuminating the scene ahead with a harsh brightness. He saw a couple of bricked-in doors, but no other openings until the far end, where the alley dumped into the next street.

The light struck his back as he moved forward, keeping to the left side of the passageway. It sent his shadow careening in front of him like a giant stick figure—the ones they used to draw in grade school when they played hang-the-man. It moved when he did, but jerky, distorted. Made him think of a body twitching at the end of a rope.

Christ! What was it that kept freaking him out tonight? Filling his mind with this crap? *Jesus.*

He kept walking toward the crumpled form, the light hitting his back an almost physical inducement to *go on, go on,* a helping hand providing a gentle nudge.

He glanced back toward the car, but could see nothing beyond the wash of headlights. Hear nothing but the soft purr of the engine he'd left running.

Shifted his gaze forward again.

The body hadn't moved. He could tell it was Lonnie by the clothes. He didn't see any blood, no signs of violence. It didn't mean shit.

He made his break across the open expanse, flattening himself against the opposite wall as he geared up for something to happen. Nothing did.

Slowly he edged down the side of the building to where Lonnie lay. Stooping to a crouch, he took his left hand from the gun and grabbed an inert shoulder, carefully rolling Lonnie over so he could see if he was hurt, or dead.

A groan greeted him. Lonnie opened a bleary eye. "Whozzat? Whassha doin' . . . ?"

Drunk. The bastard was shitfaced. What the hell had been going on? What did Swann mean by letting this happen, coming down here on her own? Didn't she know better than to let a contact get this drunk? Toss a plan out the window at a whim? Didn't she have any sense at all?

Whatever remorse he might have felt at not tailing her was canceled. She had some big-time explaining to do.

Letting Lonnie roll back onto his face, Dal worked his way down to the end of the alleyway, checked out that street and found nothing. Returned and hefted Lonnie to his feet.

"Come on, stud." Half carrying, half dragging the informant with him, he threaded the path back to the car.

"Is he hurt?" Swann asked as he pushed past the driver's door and jerked open the rear one, thrusting Lonnie ungently onto the backseat.

Dal held his answer, and his anger, in check as he slammed the door shut again, and slid in front behind the wheel. "No, he's drunk. What the hell have you two been doing, partying it up?"

"Drunk?" She jerked a glance at Talbert. "How could he be that drunk? He didn't—"

"Save it. Get in." He slammed his door for good measure.

"Excuse me? Do I detect a note of censure?" She got in and banged her own door closed.

"You goddamn right. You had no business—"

"Don't tell me about business," she cut him off. "You're the one who wasn't there when I needed you—"

Dal winced in the interior darkness.

"—and I'm the one who had to fend off Boris Karloff and the local rape gang—"

He glanced at her sharply.

"—so if anybody should be censured—"

"Are you hurt?" He flipped on the interior light, realizing he probably should have asked her that already, but *dammit!* if she was hurt she should have said so, though he probably wouldn't have, either, in a similar situation. He scanned her carefully. She looked disheveled but okay. Just mad as hell.

"No, I'm not hurt. Just angry," she confirmed. "I want to know why you weren't backing me up like you were supposed to."

He threw the gear into reverse, started to back out, remembered the emergency brake when the car didn't go anywhere. Reached down and released the lever. "Maybe we better just leave all this for now—unless there's something crucial you need to report?" The sarcasm was apparent.

She shook her head tightly. "No."

He nodded. "Great. Then we'll discuss it in the morning."

She didn't answer, and Dal took that for a "yes."

In the backseat, Lonnie snored.

Dal looped around the block and drove down a darkened side street close to where she'd parked her car, but not too close, waited for her to get out and walk up to State. Then he cruised by, keeping her in view until he saw her start her car and pull out, heading down State to turn at the intersection that would take her back to Glenwood and the interstate.

Behind him, Lonnie grunted, turned over, lapsed back into that nerve-grating snore. Dal just hoped the bastard wouldn't get sick and throw up all over the backseat before he could get him home.

Instead of turning at a crossroad himself, he kept straight on State Street, cruising on down to the alley they'd just left. Slowed to a crawl.

Nothing caught his eye. No one lurking in the dark. He drifted on past, switching his gaze to another alley about fifty yards on down and across the road. The one in the photograph. It played with his emotions as it loomed in his sight.

He pulled up to the curb across the street from it and stopped the car, letting it idle. Studied the opening.

Shades of black on black. Like the picture. Mocking him.

He sat there a minute, deciding whether to take the flashlight from the glove compartment, go on over there and check it out.

Only take a minute.

But whoever might or might not have been standing there when the photo was taken wouldn't be standing in there now . . .

Would they?

No, of course not.

Lifting his foot from the brake pedal, he sped away. He'd had enough of alleys for one night.

Listen close to what I say
Don't step in de Boneman's way

NINETEEN

Night cast its realm of shadows on the room where Maurice Martineau sat anxiously waiting for the phone to ring.

Bastards! Sonofabitches should have called in by now.

Sweat rimed the slick black skin, making his face seem to glisten palely in the lamplight, a fever-sheen of impatience, an underlying pallor of gnawing fear.

Maurice mopped his brow and tried to ignore the uneasiness that had been growing in him ever since the appointed time had come, and gone—looming ever larger in a mind beset with doubts, now that it was too late to do anything about it.

Bastards! What the hell had happened? Why didn't they call?

He threw the damp, sweat-stained handkerchief to the desk and picked up a fine Waterford crystal decanter. Splashed another healthy dose of dark Jamaican rum into a matching glass and gulped it down. It should have soothed him, warmed the chill, raw nerve endings that were screaming signals he didn't want to think about, couldn't bring himself to consider.

Not yet. Not yet. Give it more time. They could still call in. It wasn't that late. Anything could have happened.

Anything . . .

Maurice felt a sharp prick in his palms and realized he had clenched his hands, was sitting there with his eyes tightly squeezed, his nails digging into the soft, pale inner flesh of his palms. He released his breath and relaxed—tried to relax, leaning back in the comfortable leather desk chair that suddenly felt as cold and clammy as a damp marble slab. And just as hard.

He could smell his own sweat. He picked up the handkerchief again and blotted his face.

Shadows blended with light. Fear warred with anger, then self-

assurance as he thought again of the instructions he had given his
two best men:

"I want this guy dead. I don't care how you do it, just get rid
of him. But make it a clean hit, no witnesses. I simply want him to
disappear."

The pair had said tonight, it would be done tonight. A phone
call would report their success.

It hadn't come.

Not yet. Give it more time. More time.

They were good, Jean-Claude and Hector. Competent shooters,
proven on more than one occasion. They'd get the job done. They
always had.

Give it time.

Another shot of rum. Another ten minutes gone.

Fingers darting to his face, smearing sweat.

Jerky movements of a man strung out on apprehension, on the
vagaries of fate.

How many times had he had the bastard right there in front of
him, sitting right there in that chair across the desk, smiling that
little mocking smile? He could have shot him anytime he wanted
to. Should have done it yesterday, the moment he decided that it
had to be done—bastard overstepping his bounds, getting above
himself, forgetting who he worked for. There were penalties for
that.

So why hadn't he?

Maurice closed his eyes, replaying the images of that meeting,
seeing again the handsome face, the trim, well-dressed body, hearing again the extremely cultured voice of the man he was now
fully convinced had been out to get him from the first. The man
was trying to take control of the drug network that was netting
Maurice in excess of a million dollars a day.

He slammed his hand angrily down on the desktop. It would
never happen! If he had to do the hit himself, he'd show that
bastard what it meant to cross Maurice Martineau!

Maurice did not suffer betrayals gracefully.

He'd hired the bastard to do a job: get rid of the competition.
Get control of the streets so that Maurice and his cartel would

have no trouble stepping in and taking over. Somewhere along the line, the fucker had decided to go for the gold.

Maurice wasn't sure when he'd begun to sense the threat, recognize the power this man was subtly beginning to wield. The power of fear.

It was said he could make you afraid.

But not Maurice. He had this guy's number.

The fool had finally shown his true colors, thought he could intimidate Maurice with his little game. Well, Maurice would show him who was calling the shots.

Why didn't they call?

He has a way of making things happen, they said. *Or not.*

Maurice shivered.

Not that he believed it.

Any of it.

Not even yesterday in his office when—

He shivered again.

He hadn't been afraid. Not really.

But it was then that he'd decided to rid himself of the problem, before it got too far out of hand.

So why hadn't he offed the fucker right then and there and been done with it? He'd started to; Maurice remembered reaching for the drawer where he kept his gun—

Then what? The next few moments were confused in his mind. He remembered hesitating, glancing back at the man—and something in that face, something in the way those eyes were looking at him, staring at him, *into him*—

For a moment he remembered. For an insane instant he saw again what he'd seen that day—*thought* he'd seen—the shift of movement, the flicker of light: *For a moment, that face had been a skull.*

Maurice shuddered in the still silence. Superstitious nonsense! That's all it was. Word association. Trick of the light. He didn't believe all that crap. It was just a gimmick. A scam used on suckers. Boneman, *shit!*

He knew a thing or two about running a scam—didn't he have his own voodoo room set up off this one, complete with all the trappings? Voodoo paraphernalia, altar decorated with candles, herbs and fetishes strung around, conjure balls and clay pots where the souls of his enemies could be held. And in the center of it all, a ceremonial knife prominently displayed. Had quite an effect on believers and nonbelievers alike; might even say it worked like a charm.

But Maurice wasn't buying into that "boneman" routine. No way. There was no such thing.

A gimmick, that's all it was. A slick con man's gimmick.

Though he'd taken to lighting a few candles himself recently, the blue ones, supposed to grant success and give protection.

But it was all for show. A stage setting used to impress the junkers. That's all.

That's all.

The telephone rang.

Maurice nearly jumped out of his chair. There it was! Everything was okay now. Job all done. Fucker wouldn't be causing him any more problems ever again.

He swiped off the sweat that was running down his face and dripping onto the desktop and reached for the phone, taking a long, deep breath. Even managed a smile.

They'd be picking pieces of that bastard out of Dumpsters all over town for the next two months, he'd bet. What the rats didn't take care of.

"An' how you gonna like that, Mr. Boneman?" he muttered smugly. "Rats'll be gnawin' *your* bones."

Stifling a chuckle, he grabbed up the receiver, punched the button beside the blinking line.

"Yeah."

There was no one on the line.

"Hello?" Maurice felt his jaw tighten. "Who's this?"

He listened. Afraid to say anything else.

Afraid.

He could make you afraid.

After a moment he heard a click, then the dial tone.

Slowly Maurice took the receiver from his ear. The tone faded as he moved it away. He stared at it for a long moment.

The soft buzz suddenly switched to a rapid bleet. Maurice

jumped, dropped it, watched it clatter to the desk. Scooped it up again. He slammed the receiver down on the base unit.

Afraid.

Maybe it was just a bad connection. Sure, that's what it was. They'd call him right back.

The phone remained stubbornly silent.

Maurice started to pick it up again—

He couldn't make his hand obey.

Afraid.

Maybe he'd damaged the phone, slamming it down so hard. He really should pick it up and check.

But did he really want to know? He sat there staring at it, willing it to ring—afraid that it would.

Afraid.

Maurice wasn't sure how long he sat there. Time lost relevance.

A draft of wind chilling the sweat on the back of his neck brought him back to awareness. Had he left the door to the altar room open?

He turned around.

A faint flicker of candlelight filled the six-inch gap where the pocket doors stood gaping apart.

Maurice was certain he'd closed them. He was certain he hadn't left any candles burning.

But there was no way in or out except through this office, and he'd been sitting here all the time. No one could have gotten in.

Could he?

Afraid . . .

He stood, trying not to feel the tremble in his legs. No one could have gotten in. No one.

Slowly, he walked over to the doors, reached out to pull them apart.

Somewhere in the back of his mind a voice was screaming: Don't. Don't go in there, Maurice. Just turn around and run.

But his hand seemed to be moving of its own accord. He couldn't make it stop.

He slid the doors open.

Another draft of wind blew past him. For a moment, he thought he heard it whispering . . .

Listen close

He stepped into the inner room.

Candles flickered and danced along the altar. Black ones—always used for evil, or death.

The smell of incense swamped him, a too-sweet, coppery scent.

He focused on the offerings the moment he entered, but his mind would not allow him to accept them. Not until his gaze took in each detail of what he was seeing. Not until his reeling senses understood the message this was meant to convey—

Listen close to what I say . . .

Not until at last the paralysis released him and he ran screaming from the room and the two heads that had been placed upon the altar—Jean-Claude's and Hector's,

the whisper-laugh of the wind at his back.

TWENTY

JEHOVAH JONES AND THE RAIDERS FROM
THE TEMPLE OF THE LOST COVENANT . . .

J.J. studied the story sheet for a moment, then shook his head and replaced it on the floor beside him, picking up another one from the dozen or so spread out around him on the living room rug.

JEHOVAH JONES: THIS IS YOUR LIFE . . .

"Nope. Too involved." J.J. chose another.

E.C.—THE EXTRACELESTIAL . . .

"Hmmm . . . Might be fun." He considered it a moment, then this, too, was discarded with a "Nah."

All in all, things hadn't been going too well on the home front for the past couple of days. After several sessions of trying to come up with a basic list for "Jehovah Jones and the Ten Amendments," he'd only been able to come up with five—the best of which was "Thou Shalt Not Be Boring," a credo he decided he'd better take to heart and choose another story idea to work on. This one was currently going nowhere.

He reached for yet another sheet.

JEHOVAH JONES: PHONE HOME . . .

Now that might be good. He read over his thumbnail sketch of the plot:

> —There's trouble in Paradise.
> A splinter group of demigods and
> publicans is unhappy with the way
> things are being handled since the
> Lord left and has demanded an election.
> Now they've accused Peter and a band
> of archangels of breaking into their
> campaign headquarters and bugging the place.
> Gabriel is trumpeting it all over heaven,
> calling it Petergate—

"Old news," J.J. muttered with a shrug. "And do I really want to do a political satire right now?" He tossed the paper back down on the floor. Grabbed another.

JEHOVAH JONES: ROMANCING THE STONES . . .
—J.J. gets drawn into the rock music scene—

Hmmm . . .

A second sheet was stapled to the back of this one. He peeled up the top page and read:

JEHOVAH JONES: YO MAMA DON'T DANCE . . .
(Possible tie-in?)
—J.J. goes to a nightclub and meets up with a
hooker named Amazing Grace who teaches him a
few quick moves—

He quickly laid this one aside.

The next one was probably the most thoroughly outlined of the bunch.

JEHOVAH JONES
AND THE HOLY GHOSTBUSTERS . . .

He scanned the brief synopsis:

—J.J. is hired to rid the 57th Street
Mission of the ghost of Happy Jack Hoskins,
an old wino and staunch Methodist who died
of a heart attack when he heard
that the church had stricken "Onward
Christian Soldiers" from their hymnals.
Now he's haunting the mission, singing OCS
over and over and over again.

"Great. Get Gabe and Pete in on this one. Give 'em little ghostbuster suits." J.J. grinned and flipped the page over. He even had some lyrics jotted down:

When there's something odd in your synagogue
Who're you gonna call?—Holy Ghostbusters!
When your Sunday school has a pesky ghoul,
Who're you gonna call?—Holy Ghostbusters!
I ain't afraida no Holy ghosts . . .

J.J. began to get into the spirit of the thing, breaking into song on verse 2:

> "When you get a hackle at your tabernacle,
> Who're you gonna call?—Holy Ghostbusters!
> When your congregation gets a visitation,
> Who're you gonna call?—Holy—"

Somebody banged on the front door.

"Poot!" Buddy yelled from the kitchen, reminding J.J. that he needed to cover the cage.

Neighbors already? Had he been singing that loud?

Lowering his voice to a mere murmur, he continued to chant "I ain't afraida no Holy ghosts" in rhythm as he lifted himself up off the floor and shagged his way to the door. He peered through the peephole at Dal. Of course. Who else would it be at one in the morning?

He opened the door to his chronic late-night visitor. "About time. I've been trying to get in touch with you for the past two days."

"I need a drink." Dal strode into the room, not noticing the papers that littered the floor until he'd plowed through them.

"Can't you watch where you're walking?" J.J. clipped, then added "And you drink too much" as he closed the door.

"Yeah, well, so you've told me." Dal bent down to retrieve a couple of sheets that had scattered. "Hope they weren't in any particular order," he muttered, glancing at the pages. His eyebrows lifted.

" 'J.J. and the Bandit'?" he read aloud. " 'J.J. at the Bat' ?"

"Gimme those." J.J. made a grab for the papers but Dal pulled them out of his reach.

"Wait a minute, I want to read this." He went back to the first sheet. " 'J.J. is hired by Richard Simmons's evil twin Dick to deliver a vanload of Twinkies to Weight Watchers summer camp—' "

"I said, Give Me Those Papers!" J.J. swiped the sheets out of Dal's clutches, glaring at the face that grinned back at him. He began snatching the others up off the floor as Dal went over to the cabinet where until a couple of days ago J.J. had kept a modest supply of liquor. If Dal was going to drink himself into oblivion, it wouldn't be here.

"You're out," Dal said in disgust.

"There's Diet Coke and juice in the fridge," J.J. responded, and received a scowl in return.

Dal plopped down tiredly in the easy chair. "What gives, anyway?" He gave an offhand wave at the papers J.J. was gathering. "I thought you were writing about God, not yourself."

"I am—" J.J. stopped his gathering and shot him a look. "What do you mean by that?"

" 'J.J. at the Bat'?" Dal raised a sardonic brow. "Who's it supposed to be?"

"It's Jehovah Jones," J.J. snapped, irritated at Dal for pointing out something he honestly hadn't even thought about until now. How had he missed that? "So it's the same initials. So what?"

"And any relation to persons living or dead is purely coincidental?"

"That's right." He really hadn't made the connection.

Dal shrugged. "Whatever. But it sure sounds like an alter ego to me—"

J.J. peered at him closely to see if the "altar" pun was intended, decided it wasn't. Dal wasn't that sharp when it came to puns.

"—though I can't quite see you in the role," Dal was continuing to say. "Need somebody more omnipotent." He scrunched the throw pillow up to a more comfortable level, leaned his head back, and slung a leg over the chair arm. Looked as if he were settling in for the night.

"Don't get too comfortable." J.J. flashed him a frown, placing the pile of papers on the table by the couch. "I've got something to show you."

Dal grunted and closed his eyes.

"It might actually be important." J.J. turned back to his friend, regarding him impatiently. He really wasn't in the mood for Dal and his sarcastic brand of humor tonight. "You were asking me if I'd heard the word 'boneman' the other night?"

Dal raised an eyelid to peer up at him. "Yeah?"

"Well, somebody left me a note with that on it. A rhyme, actually. Looks like it might have been written by a kid or an illiterate. Some sort of dialect. I think it was Willie Dee."

Dal opened the other eye and straightened from his slump. "When did you see Willie Dee?" His voice had lost the bored drawl it took on when he was tired.

"Day before yesterday. He was out at the scene of that Davenport massacre. Little creep jumped right in the car with me."

"What did he say?" Dal's lethargy had disappeared.

"Weird stuff. Something about somebody coming to get us. He was talking crazy. I think he's flipped his lid."

"Well, the streets'll do that to you," Dal remarked with a frown. "What about this 'boneman' reference?"

"That's something really strange. Only thing I can figure out is Willie must have gotten into my car and scribbled the note while I was up at the Davenport house—notebook was right there on the seat—then he got out again, waited until I returned, then hopped back in the car with me. Like I said, crazy."

"You still haven't explained about the boneman."

"That's on the note. Willie didn't actually mention the name himself." J.J. walked over to his desk and picked up the small notebook. "He just said that someone's coming to get us, only in the note it's spelled out that it's the Boneman who's coming."

He flipped through the pages as he walked back over to Dal. Stopped walking and frowned. "That's odd." He flipped back several pages, turned them over more slowly.

"What?" Dal sounded suspicious.

"It's not here."

"What? The note?" Dal stood and came over to see.

J.J. nodded incredulously. "It's gone. It was right here, and now it's gone."

Dal took the pad. Thumbed through it. "You sure it was here?"

"Of course I'm sure," J.J. snapped. "Why would I make something like that up?"

"I meant"—Dal eyed him impatiently—"are you sure this is the right notebook? Don't be so touchy."

"Yes, I'm quite sure this is the right notebook, and I'm not being touchy. I'm mad. Somebody's been in my house."

"Now wait a minute, Harley. Why would you think there's been anybody in your house? You've just got the wrong notebook—"

"Look, Dallas. That poem was written right here in this note-book—not some other notebook—*this* notebook. Don't you think I know my notebooks? I color-code my notebooks. This one's purple. That means it's for personal notes and my own writing. Black for addresses. Manila for business. Purple for me. It was written down right here in this purple notebook, I tell you. And now it's gone."

"Only you would color-code notebooks," Dal remarked dryly while J.J. glared at him.

"A lot of people color-code their notebooks, and aren't you going to do something? What about fingerprints?"

Dal dragged an impatient hand through his hair. "Just calm down a minute, would you, and tell me what the hell it said. Then we can decide whether or not to call in the mobile crime lab."

J.J. regarded him hostilely. "Sure. Be flippant. Not your house that was burglarized."

"Christ, J.J., be sensible! Why would anyone want to break in here and steal a fucking page out of your *purple* notebook?"

"Why would anyone write that poem to me in the first place? What's it supposed to mean?"

"Maybe I could answer that if you'd tell me what it said," Dal prompted.

"It was written in crayon."

"Crayon?" Dal looked at him incredulously—as if maybe he didn't believe him.

"That's right. Red crayon. I scratched it off with my fingernail."

"Will you please just tell me what the hell it said." Dal was beginning to lose his temper.

So was J.J.

"I'm trying to remember exactly." J.J. dragged an angry hand through his own hair, began pacing, and finally went over and sank down on the couch. "The last line was 'De Boneman comin for you an me'—that's d-e not t-h-e. Here, let me write it down so you can see."

He jumped back up and went over to his desk, got a clean sheet of paper and a pen. Came back and sat down on the couch.

"I think I remember how it went now. " 'De Boneman watch,' " he said as he wrote, " 'De Boneman see,' yeah, that's it, 'De Boneman comin for you an me.' That's what it was. Here." He passed the paper to Dal.

Dal looked it over. Said nothing.

"Well?"

His friend shrugged. "I'll check into it."

"Fine. Great. What's that supposed to mean?"

"It means"—Dal got up from the chair—"I'll check into it. See ya."

"Wait a minute!" J.J. bounded off the couch in pursuit. "Wait just a darn minute—"

But Dal was already out the door.

"Who is this Boneman person, and what's Willie Dee got to do with anything, and why did he write that note to me?" he hollered at Dal's retreating back.

"I don't know," Dal tossed over his shoulder as he descended the front-porch steps.

And that, J.J. knew, was that. He'd get no more for the moment. "And don't take my car," he shouted, keeping an eagle eye on his friend until Dal climbed into his own vehicle, started the engine, and peeled away from the curb.

Only then did he go back inside the house, slam and double-lock the door.

Dal sped along the dark, near-empty streets, J.J.'s questions singing through his brain.

Who *was* this Boneman person?

What *did* Willie Dee have do to with any of this?

Why *had* he—or someone—written that note to J.J.? Then stolen it back again—if that's what had happened, and Dal had no reason to doubt J.J.'s word, though the theft did seem a little farfetched.

Questions.

Questions without answers.

Tonight he'd amassed a few of his own. Like why had Cherry lured him out into that network of back alleys; and how did Willie Dee figure in this night's deal; and what had really happened with Agent Swann, it was almost too coincidental that she'd been drawn off at the same time he had.

Questions.

Without answers.

Dal swung a left onto Nelson Drive and headed toward home.

Funny how it felt as if he were going in the wrong direction and should turn around and go back the other way.

He could have stayed at J.J.'s—had gone there with every intention of spending the night, just like always, if he hadn't been so damned restless. How often did he do that? Couple of times a week?

Habit.

But he'd just been too antsy tonight, too uptight after that run-in with Agent Swann to stick around and get embroiled in another one with Harley. He was also tired, tired as shit. Tonight had been—

What had tonight been? A strain? An adrenaline pumper? A *Far Side* cartoon?

All of the above.

He shouldn't have lost his temper with J.J. He shouldn't have lost his temper with Agent Swann. But she'd pissed him off. He was still pissed off just thinking about it, but as much at himself now as her. Might as well admit it, they'd both made mistakes, and the outcome could have been worse.

He just hoped that by tomorrow she'd be willing to forget the whole thing and not raise a fuss. In all fairness, their dual mistakes ought to cancel out.

This was why he didn't like working with a goddamn partner.

She'd handled herself pretty well, though, gotten the drop on him, sure as hell; he could still feel the shock of that gun in his gut, an icy clutch that squeezed all the way to his balls. He hadn't been expecting that.

Another mistake?

Dal shrugged. Always expect the unexpected—Standard Rule Number One for staying alive. But he'd thought she was Cherry and just hadn't anticipated the gun.

And what had happened to Cherry? She'd disappeared. There hadn't been anyone else nearby when he'd blundered out of that alley into Agent Swann. So where'd she gone?

He'd probably run right past her in the dark when he'd mistaken Swann for her on the street. She'd probably been tucked into some side hole with Willie Dee.

Willie. And what the hell was that little bastard up to? Making himself scarce out on the street; popping up in dark alleys; writing poetry? It made no sense.

Questions.

He rounded the corner at Fifth and headed toward an oasis of light midway up the block on the left-hand side. Pulled into the parking lot of the all-night package store. He needed something to make him sleep.

Went in, bought a fifth of George Dickel. It took most of his cash.

The whole time he was in there, he kept glancing around the empty store, glancing at the door as if expecting something to happen, some two-bit loser with a gun in his hand and a load on his brain to maybe burst in and start the whole thing rolling— eight ball in the corner pocket, quarter in the slot.

The clerk stared at him nervously as if he were thinking the same thing. About Dal.

Dal took his bottle and left, feeling primed, and unfulfilled, and vaguely disgusted at the knowledge that he was more than just anticipating some incident might happen; he'd been hoping it would.

He got in the car, threw George on the seat beside him, and drove out of there slowly as an exercise in control. What he wanted to do was squeal rubber and gun the car down the block.

Dal frowned in the darkness of the car's interior. He wanted a drink. Why hadn't he grabbed a shot before leaving the parking lot?

You drink too much.

J.J.'s voice—coming at him from the left side of his brain, the shriek of the harpy in it. He could hear it blossoming through his ears and setting his teeth on edge as though J.J. were sitting right here in the car with him.

Dal cocked an ear toward the passenger's seat.

"You say something, George?"

He grinned.

"Didn't think so."

Shouldn't be so hard on J.J. He meant well. He always meant well, even when he was acting like a father. Or a mother, as the case might be. Sure, he had Dal's best interests at heart, Dal didn't dispute that. And he was glad there was somebody around who gave a shit. Damn glad! If it weren't for J.J. . . .

"Might be just you and me, George," he murmured, truly thankful for his friend.

But J.J. didn't always understand.

There were times when a cop had to take the edge off, just blot everything out for a while. It was a way to cope. Not a great way, Dal would grant him that. But a way.

Like tonight.

Tonight lay like a pain in his gut, an itch beneath his skin— *a prickle on the back of his neck.*

His hands tensed on the steering wheel. Something was wrong.

Light from the occasional street lamps he passed winked across his vision and was gone. Night licked at his heels.

Eyes. Fixed on him from the dark backseat.

Suddenly Dal was sure someone was inside the car with him, had crawled in while he'd been inside the liquor store and was now hiding, waiting for just the right moment to jump him.

Keeping his hands tight on the steering wheel, he shifted his eyes from the road to the rearview mirror and back again, planning his move.

Tension—*anticipation*—became an almost physical presence in the car. Pure jazz. Dal grinned as he jerked the wheel to the left and slammed his body right and down while the car careened across the road into the far curb. He kicked the gear into park, shoved his way out the passenger door and lay flat on the ground, gun already out.

Nothing happened.

No response to his move.

Nothing.

He raised his body an inch or two. Looked around.

He couldn't hear anything; the car's engine had died, there was no other traffic.

And no one moving in the backseat.

Slowly, Dal shifted his body to the rear of the back door, reached up, jerked it open.

Gun aimed, he peered into the empty interior.

If anybody had been in there, they were gone now.

Dal panned the surrounding area, alert for any sign that his phantom passenger was on the prowl.

Phantom?

He was beginning to feel a little foolish. He straightened as a car drove by, slowed, its driver craning his neck to see what had happened. Apparently the man decided if it had been a wreck that nobody was hurt and it might be dangerous to stop. The car sped away.

Dal glanced around one more time, slammed both doors, then went around and climbed in on the driver's side, first checking the door behind him.

It was firmly shut.

Nobody had been in the car—*was he losing his mind?*

Angry with himself, he restarted the car and peeled out, the way he'd wanted to do back at the package store.

The faster and farther he went, the stronger became the sensation that someone was right behind him, staring at the back of his head.

Dal was drenched with sweat by the time he pulled into the parking space at his apartment.

"Nervous reaction. Pent-up energy. Adrenaline overload," he muttered as he swung himself out of the car, dropping a glance to the backseat once more, though he knew there was nobody there.

He saw the envelope.

The manila envelope with the photograph in it.

The picture of the alley where somebody had been standing, the same alley he'd driven past tonight.

It was as though he could feel the eyes staring up at him, their gaze piercing through the envelope, across the dark empty space.

Looking at him.

Dal reached over the seat and grabbed the envelope.

It felt cold. He shivered. *The night air,* he told himself as he slammed the car door, climbed the stairs, went inside.

The sweat had turned to ice water, chilling his skin. Goosebumps sped up his arm and over his flesh, starting from the hand that was holding the envelope. He needed a drink.

He'd left the bottle in the car.

Carefully, he opened the envelope. Slipped the photograph out.

It slid easily from its package. He dropped the envelope to the floor.

Stood staring at the photo. At the shadowy form—still fuzzy and indistinct—but definitely there.

And from the depths of that alley, from the dark recess where the face should have been, someone stared back.

TWENTY-ONE

J.J. heard the rapping on the door. He didn't want to. He was almost asleep.

He tugged the covers over his head, trying to recapture the soft, befogged state of near-slumber, but the knocking wouldn't go away. It kept on and on, steadily drumming into his skull until the murky folds of semiconsciousness receded and left him fully awake.

"Great."

He threw the covers off, got up, and shook his legs to slide his sweat pants back into place. He always slept in sweat pants, and they always rode up. But what if there were a fire and he didn't have time to put on his pants, or couldn't locate them in the smoke?

Not a pleasant thought, getting caught in your boxer shorts in front of the neighbors, the fire*persons,* and God knew whoever else might happen by. It'd be his luck for the paper to get wind of it and have Genna on the scene snapping pictures by the score. He didn't want to be a newsroom bulletin-board pinup, thank you very much.

Mumbling to himself, he headed for the door.

"Blast it all, Dal. Middle of the night. Waking me up. Why didn't you just stay here in the first place?"

He fumbled with the table lamp in the living room, switched it on.

"Twice in one night. That's too bloody much. Probably drunk by now—and you better not have a forty-dollar cab bill either."

Raising his voice on this last invective, he unlocked the front door and pulled it open.

It wasn't Dal who stood on his front porch.

It wasn't anyone he'd ever seen before.

For a minute J.J. just hung in the doorway with his mouth half open, staring at the stranger on his doorstep, trying to rechannel his thoughts. He'd been all set to start railing at Dal.

"Uh . . . Yes? Can I help you?"

A nice-looking young black man stood there, dressed as if he'd been to a fancy restaurant or elegant dinner party. He exuded wealth, poise, sophistication.

J.J. glanced past him, half expecting to see an expensive sports car or limo pulled in at the curb, but there was nothing. No vehicle of any sort. Must have had car trouble or run out of gas or something.

He switched his gaze back to the stranger's face. "Need to use the phone?"

The man smiled.

J.J. felt drawn to the warmth in that smile, the friendliness. The smile made him feel he'd known this guy all his life; give it ten minutes or so and they'd be old friends.

Then he looked into the man's eyes.

The warmth he'd felt dwindled, melting, running down his arms and legs, draining out the ends of his fingers and puddling up at his feet. He felt empty and chilled.

A cool breeze touched his face, stirring the hairs on his skin. A strange lethargy was stealing over him.

Something in the back of J.J.'s brain began to prickle. Maybe it wasn't such a good idea to throw open your door in the middle of the night to whoever knocked.

He started to step back into the house, shut the door, lock the door—*lock the door*—but his feet were oddly heavy all of a sudden, his arms and legs too thick, too cumbersome to move. His vision wavered, sending a wash of dizziness careening downward to mix with the little sparkles of light that were spiraling up.

The world went black.

Dal ran the red light at Fifth and Archer, wishing to hell he *would* see a city cop, or anybody at all on these godforsaken empty streets to keep him from feeling as if he were the only person left on earth or that maybe he'd blundered into the Twilight Zone or something.

Beside him on the seat, the manila envelope with the photograph crammed back inside rode along with him, a silent passenger mocking him as he stepped even harder on the accelerator pedal and careened breakneck off Archer onto Turner, then right onto Island Drive.

Just a little farther now.

Gritting his teeth, he hung a left on Courtney and mashed down the brake pedal, slowing for the right-hand turn onto Crestland. He pulled in at the curb in front of the small stone house and parked.

Grabbing the envelope, he jumped out of the car and bounded up the front-porch steps, banging on the door with no regard for rousing J.J.'s ire or his sleeping neighbors.

This was something that had to be done right now, and he didn't care who the hell it inconvenienced.

182

He alternated knocking and ringing the bell. "C'mon, Harley, dammit. Wake up." No way was he going to go through what was left of this night without having someone else look at this goddamn picture. No way.

"C'mon, man." He pounded some more.

Maybe it was the light. Maybe it was his imagination. But Dal had seen what he'd seen, and he had to know if anybody else could see it too. He had to know.

If he was losing it—*big-time*, from overwork, stress, *drinking too much*, whatever—it was time to face the music, or the photograph as it were—get the picture?

He felt like laughing, or swearing, or putting his fist through the wood he was pounding on.

His head was spinning as if he were halfway drunk, and he hadn't even had a damn drink since those three beers at Godiva's. Not a one.

"Yo, J.J.," he bellowed, reaching for the doorknob to give it a good shake. Maybe that would get him up, make him think someone was breaking in—

The door came open with the first jolt.

Dal caught his balance as the unexpected shift in position threatened to plunge him headfirst into the room. *What the hell?* J.J. never left his door unlocked, the man was a nitpicker about it, as he was about everything else. He'd even had the locks changed after Dal had lost his extra key that time. And refused to give Dal another one.

Frowning, he stepped inside. "Yo, Harley? You asleep?"

He peered through the lamp-lit living room into the dark hall which led to the bedroom, expecting to see his friend come stomping out, ranting and raving about Dal waking him up.

C'mon, man.

He waited for it to happen. But the house remained silent. Too silent. It felt empty.

Sudden weakness spilled over Dal like a douse of ice water. For a moment he felt trembly, almost faint, as if he were going to pass out. Nausea gushed up inside him until he could taste bitter stomach bile in his throat. He swallowed hard, feeling an unnatural tightness there.

What if someone had actually broken in here as J.J. had claimed? What if that someone had come back?

Someone's coming to get you.

"Get real, Dallas," he muttered, forcing the weakness, the nausea back down. The moment passed.

But the thought that had numbed his mind and stabbed his gut still lingered. The immobilizing thought that he'd walk into that bedroom and find J.J. lying there—lying there—

He shoved the unthinkable word aside. Nothing was wrong. Nothing had happened to J.J. He was just sleeping the sleep of the—

A sudden draft of wind from the open door behind him wandered in, chilling the sweat on Dal's forehead, chest, and back. *Don't think it—don't even think it—if you think it, it might come true.*

Until this moment, he'd never consciously thought about how much he relied on J.J. On his friendship, on his always being there. J.J. was forever lecturing that Dal had no stability in his life. He was wrong. He had J.J.

Dal laid the envelope on the table by the door, and crossed the room to the shadowed hallway, checking around him as he went—

almost like he'd do at a crime scene, looking for clues, for something out of the norm.

There was no reason for this, no reason at all, everything was okay.

Someone's coming to get you.

The living room was just as he'd left it—what, an hour ago? Less? The computer had been turned off, that's all.

His palm itched with the sudden, familiar urge to fill it with his gun. Instead of the quicksilver rush to his senses, it made him feel sick.

Balling his hands into fists, he walked down the short hallway to the bedroom, passing the bath on his right, glancing in. The Mickey Mouse night-light he'd bought after J.J.'d complained about him leaving stuff all over the floor at night revealed an empty room, shower curtain pulled back, everything neat as a pin.

No sound came from the bedroom. The door was open. It was pitch-dark inside.

He walked over to the door and stopped, stood there a moment.

He didn't know what was causing him to hesitate, giving him goosebumps, making him afraid—

afraid to go into that room

afraid to turn on the light, to see what might be there.

It was as if he had a premonition, a sneak preview of what he'd see.

Something terrible.

Horseshit! Things like that don't happen.

Of course they do.

No. Not to me. Not to my friends.

And how many times have you heard that one?

He was just being overly cautious, acting like a cop.

Acting like a cop . . .

Feeling the tightness climb back into his throat, he grimly moved to the right of the open door, reached his hand around the corner, flipped on the overhead light.

The bed was empty.

Dal felt the muscles in his arms and stomach relax. He could breathe again. The image in his mind was just a goblin—*too many murder scenes, too many dead bodies. Too much crazy shit going on tonight.*

He felt almost as though he'd been sucked into a whirlpool and the undertow had been dragging him along all night, popping him up here and there, pulling him one way, then another. A random sequence of events that felt like utter chaos, and yet . . .

And yet it almost seemed as if it were planned.

Crazy. His imagination working overtime.

The bed'd been slept in, at least for a little while, Dal saw. The covers were mussed, thrown back. J.J. always made his bed every morning, just as he always locked his door every night.

Dal glanced around. There was nothing sinister in here. Nothing out of the way.

So why was he feeling as if there were?

J.J.'s clothes were neatly folded over the chair, the clothes he'd been wearing earlier tonight. That meant he'd been to bed.

Maybe he'd just gotten up—couldn't sleep—gone for a walk. Sure, that was probably all it was, he'd gone out jogging—*at two in the morning with the house unlocked?*—maybe he'd just forgot. Or maybe he'd been hungry, gone into the kitchen.

Dal headed for the kitchen.

"Goddammit, Harley, if you've blundered around and done something dumb like hurt yourself . . ."

Visions of J.J. getting up, still half-asleep, stumbling into the kitchen for a drink, slipping on an ice cube or something and knocking himself out—or slicing himself up with a knife while trying to make a sandwich, lying there passed out, bleeding to death—

The kitchen was empty. No ice cubes. No blood.

No J.J.

The back door was locked, safety chain on.

So he hadn't gone out that way.

Maybe he *had* gone jogging.

Dal strode back through the house, turning on lights as he went, not even attempting to be quiet as he looked into every room. The house was empty.

"Shit." He returned to the living room and stood there a minute, thinking, pissed off and restless and still a little bit scared. Then, cursing his stupidity, he went outside and checked the driveway for J.J.'s car. Sure enough. It was gone.

He stormed back in.

"Probably went to the fucking store for some fucking bread," he muttered, feeling no better for slamming the door behind him.

"Probably come driving up in half a fucking minute and accuse me of breaking into his fucking house."

He flung himself down onto the couch and stretched out, feeling a little stupid and a lot irritated and generally rattled and off balance. God, he felt as if he'd run a fifty-mile race.

He closed his eyes, thinking about the hard time he was going to give Harley when he returned. Nice to be on the doling-out end for a change. *Leaving his door open. Going out for groceries in the middle of the night . . .*

The phone woke him.

Dal squeezed his eyelids against the brightness stabbing at them, wishing he could squeeze his ears shut, as well.

The ringing persisted.

He opened his eyes halfway, and for a moment wasn't too sure where he was or what he was doing here.

Then he remembered. Apparently he'd fallen asleep waiting for J.J. to come home.

"Damn!" He levered himself to a sitting position, wincing as his back muscles protested the sudden move, rolled his shoulders to get some of the stiffness out as he jumped up to go check the bedroom, ignoring the phone.

Had J.J. ever come in? He hadn't heard him. And the usual pillow and blanket his friend stuffed around him when he passed out on the couch were absent.

Something was wrong.

The phone continued to ring.

One glance at the bedroom told him all he needed to know. J.J. had not returned. The room was as he'd seen it last night. Bed empty. Clothes folded over the rack.

A quick-flash of fear shot over him, then subsided.

The ringing phone broke through his fugue.

Christ! It was probably J.J.

He dashed over to the desk, jerked up the receiver. "Hello? J.J.?"

The line was open, but nobody said anything.

"Hello, hello? Who is this?"

Dal thought he heard a soft laugh, then after a minute a click. Then the dial tone.

Something about that chilled him, and he didn't know why. Unease turned to anger.

"Shit. Goddamn wrong number." He hung the receiver up again, none too gently. And almost immediately picked it back up.

Dialed the newspaper. Maybe J.J.'d been sent out on a late-breaking story last night. Maybe he'd gone straight in to work.

But nobody at the paper had seen him. A check with the city editor showed that he hadn't been in, hadn't been called out on a story, not today, not last night.

Dal hung up.

Where the hell was he? Was something wrong? He'd sensed it last night, he just hadn't wanted to admit it. *Still didn't.*

Was he overreacting? Maybe. Hopefully.

But what if something had happened?

187

Worry hardened in him like a rock. It was times like these when he cursed his insider's knowledge of disasters.

He picked up the phone once more, called Andy, asked him to check out all the hospitals, all the accident reports, the entire routine. He couldn't bring himself to say "morgue," but it hung in the air between them and he knew Andy would check that too.

"I'm on my way," Dal said, and hung up.

Taking a quick pass at the bathroom, he took a leak, splashed his whole head with water, tucked in his shirt.

Went into the kitchen and penned a note: CALL ME IMMEDIATELY WHEN YOU COME IN. Stuck it on the fridge.

Glanced at Buddy's cage.

Better check his birdseed, give him some fresh water. He pulled off the cover.

Buddy lay on his side at the bottom of his cage. Eyes open, body stiff.

Something froze inside Dal.

He lifted the wire closure, picked up the little bird. Buddy had been dead for some time, the small, fragile body was cold and hard. The soft blue-gray feathers felt as dry and lifeless as the corpse.

What had happened? What had killed the little bird?

There was something bad about this. Something totally bad.

Wrapping the little body in a dish towel, Dal headed for the door. The sense of being caught up in a whirlpool returned. A giant whirlpool where he was spinning around and around, trying to keep his head above water and gasp for air.

Something was wrong. Something was very wrong.

About to reach for the doorknob, he glanced at the manila envelope with the picture in it, lying on the table where he'd tossed it last night. He hadn't thought about it since.

Not till now.

The urge to open it spread over him, and he had the uncanny sensation that the shadow image might be clearer now, might be—

No. That was too crazy. That was totally insane.

But he couldn't bring himself to look.

Picking the envelope up, he took it and Buddy's corpse and left the house, leaving the door unlocked behind him.

J.J. would be furious if—*when* he came home. Dal could live with that.

Mama, Mama, take my hand
Save me from de ol' Boneman

TWENTY-TWO

Darkness pressed down on J.J. Heavy and silent, as if he were deep within the bowels of a cave. He could feel the weight of it massed around him, rock-solid and impenetrable, trapping him in some sort of black pocket where nothing moved, there was no hint of light or sound.

What was going on? Why had he been brought to this place, wherever this was?

He felt—nothing. Not hot or cold. Not sick or well. Reasonably comfortable, or at least not uncomfortable. Nothing hurt.

That was on the plus side.

On the minus: He couldn't feel his toes.

He'd been trying to, ever since consciousness had crept back in about ten minutes to a century ago, trying to regain some motor control over a body that was totally unresponsive. Nothing worked.

Or if it did, he couldn't tell.

He thought his eyes were open, but the need to blink was absent. He couldn't be sure his eyes were actually open. Maybe he was blindfolded and just couldn't feel the tape, or whatever it was.

He couldn't even be sure he was really awake—except that he was.

He took it for granted that he was breathing, though he couldn't feel his chest at work or air being drawn in through his nostrils or mouth. Couldn't even tell if his mouth was closed or open.

He could think, though. His mind was surprisingly clear and sharp. Whatever that man had done to him—or given him, *now there's a pleasant thought*—seemed to be affecting only his ability to move. And feel. He couldn't tell what he was lying on, whether it was hard or soft, ground or floor. Might even be a bed.

It was sort of like lying motionless in a tub of hot water until temperatures had equalized, until you couldn't tell the difference between the porcelain, the water, or the air against your skin. They all felt alike.

Maybe he'd been tied up so tight that the circulation was cut off and his entire body had gone numb. Maybe that was it.

He tried concentrating on determining what was beneath his prone body, focusing his total senses on it.

That didn't work either. But feeling was bound to come back eventually whenever the drug—if it was a drug—wore off.

The thought of an unknown, probably dangerous drug at work in his body was grim. What about lasting conditions? Side effects? Had the needle been clean?

Funny, he didn't remember feeling a needle prick him, or the man ever being close enough to do it. At least he didn't think so. That part was rather muddled. Maybe the guy hadn't been alone.

He knew he should be afraid, but he wasn't. Not yet, anyway. Right now he was more interested in the who, what, when, where, why, and how. Reporter's job—right?

That man, J.J.'d never seen him before. It didn't make sense. Why would somebody want to kidnap him?

J.J. didn't get the sense of anyone being nearby. Apparently his captors had left him here to awaken in his own time. But they were bound to check on him eventually.

Then what? Should he fake being asleep? Make them think he was still helpless, then try and make a break for it? Providing the paralysis had worn off by then, of course.

Choices.

What would Jehovah Jones do in a situation like this? More to the point: What would Dal do?

Whatever it was, J.J. doubted he could do it. Dal was trained; he was not. Playing cops and robbers for real was not his forte. Still, it was only logical that he try to come up with some sort of plan that might stand a chance of getting him out of here reasonably intact. Or would cooperation be the better course?

Choices.

What should he do?

Be afraid, for starters.

Maybe he was in shock and his mind had thrown up a protective shield that was letting him consider his plight objectively without the debilitating factors of panic and terror entering in.

Maybe it was his reporter's analytical process at work. If they'd wanted him dead, he'd be dead already, right?

So what was the deal? Had he written something that someone didn't like? Been privy to any sensitive or off-the-record information that might set him up as a target?

What?

Guess we just wait and find out, J.J. thought, for the first time pondering the possibilities of what that might entail.

Suddenly, an unsettling thought struck him: He'd seen that guy's face. In all the stories and books he'd read, in all the crimes he'd reported on and all the research he'd done into such events, one fact stood out above the rest: Criminals don't like to leave eyewitnesses who can identify them.

For the first time since J.J. had woken up, he was scared.

TWENTY-THREE

Jackie parked the Mercedes station wagon in the restricted lot and headed toward Phoenix City PD's brown brick building. Warm morning sunshine beat down on her back and shoulders, doing its best to chase away the chill that filled her body. Not succeeding.

The argument she'd had with Philip when she'd returned home

in the wee hours of the morning still rang like an echoing death knell down the back roads of her brain.

He'd been waiting up for her. She'd been primed for the confrontation.

It had left them both shaken. And Jackie knew, with a certainty that brought nausea to the pit of her stomach and tightness to her throat, that they were near a crisis in their marriage.

That thought left a bleakness in its wake, so that she wasn't actively aware of Detective Reid coming out of the building and striding toward her until he'd grasped her arm.

"I want to talk to you." He swung her around in the opposite direction and began pulling her along.

"Now, just a minute!" She started to shake his hand off, feeling last night's anger rekindle and mix with this morning's precarious control.

He jerked to a halt and turned to look at her. "I haven't got a minute," he said, not releasing her, and there was so much fury and raw emotion in the words that Jackie felt a moment's hesitation.

Then her own rage took hold. "If this is about what happened last night, forget it! As far as I'm concerned we can go in there to your captain right now and spread this whole thing on the table."

She'd decided on the drive over this morning not to make waves about what had happened last night. They'd both been at fault, and luckily nothing serious had come of it. They should be able to work it out between themselves. But if he was going to—

"Listen to me," he said, gripping her arm even tighter, fingers digging through the thin linen blazer and cotton shirtsleeve into her flesh. She didn't think he realized he was doing it. "I've got to talk to you. And I don't have time to stand around in a parking lot arguing about it."

She searched his face, reading worry and determination in the set features, the black holes of his eyes. This wasn't about their altercation last night. This was about something else entirely.

"Please," he said tightly, and it was obvious he was fighting some inner demon—and just barely keeping it in check.

Jackie knew about those. She gazed into his dark, thickly lashed eyes, now rimmed with bruise-colored shadows, and wondered what the hell this was all about.

Nodding once, she went with him to his car.

They fought the morning rush-hour traffic. Dal narrowly avoided several rear-end collisions by slamming on the brakes, then swerving into another lane and gunning the car forward again. Jackie held on to the door handle, and her temper, with tight control, gritting her teeth at every near miss. She damn sure hadn't bargained for getting herself killed when she'd agreed to go with him. After half a dozen blocks, he turned onto a side street and headed into a more residential area, leaving the main city congestion behind.

"Where are we going?" she asked, when she was able to relax enough to talk normally.

"To a friend's house." He didn't take his eyes off the road, which was probably a blessing. He hadn't slowed down a bit. "He disappeared last night and I think something's happened to him. It may be tied in with this case. I need your help to find out."

She studied his profile, drawn with worry and concentration, as they sped along the quiet residential street, and wondered what kind of help he had in mind. He was still an unknown quantity—and a loose cannon at the wheel, maybe even at the job, she decided. Last night had done nothing to reassure her on that front. She'd have liked to question him further, but at the rate of speed they were traveling, thought it might not be wise. So she leaned back against the seat and they rode the rest of the way in silence.

In a short time, Reid pulled in at the curb in front of a small stone house. "Still gone," he muttered as he threw open his door and jumped out. "At least, his car is."

Jackie followed Reid, and they threaded the short stone walkway to the porch stairs, where he took them two at a time, then preceded her into the house.

"J.J.?" he hollered as he strode inside. No one answered.

It was cool and still inside. Jackie shivered at a little touch of apprehension that came out of nowhere to brush a few goosebumps across her arms. The house held a feeling of unnatural emptiness.

What an absurd thought. She rubbed her skin. It was just a breeze.

Reid had left the door open behind them. "So I can hear his car drive up," he'd said, more to himself, Jackie thought, than for her benefit. She watched him quickly check out the rest of the house.

He was a bundle of nerves and pent-up energy, and she followed his trek through the rear of the house by the impatient sounds of doors being wrenched open, banged shut, a shower curtain jerked back, furniture being jostled aside.

His face told the story when he returned. He headed toward the kitchen.

Jackie moved from the spot just inside the front door where she'd been standing and followed him out. He was standing by the refrigerator, staring at a note stuck to it by a smiley-face magnet: CALL ME IMMEDIATELY WHEN YOU GET HOME. For a moment he just stood there, as if uncertain what to do next, what action to take.

This was a man who needed to keep moving. It was as though each moment of inaction drove a nail in his gut.

"Reid?"

He turned around, gestured to a kitchen chair, and she walked over to it but remained standing.

"Are you ready to tell me now what this is all about?"

He pulled out another chair and sank down onto it, rubbing a hand across his forehead. "I need to know what happened with you and Lonnie last night. Everything. In detail."

She stood there, not particularly liking being treated as an interrogation subject. "I'd really like to know what this is all about, Detective Reid."

With a curse of exasperation, he slammed his hand to the table and glared up at her. "Look, I haven't got time to go through it all right now. Christ! I'm not even sure I know myself. But believe me, my friend may be in real trouble, and it looks like I'm the only one who's going to do something about it. And if you think I'm going to wait around here until something else happens to prove my point, or maybe it turns out to be too fucking late to do anything at all, then you're as big an idiot as that goddamn Cutter. Now are you going to help me or not?"

The remark about Cutter provided some insight into his anger. She studied his face and saw desperation beneath the anger, and something else: fear.

She pulled out the chair and sat down. "Where shall I start?"

Reid shrugged impatiently. "I don't know. The beginning. Did Lonnie say anything during the drive over to State Street?"

Jackie shook her head. "Very little." She went over their conversation, trying to recall every detail. He made no comment about the pass Lonnie had made.

"How about while you were in Godiva's? You were there for almost an hour and a half."

Jackie clamped her teeth on the rebuttal that it had been forty-five minutes, tops. "We didn't talk much. Too loud." She relayed what she could remember.

"What about after? Where did you go?" He rubbed his forehead again, dragged the hand through his hair.

She began to relate the events, turning her vision inward and trying to relieve every moment of last evening. She could tell it wasn't what he was looking for from the way he kept rubbing his forehead and closing his eyes for longer stretches of time. He looked dog-tired, and she wondered if maybe he'd fallen asleep—until something she said caught his attention.

"Wait a minute." He looked up at her. "Did I hear you mention Willie Dee?"

She nodded. "That's the name Lonnie gave me. Told me he was nobody to worry about, just a street person. But . . ."

"But what?"

"I don't know. I thought at the time that the little man might be setting us up. He was just too . . . cooperative."

"Willie Dee," Reid murmured, his look turning thoughtful. "It keeps coming back to Willie Dee."

"What do you mean?"

Reid shrugged again. "It's just that he seems to keep popping up all the time. First with Cherry. Then me. Now you and Lonnie. Even J.J. said Willie got in the car with him out at the Davenport house . . ." His voice faded out, his expression puckering to a frown.

"Do you think he's behind these drug murders?" Try as she could, she had trouble with that one. But she'd seen too many unlikely looking killers to be thrown off the scent by someone's innocuous appearance.

Reid shook his head. "No, I don't. But I'm willing to bet he knows something about who and where that person is. C'mon." He jumped up, anxious to leave.

"Wait a minute." She got up, not quite as ready to jump as he was. This hotshot with his Action Jackson attitude could get them in some real trouble. Whatever had happened, it was obvious he'd become emotionally involved.

"Just what are we planning on doing here?" she asked him. "Where do you think—?"

"I don't think, I know. I'm going to find Willie Dee. And when I do, I'm going to get some answers. Now are you with me, or do you want to call a cab to come take you back to the station?" He gestured impatiently toward the wall phone on his way out.

Against her better judgment, she followed him out to the car.

Scared.

He was scared.

The fear, once admitted, swooped in like a tornado, whipping around him, buffeting, beating, spearing lightning bolts through his body like jagged ice splinters driven on a merciless wind.

J.J. had never been so scared in his life.

Darkness surrounded him, sank down on him. It gagged his mouth, blindfolded his eyes, pressed in until he thought he could feel it entering his pores, crawling under his skin—

Dal, man! Get me out of here! Please come and get me out of here!

But would Dal even know he was gone? Days often passed between visits; no telling when Dal would be back. And they'd had that argument. It might be next week before somebody missed him, when he didn't show up at work.

Silence deafened him. His mind was screaming bloody murder, but no sounds were getting out. He couldn't hear a thing—no noise, no lights, no evidence that there was anybody in his little corner of the world but him.

Will somebody please come and get me out!

He couldn't stand it. He couldn't! What was going on? Why couldn't he hear anything—*feel* anything?

Minutes passed. Hours—*days.* And still nobody came.

J.J. began to wonder if he was becoming deaf to his own mute pleas, losing the ability to think rationally because now the darkness felt as if it were seeping inside his head, filling him up with gummy blackness—as if he were being embalmed.

Get me out of here!

He was choking on it. Drowning in it.

Out!

Deep inside himself he moaned, trying to push back the monstrous panic and grab the mouse of sanity that was threatening to skitter away.

Dal? Somebody! Where are you?

Where am I?

That thought cut through the rising waves, giving him a thread to hang on to. A piece of the madness to focus on. Maybe if he took this thing piece by piece he could keep from going crazy.

Where would they have put him?

A basement? Was it getting colder? Did it feel damp?

He'd begun to have the sensation of deepening coolness a while ago—how long? he didn't know—but now he began to wonder if it didn't feel damp too.

A basement. Sure. It could be a basement. Couldn't he smell the dirt?

Maybe if he tried very hard . . .

Nothing. There was nothing. No smells to go with the no sounds and the no light.

He was losing it.

Steady, J.J. Keep it steady.

The drug would soon be wearing off. It had to. How could he be feeling cold and damp unless it was starting to wear off?

Please let it be wearing off. He tried to move his toes.

Nothing.

Maybe it hadn't really been that long. Maybe it just seemed like a long time going past, locked here in this basement in the silent dark.

Again he tried to move his toes.

Don't think about it. It'll come. The drug is wearing off.

It's wearing off.

He could feel the cold, the dampness. Almost smell the basement dirt.

Couldn't he?

Or was he conjuring it all up in his mind? Like a prisoner in solitary confinement painting mental artwork on the barren walls of his cell.

Were there rats here? Rats lived in basements, didn't they? What would he do if they started crawling over him? Biting him? He wouldn't even feel it.

Oh, God, somebody come and get me out of here.

Don't lose it, J.J. Don't lose it, man. Think about something else—anything else.

Jehovah Jones. What would Jehovah Jones do in a situation like this?

The thought made him want to laugh. Laugh and laugh and laugh. *What good is God if He isn't God anymore?* J.J. wondered. He tried to laugh, tried very hard. But he couldn't tell if he was laughing—crying—maybe neither.

Were his eyelids squeezed shut? He tried to feel the muscles straining in his face. Imagined a tear leaking from one corner and tracing a ragged pathway toward his left ear.

But there was nothing. And the panic rose again, sending jolts of fear forking through him, ebony lightning bolts splitting the silent dark.

They split up, working State Street, asking questions. Dal had told her to meet him back at the car at three. It was nearly that now.

He'd gotten here first, and stood beside the car, waiting impatiently for her to show. He'd parked on a side street, far enough away to avoid their being seen together by anyone who counted. They'd walked in separately.

She'd made him stop at a K Mart on the way over, gone in a classy woman and come out a punk street kid—jeans and rock-star T-shirt, neon sneakers and a red plastic purse dangling on the end of a silver chain.

"No sense blowing my cover if I don't have to," she'd told him, and he'd felt vaguely annoyed with himself that he hadn't even thought of that.

He'd watched her transfer her .25 automatic from the expensive leather purse she'd been carrying to the cheap new red one and sling it bandolier style over her shoulder. It was barely big enough to hold the gun.

She'd also done something to her face, changed the makeup or maybe washed it all off, or something. Whatever she'd done had peeled ten years off her age, made her look vulnerable and street marked at the same time, that and the hair. She'd frizzed it, pulled it into a sideways ponytail high up on her head, put something in it that made it look oily around the roots, brassy, and in need of a wash.

So far, he'd seen three versions of Agent Swann, and wasn't at all sure that he'd seen the real one yet. Probably never would.

During the drive over, he'd given her a sketchy idea of why he thought J.J. might be involved in this, including Willie Dee's odd visit at the Davenport multiple and his cryptic threat—*someone's coming to get you.* Then there was the childish rhyme about this boneman, whatever that might mean, leading up to last night's visit to the house. He could tell she wasn't wholly buying it; but then, she didn't know J.J. as he did, and wouldn't put as much credence in what he knew was totally uncharacteristic behavior on J.J.'s part.

He didn't mention the photograph. That would have been enough to make Jackie question his sanity for good, as well as his ability to continue handling this case or any other. The only person he'd shown the photo to was Andy, first thing this morning. The shadowy image had been gone.

Dal still didn't know what to think about that. He'd been so sure. Maybe he *had* been working too hard lately and his eyes *were* playing tricks.

He didn't know. All he knew was that somehow J.J. had gotten tangled up in whatever was happening on the streets and it was up to Dal to find him.

Other than Andy, nobody down at the station was going to be able to give him much help, at least not officially. Anger flamed at the memory of Cutter's asshole comment: "There's no proof he's involved, Reid. Probably out on a story or off getting himself laid or something. You know the rules. Forty-eight hours on a missing-person report, and we haven't got the available manpower to go off investigating something like this on a whim." It had been all Dal could do to keep from hitting him.

The chief was out of town.

So that left it pretty much up to him to find J.J., and he just hoped to hell his buddy *was* out on a story or off getting laid or something of that sort.

He spotted Swann walking up the sidewalk, looking like a rebellious teenager playing hooky or a street kid on the bum. Even her walk was different. Maybe she'd taken drama courses. Done theater. He'd have to ask her to teach him a few of those tricks. Sometime, when the world was right again.

"Anything?"

She shook her head as she reached him. "Nothing at all. People looked at me as if they didn't even speak the language."

"Dammit." Dal felt anger stab at his gut again. He'd met a stone wall too. Everyone on the street seemed lobotomized. Nobody was talking. Nothing was being said. The few times he'd mentioned the word "boneman," people had looked at him as if he were carrying the plague.

He'd hoped Jackie might have better luck than he could playing the cop. At least that way they'd been able to cover both sides. Now he didn't know what the hell to do.

"Let's go back to the house," he said. "Maybe J.J.'s come home by now."

"Maybe so." The way she said it didn't sound overly optimistic; the feel of the street must be getting to her too. He winced as his own doubts came flooding in. He didn't want to hear them voiced. But she got in without another word and they drove off.

J.J. had not returned.

Dal called Andy, who'd been running some checks but had nothing to show for it. The unofficial APB Dal had put on J.J.'s car had netted no results, and Andy had extended it to the new shift. At least all units rolling would keep an eye out for J.J.'s vehicle and report in if they spotted it. Whitaker was coming by with his print kit after he got off duty.

And beyond that, there was nothing much else they could do.

The doorbell rang. It was Whitaker. Belcher was with him.

Together they covered the interior and exterior, and picked up a few things. But it didn't look good.

"We'll run it through," Whitaker said as they left, and Dal knew that everything these two lab guys could do would be done quickly and thoroughly.

It was now after five o'clock.

"I'm going back out." He couldn't stand sitting around here another moment. "Want me to drop you back at your car?"

She shook her head. "I'll stick around a while."

He nodded. "Thanks" was all he could say. It sounded trite to his ears, but he meant it.

They went back out to the car, and she offered to drive—did he look that beat? He let her. They didn't have that far to go and he hadn't had anything to eat all day, so maybe his stomach could take it.

She proved to be a good driver. He found himself beginning to relax, and decided that maybe Swann might be a pretty good man to have around.

They made a pass by Lonnie's rooming house, as they had earlier, but he still wasn't home. Dal began to speculate if maybe he, too, had been snatched, or had he just "disappeared" for a while to keep out of the way? The latter was probably the case, though Dal wasn't dismissing the other possibility.

Or was he seeing shadows where there were none? Like that image in the photograph.

God, he was tired.

"By the way"—Swann startled him out of a near doze—"mind telling me what happened to you last night after Lonnie and I left Godiva's?"

He rolled his neck and felt the stiffness that had gathered there, flipped on the air conditioner and welcomed the sudden blast of cold air. "I got lured into a chase by a hooker named Cherry Pye. She's the one who gave me that bad information on the dude named Poppy, said he killed Coley Dean. Said Willie Dee had told her that."

He frowned. Good ol' Willie. "Anyway, she led me a merry chase through a back-alley maze that must have taken me around in circles until I wasn't sure where the hell I was. Didn't really know until I piled out of that alley into you." He hesitated a moment. "You scared the bejesus out of me, by the way. Wasn't expecting Cherry to have a gun."

She gave him a quick sideways glance.

"Just thought you'd like to know," he murmured.

She made no comment.

"Willie was in there too," he added, and they traded another look. "Like I said, he keeps popping up."

She glanced back at the road. "Would this hooker of yours happen to be a bleached blonde? Cherry-red lipstick and nail polish?"

Dal nodded. "That's her."

"She was in the ladies' room at Godiva's, came in after I did. I'd forgotten about that."

"What did she say?"

Jackie shook her head. "Nothing. She just stared at me for a minute, then went into one of the stalls. I left before she came out again. She couldn't have known who I was."

She made the right turn onto Glendale, apparently pretty good with directions—he hadn't had to prompt her yet.

"That sounds about right. I must have caught her just as she was coming out again."

They lapsed into silence.

"Ask around for Cherry while you're at it," he said as she pulled in to the curb a couple of streets over from where they'd parked earlier that day. "It'd do better coming from you. I'll check for Lonnie. Let's stay in sight of one another this time. I'll work one side of the strip, you work the other. If we need to, we'll swap."

She nodded, and they went their separate ways, Dal feeling the fear coiled up at the pit of his stomach like a snake ready to strike.

There was something wrong with this, something bad wrong. And it was getting wronger by the minute.

Daddy, Daddy, come and stay
Make de Boneman go away

TWENTY-FOUR

The panic had passed for the moment. But fear still clung to J.J. the way a drowning person grasps at the slippery underside of a capsized boat. Any minute now he'd be pulled back down again, back into that rising sea of panic.

He didn't know how long he'd been here. Time had lost all meaning. It might have been an hour, a day.

Feeling and emotion were absent, except for fear, of course, which was doing quite nicely, thank you very much. But he wouldn't think about that. Soon somebody would come for him. It had to be soon. They couldn't leave him here forever, could they? There was no reason for it. No reason at all.

Did he have to go to the bathroom? That might have given him some indication of how long he'd been unconscious, but he couldn't feel anything down there, either, and he quickly shut the door on that particular thought. Like a slippery slide, it led back down into the sea, and he had to keep his head above the panic, keep treading the waves so he could think straight when they came to get him—

—*if* they came to get him—*Why didn't someone come to get him?*

Maybe that was their intent, leave him here until he was a gibbering idiot who'd do anything they asked.

But what on God's green earth could they possibly ask for? What did he have, what could he do that might give someone cause to kidnap him, lock him away like this? He didn't know that man who'd appeared at his door, could swear he'd never seen him before. It made no sense. None at all.

What use could he possibly be?

Careful, J.J. Watch out for the rising tide.

He blanked his thoughts for a moment, and maybe slept a little because, suddenly, when he came to again, the darkness didn't seem quite as thick as it had before. It seemed to be lightening up around him, like a dimmer switch being slowly turned, melting the darkness from pitch-black, into sooty, and finally to charcoal-gray.

He blinked. His eyelids were working! He could feel them. He could see the light!

Was he dreaming? Was this some sort of hideous dream and in a minute he'd wake up and find himself back in the dark again, alone in that silent dark? Maybe this was all a dream. Maybe he'd wake up back at his house, in his bed.

Let that be it—please, God! Let that be it.

But that wasn't it. He could tell as the light continued to grow, up from gray to murky yellow, then warming to a soft constant glow like muted lamplight or the dusky gold of candles.

He sat up, flexing his body experimentally. It felt miraculously light. Light as a feather. And strong. No obvious ill effects from the drug. *Thank you, God.*

He looked around. He wasn't in a basement after all. He was in a bedroom. Large, with high ceilings. Old, but in good repair, and furnished with obvious wealth, though a bit on the ostentatious side. He'd never been here before, he'd swear to that, and hadn't a clue as to where he was.

Another thing: The room was empty.

So who had turned on the lights?

Antique sconces lined the gilt and red flocked walls, but the bulbs were strictly modern: K Mart blue-light special, four in a pack for a buck ninety-eight. Someone, somewhere had turned them on.

Carefully, J.J. swung his legs over the side of the bed, and gasped as his bare feet met the icy hardwood floor. Of course, he hadn't had his shoes on when they'd kidnapped him—thank God he'd been wearing sweat pants.

He sat poised there a moment, waiting for his body, and his senses, to adjust; but mostly waiting for something to happen, someone to come. Where were they? What were they waiting for? He listened intently for some sound, some intrusion into the stillness that would give him a clue as to what was going on.

There was nothing.

"One way to find out what's up." He experienced a moment's

dizzying relief when he heard his own voice. He'd been more than half afraid he'd find himself mute.

But everything seemed to be in good working order again. He flexed his arms and legs once more to make sure, rolled his shoulders a couple of times. Stood up. A minor rush of blood to his feet and legs sent a smattering of pinpricks sprinting all the way to his toes. But in a moment that unpleasantness was gone.

Now to get out of here.

Carefully, he went over to the closed bedroom door, put his ear next to it and listened for any telltale noise beyond.

Nothing.

Slowly he turned the handle, sure he would find it locked. With a soft click, the door eased open. He held his breath, afraid to pull it any wider, afraid of what might be lurking on the other side. But when an eon passed and nothing happened, he drew up his courage, cracked the door several inches, and peered into a hall.

The hall was empty, at least what he could see of it. A rich burgundy-colored carpet runner covered most of the wood floor and stretched left and right. It had once been luxurious, but now it was old, worn through in spots. The walls were paneled in dark, heavy walnut; they looked almost black. More sconces lit the corridor, giving it a low, lustrous sheen. But there was a layer of dust on everything, as though no one had bothered to clean it for months. He spotted a few boxes stacked against the far wall. Maybe whoever lived here was just moving in. Or out.

Did it really matter?

J.J. widened the crack another inch or so, stuck his head out and glanced left and right. The hallway was truly empty. Other closed doors lined both sides, and he could see the top of a staircase off to his left. Where were his captors?

This was strange. Too strange.

He darted out into the hall and across to the door opposite, grateful for the thick carpet that muffled the sound of his footfalls—just in case they didn't know what he was about. Gingerly he tried the knob. Locked.

He did this with each of the other doors, making his way closer to the staircase with every move, careful not to give himself away. All were locked. Flattening himself against the corner of the wall next to the head of the staircase, J.J. stood listening for sounds from below. It was as if he were alone in the house. After a moment, he risked a peek around the edge.

The narrow stairs descended to an intermediate landing, made an abrupt right-angle turn, then continued on down. He couldn't see the bottom of the enclosed stairway.

The silence was unnerving. He should have been able to hear something by now, see someone, but there was nothing, and J.J. felt the ever-present fear lurch forward again, almost paralyzing him.

Had they heard him coming? Were they hiding down there, waiting to jump him when he went by?

That was too crazy. Why would they do all this? Why wouldn't they just come get him in his room?

What was going on?

He felt as if he were being watched; eyes in the walls. Like those two-way mirrors they used in retail stores to spot shoplifters, or those stately portraits with peepholes in the eyes, more in keeping with this decor. But there were no portraits hanging on the walls, no mirrors that he could see.

Still he felt as if he were being watched—and maneuvered; manipulated like a laboratory rat in a maze.

Creepy feeling. Creepy.

Was there another way out of here?

He glanced back down the hall, noting the solid walls on both ends, the locked doors. That way was closed to him. There was only one way to go. Down.

So, okay. If this was their way of prompting him down the stairs, he guessed he didn't have much choice. Quashing the fear and uncertainty, he stepped out into the empty space at the top of the staircase.

Immediately, he felt the icy clutch of fear. It was like stepping out on stage in his underwear, utterly terrifying, totally exposed. But no one challenged him, and he had no sense of anyone lurking below him on the stairs. Taking a deep breath and holding it, he cautiously began to descend.

At the landing, he stopped, listened some more. Breathed. Still there was nothing. No movement, no sounds.

Maybe whoever had brought him here had simply dumped him in that room up there, thinking he'd be out for longer than he was. Maybe there was nobody home right now but him.

And maybe there's such a thing as the Easter Bunny too. And Santa Claus, and the Tooth Fairy, and she's the one who turned on the lights and unlocked your door.

Nervously, J.J. continued on down, feeling the fear congealing into a solid lump that stretched from groin to throat. Never had seconds seemed to crawl by so slowly. Never had a distance seemed so long. At any moment, he expected to be confronted by the ones who had brought him here, that man who'd knocked at his door.

Nobody appeared.

The staircase dropped into a small entry hall. J.J. studied the layout for a moment. The place looked like an old town house, or one of those old Victorians over on the south side of town. A number of agencies were restoring old houses around the city as private residences or elegant office facilities for the rich and trendy.

He must still be somewhere in the city, though it seemed like he should hear some traffic noise, even in the semiresidential sections of town.

The front door loomed to the left of the stairs. It was solid and looked brand-new, plenty sturdy, he'd bet. A shiny new lock caught his eye; looked like a dead bolt. There were no windows in the foyer, but a peephole had been installed in the front door at eye level.

Across from him, sliding pocket doors were closed. Maybe a living room. No light shone through the cracks. The only other door looked like a coat closet.

Unfortunately, the thick carpeting ended abruptly at the bottom of the staircase. The original hardwood floors would have been beautiful, but they were badly scuff-marked, and certainly wouldn't absorb sounds.

Four paces, J.J. estimated, five at the most, and he could reach the front door.

What if it were locked?

Of course it's locked! the panic shouted. *Do you really think they'd be stupid enough to leave the front door unlocked, you imbecile?*

But locks on the front doors of houses are installed to keep people out, not in.

He stood there a moment, poised on the second riser from the bottom, debating his course of action. The longer he stood there, the surer he was that someone else was standing nearby, just around the corner from him, waiting until he descended these last two steps to grab him. His flesh crawled with the feel of it, the certainty that he was not alone, that whoever had brought him here was not about to let him leave this place so easily.

Why were they doing this? Why?

Holding his breath, he descended the final two steps.

The downstairs hall was empty.

A flood of relief washed over him as he hurriedly crossed to the front door. The relief was short-lived. The lock was a double dead bolt, no key in sight. He looked through the peephole and could see an empty street out there, a few parked cars. It was still night.

So close, he was so close. He could have shouted with the helplessness, the unfairness of it. What could these people possibly want with him? Who was doing this? Why? It had to be a mistake, some kind of stupid mistake. They thought he was someone else, that had to be it.

He stood there a moment trying to compose himself, not doing too great a job.

Still, no one had stopped him yet. Maybe it wasn't all over till the fat lady sang.

Silently, he moved over to the closed pocket doors and tried them. Locked.

Stay calm, J.J. Stay calm.

He glanced down the hall. Light shone at the rear, a medium-bright glow spilling from a half-opened doorway on the left. Another sliding pocket door. Beyond that, a single door probably led out to the kitchen, and with luck the back way out.

If he could just make it down the hall.

Quietly, cautiously, he threaded the short hallway, hardly daring to breathe and just waiting for the old wood flooring to betray him.

But he managed to make the journey in silence, and at the edge of the open double doors he stopped, again listened. Everything was quiet.

He decided to risk a quick peek.

The room appeared to be empty.

He'd meant to keep going, after checking to make sure there was no one inside this room who might stop him. Then through the back door and out into the kitchen and away from this place. Smash a window if he had to. Break down the door. Would it matter by then how much noise he made?

Then he saw the telephone. It was right in the center of the desk.

Uncertainty struck again. What would be best? Go for the door? Go for the phone? What should he do?

Did he dare to risk making a call?

Did he dare *not* to? What if the back door had a dead bolt like the front? What if he couldn't break it down?

What if they were watching him right now and betting on his choice?

"Come into my parlor . . ."

He couldn't close his mind to the idea that he was being set up. It was just too pat. He was being herded from point A to point B with a devious sense of design, being poked and prodded through corridors, down staircases.

A rat in a maze.

And was that phone the cheese?

Grimly, J.J. made his decision: go for the bait. It was just too tempting to pass up.

He ducked into the room. If he was wrong about the setup, he might never get a better chance.

The room was an office of sorts, with the desk sitting in the center of the floor, a big leather chair drawn up to it. The rest of the room was furnished with comfortable sofas and chairs.

Windows lined the far wall, but he could see from here that they were fitted with fancy wrought-iron burglar-proof bars.

Another door opened off this room, some sort of anteroom beyond. He could see light inside there, too, through the cracks. Flickering light.

Still no sounds.

He hurried over to the telephone, keeping a wary eye on the

opening behind him, afraid to close the sliding doors because they might squeak and then someone would hear.

He grabbed up the phone, squeezing his eyes momentarily shut in heady disbelief as the dial tone sounded in his ear.

He carried the portable phone over to one of the windows, peering out as he punched in 911. It was still pitch-dark outside, so he couldn't have been here that long. A streetlight gleamed dully at the nearby corner, and J.J. could see that the area was a slum. No wonder they had dead-bolt locks and burglar bars.

Light shone faintly on a street sign. He narrowed his eyes to read what it said: 57th Ave. So. and D St. *Please let that be right.*

"C'mon, people, c'mon." He squeezed the phone, waiting through those endless seconds for the first ring—

A busy signal. He couldn't believe it. The buzz drummed vindictively in his ear. *No. Please, God, no.* He mashed the button and tried again. This time the busy signal was immediate.

A busy signal on 911? That wasn't supposed to happen!

Desperately he punched the trio of numbers a third time. His hand was sweaty and trembling. His fingers felt frozen to the bone. What was going on here?

The busy signal sounded once more.

He felt like throwing the phone against the wall, banging his head along with it. His insides were churning like a lava pit. He could taste the burning bile.

Quickly he punched in the police department number, hoping he could remember it right. His mind had tilted crazily.

Busy.

J.J. could have cried with frustration. Could have sat down and cried.

Instead, he took a deep breath, let it out slowly as he dialed Dal's home phone number.

Thank God. It wasn't busy. He listened as it began to ring.

Three times . . . four.

It continued to ring.

"C'mon Dal, c'mon . . ."

Seven . . . eight . . .

J.J. squeezed his eyes as he breathed the prayer softly again and again.

And the phone continued to ring.

Dal wasn't home. Or he wasn't answering. One and the same. J.J. mashed the button down.

Again he tried the emergency number—busy; the police department—the raucous *buzz-buzz-buzz* spit in his ear.

And then he thought of something.

Gripping the phone to keep from dropping it, J.J. punched in his own telephone number. There was the off chance that Dal had come back to his house tonight, was there right now, asleep on his couch. And even if he wasn't, there was the answering machine— that would be better than nothing. He could leave a message, then get outa here. "Let him be there," J.J. whispered. "Please, God, let him be there."

For an abstract instant it struck him ironically that he'd probably prayed more tonight than he had in—Lord, he didn't know, *years,* possibly. *Takes a crisis,* he thought. *People always come back to God in a crisis.* Did that mean that down deep he really, truly believed He was there?

"Not the time for philosophical self-examinations," he murmured as he punched in the last number and held his breath waiting for the phone to ring.

"Be there," he whispered. "Please, God—or Dal—or somebody. Be there . . ."

The phone was ringing.

Dal heard it the moment he reached the front-porch steps. He took them two at a time and was through the door and scooping up the receiver in seconds.

"Hello? J.J.?"

But the voice on the other end was Andy's. "Sorry, man. I guess that means he hasn't come home yet."

Dal wavered between relief that Andy didn't have any bad news to impart, and disappointment that he didn't have anything good to report either. "Nobody's spotted his vehicle yet?"

"Sorry. But I have got some information for you, though I don't know if it'll be of much use."

"Go ahead."

"Lab report on the dead bird drew a blank. They don't know what killed him, there was nothing out of the norm. Apparently he just died. And that follow-up I did on Poppy—remember him?"

Dal grunted affirmatively.

"Seems there was no autopsy performed because the body disappeared from the morgue. And get this—it was the ninth such disappearance in a month."

"The hell you say."

"I swear. Got it direct from Lancer down in forensics, they're keeping it quiet, think maybe there's an organ-legger ring starting up."

"Shit." There were some sickos out there. It sure didn't make Dal feel any better. "Anything else?"

"Yeah. Got a call from Dr. Grimes, the ME on the Coley Dean murder. Said she promised to keep you directly informed. They can't identify the dust particles found on the victims' bodies. We may be looking at an unknown drug here."

"Christ. That's all we need now."

"Oh yeah, and the lady down at the public library found a reference to the term 'boneman' in a book on myths and fables."

Dal pricked up his ears.

"It's a Haitian term," Andy told him, sounding as though he were referring to his notes. "Rather obscure, sort of an equivalent of our boogeyman, it seems. He's described as a kind of ultimate voodoo witch doctor or sorcerer, someone who practices the darker arts. He's sometimes called the 'ghost who walks among us,' and comes to collect the dead. He's supposed to have total power over them."

"Nice-sounding fellow," Dal murmured.

"The origin of the term is unknown," Andy continued, "but the author suggests that it's a euphemism for 'devil' or 'death.' Sort of the Haitian version of the Grim Reaper."

Dal felt a vague chill run down his spine. *He's coming for you. Coming for you all.* "That it?"

Andy gave an almost imperceptible sigh. "I'm afraid so."

Dal glanced at his watch. Almost midnight. "What are you still doing at work, anyway?" he asked tiredly. "You should have gone home hours ago."

"Thought I'd stick around a while. Maybe get something in from one of the patrols."

Dal managed a "Thanks, but go on home. They'll let me know if they have anything."

"Right. See you tomorrow."

He replaced the receiver. Andy was due a month's supply of Snickers bars for this.

Outside a car drove up.

Dal went to the door, raking a hand through his hair as he saw Agent Swann's blue Mercedes pulling in at the curb, not J.J.'s bottle-green Ford Explorer. What was she doing back here? He'd dropped her by the police lot and assumed she'd be halfway home by now.

He watched her get out and walk up the steps. She was still dressed in her K Mart street-punk outfit and was carrying a bulky McDonald's sack.

"May I come in?"

He nodded and stepped aside.

"What're you doing back here?" He followed her into J.J.'s kitchen.

She shrugged, held up the sack. "Thought you might be hungry."

She was right. He was. He couldn't even remember when he'd eaten last, and suddenly the urge to do so overwhelmed him. Maybe it was the smell coming from the sack.

"You eat junk food?" he asked as she placed the bag on the table in front of them and opened it. Somehow that surprised him. She seemed more the salads and designer-water type.

"They make good salads," she said as though reading his mind, and he grimaced at the thought of what the bag might hold.

But what she pulled out of the sack was three Quarter Pounders with cheese, two giant-sized orders of fries, four half-pints of milk, and a couple of apple turnovers.

He frowned at the milk, but sat down and began to eat, not talking, just wolfing it in.

He'd finished his before she was halfway through with hers, and she pushed the rest of her fries, and her apple pie, toward him, along with her second carton of milk. He didn't turn it down.

"Better?" she asked as he finished the second pie.

He nodded. "Yeah. Thanks. I owe you a dinner."

She smiled, and he recalled what she'd said that night he'd met her about always trying to have dinner with her husband and son. "Shouldn't you be at home right now? Won't they be wondering where you are?" He wasn't sure why he said it, didn't even know why he'd thought about it, he didn't normally consider such things. *Cops shouldn't be married, didn't need to have families at home worrying about where they are, what they're doing.*

Maybe this whole thing with J.J. had made him more aware of what it meant to have someone who worried about you.

"I thought I'd stick around a while," she said. "Unless you'd rather I didn't?"

"No," he said quickly, "don't go." He didn't want to be here alone right now. He didn't think he could stand it. "Did you call home?" he persisted.

She gave him a funny look, and he mumbled, "Sorry, I shouldn't ask that. None of my business."

"I called," she said.

He got up and went into the living room, restless for something to do, somewhere to go.

The papers J.J. had spread out all over the floor last night were still sitting on his desk. He went over and riffled through them. "Jehovah Jones: This Is Your Life." "E.C. the Extracelestial." "Jehovah Jones: Phone Home."

Phone home.

Dal dropped the sheets and sank down on the couch where he'd spent so many nights. Where he'd slept off too many drunks and taken out too many frustrations on J.J., usually during the wee hours between midnight and dawn.

He'd never really given much thought to what J.J. might be

feeling at those times. He'd been much too busy helping himself to J.J.'s groceries, sticking out his hand for a loan, turning a deaf ear to the lectures, a blind eye to the expressions of worry and concern. "That bike's gonna get you killed." "Why don't you get some stability in your life?" "You drink too much."

With a start, Dal realized he hadn't had a drink in at least twenty-four hours, not even a beer.

"Harley, my man, just get your butt home okay and I swear I'll never touch another drop," he murmured, slinging an arm over his eyes as he leaned back on the couch.

"Tell me about your friend." Jackie had come into the living room.

"Harley?" He glanced up at her as she sat down—on J.J.'s chair. Dal tried not to wince.

She nodded. "Why do you call him that?"

Dal smiled faintly at the old memory. It was something he hadn't thought about in a long time. "It happened when we were kids, I don't know, about fifteen or so. I had a trail bike. Not supposed to ride it in town." He looked at her with an ironic grin. "No license.

"Anyway, one night I decided to sneak out and go get some beer. It was late, a school night. I talked J.J. into riding with me. I was always getting him into trouble. So we got the beer, bribed some wino to go in and buy it, and were on our way home again when the cops saw us. They gave chase. I, being fifteen and fearless, decided I could outrun them. It was a wild ride, let me tell you, J.J. hanging on for dear life. They probably would have caught us, though, if I hadn't veered off the road and into the woods. Wrecked the bike. Lost the beer. Broke J.J.'s arm.

"He vowed he'd never get on another bike again as long as he lived. So far as I know, he never has." Dal shrugged. "I started calling him Harley after that. I guess it just stuck."

She smiled at him warmly. "It sounds as though you two have been through a lot together."

He nodded, unable to speak for a moment due to an uncharacteristic lump that had suddenly appeared in his throat. He swallowed against it. "If anything's happened to J.J.—"

He got to his feet, started pacing restlessly. "I've got to go back out. Check the streets again. Do something."

"Look." She got up too. "We've been all over the streets a dozen times. You've put the word out, given this number. What if someone calls?"

"You can stay here."

"And how will I get in touch with you?"

"Call the department, they'll get me on the radio," he said impatiently, running a hand through his unkempt hair.

"And are you planning on staying in your car the whole time?"

He looked at her sharply. "I need to be doing something."

"There's nothing to do at the moment. You're tired. Why don't you stretch out on the couch and get an hour's sleep? If nobody calls, we can go back out. It'll still be prime time on the streets, maybe we'll have more luck then."

Dal raged at the helplessness he felt, the frustration of knowing she was right. "An hour, no more."

She nodded. "I'm going to take a quick shower, get out of these clothes. I'll wake you in an hour."

He believed her.

He watched her go out to her car, get some clothes and a makeup case. She went into the bathroom and shut the door. In a minute he heard the water start to run.

He stretched out, feeling an alien discomfort on J.J.'s couch. But he was too tired to let it bother him much. The sound of the water was a soothing drone.

Just an hour. He'd sleep for one hour, then go back out and search for Cherry Pye and Willie Dee . . . and Lonnie too . . . *and J.J. most of all . . . and some dude called the Boneman who was like a shadow in the dark, a grinning death's-head atop a flowing black cape that billowed out larger and larger, closer and closer, blowing and swelling and rippling on the wind that came in sudden gusts, parting the cape and folding it around and around Dal so that he was trapped inside with the bones, the hard, cold bones—*

Dal tried to jerk away from the nightmare, not fully awake but aware he was dreaming, fighting the black folds that were still trying to wrap around him and drag him back down.

Somewhere he could hear a phone ringing—

Phone home, J.J. Phone home.

The sound was muffled by the heavy folds of the cape. It echoed in his ears, getting mixed up with the sounds of a waterfall nearby.

Dal fought through gummy layers of sleep toward the sound. He knew he was still dreaming and needed to wake up—*wake up and answer the goddamn phone!*—and he was trying, trying, but the Boneman was holding him down, curling his skeleton's arms around him and hugging him tight, wrapping him up in the thick black cape so he couldn't move, couldn't see, couldn't even breathe, and now he was stripping the flesh from Dal's body, turning him into a boneman too—

Dal wrenched himself awake, halfway falling off the sofa and stumbling over to the phone that was still ringing.

At the same time, a half-dressed Jackie threw open the bathroom door on her way to answer it.

Dal jerked up the receiver and mumbled, "Reid."

"Dal? Dal, thank God! Come get me. I'm at Fifty-seventh and D Street. South side. Hurry."

"Harley? Harley, what's going—?"

The line went dead.

Dal stood there staring at the phone, and the last residue of sleep fell away. He slammed the receiver down.

"Fifty-seventh and D Street." He headed toward the door, grabbing his shoes as he went, hearing her follow.

He pulled on his shoes as they rushed toward the car, and she was still buttoning her blouse and zipping up her pants as he gunned the vehicle to life and tore off down the midnight-quiet street.

Hurry, J.J. had said. *Hurry.*

TWENTY-FIVE

"Did you complete your call, Mr. Spencer?"

J.J. whirled around, clutching the phone to his chest like a life preserver. It had gone dead in his hand as he'd been talking to Dal, but he still clung to it. He needed something to hang on to.

The handsome black man who'd come to his house in the middle of the night was standing just inside the sliding panel doors.

"You're too late," J.J. said defensively, hugging the phone, trying to sound aggressive and not to shake. "I've already called for help. The police are on their way." He took a step back from the desk as though to put more space between them.

"Are they really, Mr. Spencer?" the man remarked, and J.J. felt a tremor go through him. It was as if the man knew about the calls, knew about the busy signals—

had somehow caused them?

No. That was crazy, too crazy. That was impossible.

Besides, he'd gotten through to Dal, hadn't he? Dal would be here. Dal would call for reinforcements—

or would he? What had he said to Dal? He tried to remember. The address, he'd given him the address, told Dal to come get him, to hurry. Had that been it? Had he mentioned the kidnapping? The danger? Had he drawn his friend into a trap?

The man smiled, as though following J.J.'s thoughts. "Shall we sit down and wait for them, then, Mr. Spencer?" He gestured politely to a comfortable chair.

J.J. felt frozen to the spot. His mind was a morass of conflicting data, indecision. There was something about all this that went beyond the obvious act of kidnapping, this crazy psychopath. Something . . .

"So many questions." The man shook his head in tolerant amusement. "All will be answered. In time."

His voice was well modulated, obviously refined. Not at all what J.J. expected, though exactly *what* he had expected he wasn't quite sure. Street slang maybe, something down and dirty, hard and mean. Somehow, this chilled him more.

Slowly, the man began to walk toward him.

Tension gripped J.J.'s already numb body. He wanted to run, but there was nowhere to go except through those sliding doors, and to do that, he'd have to get by the man.

The guy was by no means a gorilla, but looks are deceiving, and J.J. did not relish the idea of a fight—he'd never had one, not since that time when he was twelve and Eddie Craddock had tried to beat him up but Dal had come along and gotten into the fray and the worst J.J. had come away with was a black eye. No, he was no fighter, and this man could have a gun or a knife. Better try and stall him, play for time until Dal came.

Dal would know what to do. He knew how to handle himself, wouldn't let himself get hurt—J.J. tried to believe that.

He held his ground as his captor approached, looking for all the world as if he had all night and well into the next day, appearing to be totally unconcerned that the police might be here at any moment.

Will be here at any moment, J.J. reassured himself silently, telling himself that Dal would have called them.

"What's this all about?" J.J. demanded, shying away from looking directly into those dark eyes, dark as pits. There were things he didn't want to see in those eyes. "Why did you bring me here? What do you want?"

"A momentary amusement, Mr. Spencer. Nothing more."

They might have been conversing about the weather, or making idle small talk at a cocktail party. It was crazy. But suddenly J.J. was more afraid than he had ever been before. Afraid of this man in a way he couldn't explain, and wasn't sure he wanted to.

"Who are you?" he asked, and his voice was barely audible—if, in fact, he had voiced the question at all. He didn't want to. But the words had come of their own accord.

The man stopped walking, stood across the desk, regarding him with mild interest. "Why, I'm what you fear the most, Mr. Spencer. The face of your own mortality."

J.J. felt the fear lock up his throat. "What do you mean by that?" he managed to force out hoarsely, and the coldness filling his body hardened to a block of ice. "Are you planning to kill me, then?"

The man just smiled, turned, and strolled over to the window and stood looking out.

When Dal drives up, is that when he'll do it? J.J.'s mind reeled, unable to comprehend any of this. *Is that when he'll kill me?* But why? What had he done?

He glanced back at the open door to the hall. Could he make it? Could he dash through that door and back upstairs and lock himself in that bedroom until the cops arrived? Or maybe go for the rear exit—an unknown factor but closer. Most of all, could he do either before the lunatic behind him pulled out a gun and shot him in the back?

He switched his gaze to the man again. He still hadn't moved. Just stood there, staring out the window.

J.J. wondered if he could see their reflections in the glass. He decided to test it. He might not get another chance.

He eased backward. The man didn't move. He took another experimental step toward the door. A loose floorboard creaked.

"You don't look like a murderer." J.J. said the first thing that came into his mind, trying to camouflage the noise of his footsteps, watching the man's profile for the slightest move.

The man remained standing as he was, gazing out the window. Another step . . .

It was a strong profile, aristocratic looking, with a straight, thin nose and full, but not overly generous lips. His skin was smooth and shone golden in the soft lamplight.

But then, as he turned to look at J.J., freezing him to the spot, it seemed to pale suddenly, grow ashen, thinning to transparency that allowed J.J. to see through the flesh to the bone.

He was looking at a skull.

"Death has many faces, Mr. Spencer," the voice said, and the

words were coming toward J.J. down a long, hollow tunnel, floating on a dry, hot wind.

He tried to move, tried to run, but he couldn't feel his hands,
couldn't feel his toes. The room was receding, zooming back in a
sudden, dizzying burst of speed. He could still see it, captured
there in the soft glow at the end of the tunnel that was one eye
of the laughing skull, but it was dwindling now, becoming a
pinprick in a dimming blur of light . . .

*and he'd been dreaming, dreaming after all, dreaming about coming
down here and phoning Dal and getting away, dreaming in that upstairs
bedroom, dreaming in that endless ebony void.*

The wind blew harder, shrieking past and drawing him down
into a maelstrom that was taking him back, back into the darkness.
Back into the silent, empty night.

A brisk wind had sprung up out of nowhere.

Jackie watched the trees nodding silently as the car raced by.
There'd been no lightning yet, no rumble of thunder across the
deep midnight sky. Yet the darkness hung thick and heavy, clouds
gathering fast and low and making the air feel charged with the
threat of an impending storm.

The wind rose. Jackie could feel it shove against the car every
now and then as though trying to push them off the road. Above,
the trees bucked and swayed. She held her breath as a volley of
leaves and small twigs rained down around them, tensing for the
moment a limb would crack and come tumbling down in their path
or land right on top of the car. They were going too fast to stop.

"Hurry." Dal muttered the word again, and she knew he wasn't
aware that he kept saying it, nor was he paying much attention to
the building storm, other than to grip the steering wheel even
tighter each time the wind nudged the car.

He sat leaning forward, hands clamped to the top of the steering
wheel as though the force of his body weight could make the car
go faster. Like the high-beam glare of his headlights, his gaze
stayed fixed on the road.

Luckily there'd been almost no traffic; Reid was doing nearly
seventy and they'd already run two red lights in the past four

blocks. At least he'd stuck the emergency light up on the roof. Its flashing blue beam swept the darkness ahead of them to signal their approach. But he wasn't using the siren.

Jackie clung to the door handle as Dal jammed on the brakes and sent them skidding around a turn. Something had been bothering her ever since they'd left the house, something other than Dal's driving; she gripped the handle tighter as the car fishtailed for a second before gunning forward again.

Why had J.J. called his own phone number? He couldn't have known Dal would be there. Unless he'd tried to reach Dal at the station house or at home first and then just taken a chance. But if he was in such urgent need of help, why waste precious time trying to reach Dal at all? Why wouldn't he have simply called the police or 911?

Panic? Maybe. People do strange things under stress, take totally inappropriate action.

But it still seemed odd.

She knew there'd been no direct call to the Phoenix City PD because someone there would have notified them at the house. And 911 should have relayed the call. Of course there was always the chance that there'd been a mix-up and it just hadn't come down the tubes yet, sometimes these things took time. It just seemed odd.

She took the small Beretta from the bag she'd grabbed on her way out the door and placed it in the pocket of her linen jacket, wishing she had her .357 Magnum instead. Remembered the .12 gauge pump under the dashboard. If Reid didn't get it, she would. She didn't know what they might be walking into, had no clue whatsoever. She only had Dal's word for it that it had actually been his friend who'd called—it'd been a very brief call, and Dal had been half-asleep. Probably it was, but who was to say J.J. hadn't had a gun to his head, or been tricked somehow into making that call. Farfetched? Maybe. But Jackie wasn't about to let what had happened last night happen again.

Apparently Reid's friend hadn't said anything about the nature of his problem, only where he was and that he needed help and to hurry. Beyond that was anybody's guess. A wrong guess could prove fatal.

Jackie winced as a gust of wind blasted the car just as Reid flung it around yet another corner. For a moment it seemed as if the car might actually leave the road. Then it righted itself, slamming her into the door and cracking her shoulder up against the hard metal edge of the window. She'd have a king-sized bruise by tomorrow, something to explain to Philip.

Philip.

Was he awake? Listening for the sound of her car, waiting for the phone to ring? He'd told her once, before their cold war, while they were still trying to hang on to some level of communication, how much he hated to hear the phone ring at night when she was out on a case, how he had to steel himself to pick it up and say hello, prepared to hear that she'd been hurt or killed. Every time. She'd forgotten about that.

Or disregarded it. How had she dismissed his concern so easily? She glanced over at Dal, seeing the lines of worry etched in his face. He cared deeply for his friend, loved him, she realized. She didn't have a friend that close, hadn't for years; she didn't have time for friends. Oh, the people she worked with cared; but danger was part of their job, they knew the risks they took, what the bottom line could be. There wouldn't be anyone out there who'd fear for her like this, not on so personal a level. Except Philip.

She wondered if Jason was sleeping, if his window was closed against the coming storm, if he'd asked for her when his dad had tucked him in tonight. Or was he beginning to stop expecting her to be there because so often, too often, she was not?

The thought hung in her mind and wouldn't go away. Was she missing moments in her child's life that she was going to regret someday? She'd chosen to have Jason, his birth was something they'd planned. But then, when it came time to give up her job, she'd balked. Why? Was she so afraid of becoming lost in the housewife-and-mother routine that she was willing to push it totally aside? What was wrong with being a housewife and mother? Wasn't it okay to choose that?

"We're almost there." Reid's voice broke through her mental fog, brought her back to the cold, hard night.

He'd turned off the flasher, dimmed the headlights to low, and cut their speed by half. As they made a left turn, he slowed even more, and flicked the headlights down to parking beams.

"There it is." He nodded toward the next street.

The area was an old residential section, once a respectable, even wealthy part of town, she'd guess, now decayed into tenements, with a few CONDEMNED signs here and there. A true slum. Trash littered the broken pavement of the sidewalks and street, and the wind made small tornadoes with it, whipping it back and forth in front of their car.

The street appeared deserted. A few cars were parked along the curbs, mostly junkers; anything decent would have been quickly picked clean. There was no one around, no lights in any of the structures, except for one.

"There, that's got to be it." Reid indicated the lighted window. Thick iron bars gleamed darkly on the outside of the dingy glass.

"Why that one?" she asked, suspicious at once of the lighted windows in an otherwise dark street.

He shrugged impatiently. "We've got to start somewhere. Radio in our position, tell them we're checking it out and if they don't hear back from us in, say, twenty minutes, to send in some backup."

He drew the car to a standstill at the opposite curb, a good hundred yards away from the house on the next corner. Cut the engine, killed the lights. Opened the door to get out. The overhead light didn't come on, and she guessed he'd screwed the bulb partway out some time or other; the lights on the dashboard were controlled by a switch.

She finished speaking into the radio and replaced it, heard him murmur "Bring the shotgun" as he climbed from the car, easing the door closed behind him. It made a soft click as it caught halfway. He'd unholstered his big automatic.

Grabbing the 12 gauge, she followed him out.

For the first time that she could remember, Jackie had a bad case of nerves. Her hands felt clammy, and she wiped first one, then the other down the sides of her slacks.

The wind had died down some, but an occasional gust whipped by, hot and dry, stinging her face and hands with grit picked up from the street, making her squint up her eyes. She could feel her heart thudding in her chest and throat, hear it pounding in her ears, and imagined she could feel the blood rushing through her veins.

Cautiously, they approached the house. Sweat trickled down her sides. It stuck like glue in her armpits, and the damp waistband on her slacks had begun chafing her skin.

Reid motioned for her to let him go first, and she readily complied. She didn't want to go first, didn't want to go at all. What she really wanted to do, Jackie suddenly realized with stark clarity, was go home to her husband and son. She had the horrible, uncanny thought that if she went into this house, she might never come out again.

Get hold of yourself, Jackie. She forced the destructive thought away. What was the matter with her? Was she losing her nerve?

She remembered something an instructor at the academy had once told them: "If there's reason to think it, there's reason to believe it." It's okay to be scared, he'd said. But once you stop controlling that fear, start letting it control you, you're in trouble.

In all the situations she'd ever been in, she'd never so badly wanted to turn around and run.

Gripping the shotgun in both hands, she flattened herself against the side of the house next to the lighted, barred window, while Reid looked in. He shook his head—apparently the room was empty—motioned her with him toward the front door.

Once there, she waited again, pressed to one side of the rough clapboard facade as Reid climbed the few stone steps that led directly up from the sidewalk. A rickety iron handrail lined either side.

He put his ear to the door a moment, then reached for the knob.

The door swung open, not making a sound.

He disappeared inside.

Jackie waited for him to reappear, but he didn't, and after a moment's hesitation, she realized he wasn't going to. Gritting her teeth, she raised the shotgun and followed him in.

The smell hit her as soon as she crossed the threshold, a thick, sweetish aroma that made her want to gag. She melted left, going low and quickly scanning the murky interior while the sickly aroma flowed over her, coating her skin, clogging her nose. It was a smell which, once imprinted on the olfactory senses, couldn't be erased. The smell of Death.

Reid had already advanced to the rear of the short hall, where an open doorway on the left spilled light into the darker corridor. He stood flattened against the wall just this side of the opening, weapon gripped in both hands at hip level, preparing to move into the room. He wasn't wasting any time.

Jackie glanced grimly from the shadowy staircase on her right to the closed panel doors at her left. No time to check them. In a practiced move, she began advancing quickly down the hall toward him, keeping her back to the opposite wall and her eyes roaming the distance from the front of the house to where he stood.

Her heart was jamming her throat. The shotgun felt gawky and unfamiliar in her sweat-clogged palms, though she regularly qualified in all types of firearms use.

The all too present thought that she might not make it out of here, that this time might be *the* time, came barreling at her with the force of a 12 gauge shell. She'd been afraid before in tight situations, but nothing like this. This wasn't the kind of healthy fear that kept you alert, kept you smart. This was sheer turn-and-run terror. And Jackie had to force herself to keep edging down the hall.

The smell got stronger as she neared the open doorway.

It was all she could do to keep breathing. She tried breathing through her mouth, but that didn't help; the smell still came inside her, only now she could *taste* it.

For one dizzying instant, she thought she was going to throw up, lose that Quarter Pounder and fries right there on the hardwood floor. She swallowed convulsively, tasting bile. She imagined what Dal must be feeling right now. If asked at that moment, she'd bet they'd find his friend inside—dead.

It seemed an eternity, yet she knew only seconds had passed as she moved into position, prepared to provide backup for Reid if he needed it. She wondered if he even remembered she was here, he was so focused on his own move. He hadn't looked back once since she'd entered the house.

Without a glance her way, he swung into the opening, immediately throwing himself into a crouch at one side.

Nothing happened. No shots were fired as Jackie quickly switched to the space Dal had just vacated, then across the opening to the opposite side, still keeping a lookout toward the front of the house.

Nothing stirred. Not in the front, not in the back. And not in that room.

She'd gotten a quick glimpse of the interior as she'd bolted across the opening. Looked like a study or office, big desk sitting in the center, a few chairs, a sofa, some small tables grouped around the sides.

No obvious signs of violence, no blood she could see. Most of all, no body.

The smell said otherwise.

She'd spotted another room, looked like a small antechamber of some sort. There'd been a glimpse of flickering lights.

She swung around the door frame and took up a position just inside the office as Reid darted over to this smaller opening, going through the same routine as before, but not for long. He ducked into the room.

Jackie remained where she was, watching the entryway, covering their backs until she heard Reid make a choking sound, then curse.

In an instant she was there, shotgun at ready.

He came bursting from the room, nearly knocking her down as he rushed by, shouting "Get help" as he continued into the corridor. He was making no effort to be quiet now.

Jackie glanced into the inner room—and caught her breath.

The scene was like something out of a horror movie. An altar, set with lighted candles, dominated the central space. Bottles and jars filled with unspeakable things, some looking like human organs, sat in rows upon the shelves lining the walls. Feathers and bones hung in bunches all around. A human skull leered down from a niche, staring at a collection of shallow bowls which held liquids and powders and pieces of decaying raw meat—from what kind of animal, Jackie didn't want to speculate.

All around her, the heavy scent of incense and putrefaction and blood.

But all this faded into the background as her gaze was caught and held by two pairs of staring, lifeless eyes, two severed heads that had been placed on either side of the altar, faces turned toward the door. Blood had coagulated in pools around the ragged throats, dark strings of it leading down to two puddles on the floor. The bodies of the two men were nowhere in sight.

Reeling back from the horror chamber, Jackie stumbled to the desk where she'd seen a phone, only just remembering to pull out a handkerchief and cover the receiver before picking it up. She hadn't expected the phone to be in working order, but she heard the dial tone loud and clear and felt an almost giddy relief at this tenuous connection with the outside world.

Nothing she'd ever seen compared to this, nothing.

She made the call as quickly as her numb fingers would allow, her whole body had gone cold as ice; gave the code that would have the whole range of emergency personnel here in a matter of minutes, then dashed back out to the hall, trying to banish the afterimage of that altar. Like the glare of a flashbulb, it kept swimming before her, blanking her vision as she ran toward the stairs.

Reid had gone up them. She could hear him moving around up there, kicking in doors and shouting for J.J., his voice raw.

She followed him up. This thing wasn't over yet.

Empty rooms, their lights on, their doors hanging open, lined the corridor on either side and served to shed more illumination into the hallway. She checked out each one she passed, making sure no one waited to surprise them. She doubted that Reid had given them more than a cursory glance. Some were haphazardly furnished, others piled high with boxes and shipping crates.

It looked like a drug house to her.

Shotgun ready, finger poised on the trigger, she wasn't about to forget that whoever was responsible for the horror chamber below might still be in the house.

At the end of the hall, Reid burst in the door to another room and dashed inside. "Oh shit, Harley, shit, shit," she heard him say.

She ran forward, bracing herself for what she was about to see.

The bedroom was lavishly furnished. Reid was at the bedside, bent over the still body of his friend. She saw him strike the bare chest sharply, lift the head, clear the air passages, then desperately begin giving artificial respiration.

Useless. She could tell from here. That man had been dead for some time, the body already pale, almost waxen looking, with that bluish-gray cast that signaled postmortem lividity. Filmy eyes stared sightlessly into space.

She went over to the bed, going around to the opposite side. Dal struck the chest again, began pumping. "C'mon, J.J. C'mon, man. Breathe, goddammit! Breathe!" He glanced up at her. His face was a wound. "Help me. We've got to get him going." He was panting for breath, pumping away.

Jackie bent down and placed her fingers on J.J.'s neck, felt for a pulse.

There was none.

The skin felt cool and like it had begun to toughen.

She looked at Reid, knowing it was useless, knowing there was nothing they could do.

"Dal, he's gone—"

"No he isn't!" Reid glared at her. "He'll be okay. He'll be okay."

In the distance, a siren wailed.

She watched him continue to work as the sirens got louder, as brakes squealed to a halt outside the house and people rushed in.

Shouts spread out below them. Doors banged. Footsteps climbed the stairs.

More shouts as they poured into the room.

Police first, their guns drawn, then paramedics wielding stethoscopes and black equipment cases. They had to pull Reid away from the corpse as they went about their work, movements growing slower as they saw the lifeless form, but going about the business of checking for vital signs anyway. At last they gave it up and started putting their equipment back into the cases.

"Wait a minute! What the hell do you think you're doing?" Dal grabbed one of the paramedics by the arm and jerked the man around. "Don't stop, goddammit! You can't stop!"

Jackie started to go toward them.

But the paramedic seemed to judge the situation and said qui-

232

etly, "Look, man, this guy's dead. His body's already started to cool and turn hard. He's been dead for hours."

Dal was shaking his head desperately. "No. No, that can't be right. That's impossible. He called me less than an hour ago."

"Not this guy." The paramedic slowly removed his arm from Reid's grip, which had slackened. The hand fell limply away. "Maybe somebody was trying to make it sound like him, I dunno. But this guy's been dead a while, five or six hours, minimum. I'm sorry."

The emergency medical team returned to their work.

Jackie walked over to Reid. He looked stunned—shell-shocked.

She placed her hand on his arm. "Somebody's playing a cruel game with you—"

The look he turned on her was outraged. "It was J.J. You think I don't know his voice?"

She offered nothing more. The phone call had been brief, he'd been asleep, there was room for error. Maybe it had been a recording.

But this wasn't the time to point these things out. "C'mon, let's get out of here."

She gripped his arm, wanting to steer him out of the room. He didn't need to see the procedures that would come next: the guys from the crime lab gathering evidence, the photographers, the coroner's exam, the ambulance crew wheeling in their snow-white stretcher with a black body bag lying on top. It was enough that he knew the routine.

"Give me the shotgun."

"What?" Jackie let go of Reid's arm and backed up a step as he grabbed the 12 gauge pump. She started not to relinquish it, but something in his expression said she'd better let go.

"Reid, don't be a fool!" She followed him to the doorway, out into the hall. "You can't go after whoever did this now. You don't even know who it is."

He ignored her, pushing past the lab crew that was coming down the hall, and disappeared down the stairs.

De Boneman here
De Boneman there
De Boneman be most anywhere

TWENTY-SIX

Dal ran from the brutal scene, leaving the flashing emergency lights, the gathering crowds, behind him.

Someone yelled his name as he bolted past, but he didn't stop, just kept running. Jumped into his car and screamed away from the curb.

In a moment he was alone, racing along the dark, silent streets as if the devil himself rode his back.

Alone.

But he wouldn't think about that now. Wouldn't think about the time he and J.J. got "lost" on a school nature hike and ended up at cheerleader camp where they hung out all day. Wouldn't think about that summer they'd worked as busboys at Myrtle Beach and lived on pizza and beer and met a new round of women every week. Wouldn't think about the white-water rafting trip they'd been going to take for the past three years, or the trip to Seattle to visit J.J.'s folks—his folks, he'd have to tell J.J.'s folks—*no, wouldn't think about that.*

Dal felt the tears rolling down his face. Reached up and savagely brushed them aside.

He wouldn't think about any of that now.

Later. There'd be time later to think about all these things and more. Too much time.

Right now was good for only one thing—find the person who'd murdered J.J. and kill him.

Fury rose up in Dal until there was no room for anything else. No room for grief or pain. Only hate.

He was going after Willie Dee—if he had to go through every piece of scum on State Street to do it. Whatever it took, however far he had to go, he'd get some answers this time. Somebody out there knew where Willie was, and they were going to tell him. It was as simple as that.

Willie was the key. Willie knew who was behind all this, Dal was willing to bet his life on it.

He caught the beltline and whipped out into traffic right in front of a tractor-trailer rig pulling a piggyback load. The truck driver gave him a long blast on his air horn, but by then Dal had the car over in the fast lane and had boosted his speed up to ninety. He had the blue emergency light on the seat beside him, but hadn't taken the time to turn it on. He did that now, set it out on the roof; he had the radio if a traffic cop got on his tail.

Wind screamed past the windows. Fury sang in his veins as he tore through the bitter night.

He played the lanes, whizzing by cars on the left, then the right, until he came to the Glenwood exit. Took the off ramp at double the maximum safe speed.

At the intersection he slowed just enough to swing a left, then floorboarded it again until he came to the State Street turnoff. He cut a right.

The street was lit up like a K Mart Christmas tree—

what would he do this Christmas? He never bothered putting up a tree, J.J. always did it

—and the lights ran together like blood. Conversations and laughter crackled like static on the wind, the music raucous and off-key. It was obscene that people should be laughing and talking, going about their tawdry little lives, while J.J.—

He slammed on his brakes and pulled over to the curb and parked. Grabbed the shotgun. Got out and headed up the street.

People parted for him when they saw the shotgun.

First he'd check Mel's Diner. Willie liked to hang out there, had something going with one of the waitresses. Dal had talked to her earlier, and she'd sworn she hadn't seen Willie in days, but maybe he hadn't made his position clear. Maybe she hadn't quite understood just how serious he was. He'd clarify that this time.

The crowd began to thicken and surge around him, few noticing the gun until he was right up on them or already moving past. A little ripple of commotion spread in his wake, morbid curiosity, most likely, people wondering what the action was, where it might take place. A few slid away, not wanting to get caught in it.

Somebody bumped him. He glanced to his right—and stopped short. There, across the street, staring directly at him, was Willie Dee. The little bastard grinned.

Dal took off, running, dodging a pickup truck that rattled by, then a cab. The cab driver shouted something at him, but by then Dal was halfway across the street, trying to get around a garbage truck that was doing its nightly rounds. By the time he made it to the opposite sidewalk, Willie was gone.

Then he spotted him again, half a block ahead and moving away fast.

Dal began running once more, jostling people aside, jerking his arm loose as somebody who didn't like being shoved tried to grab him. "Police! Clear a path!" he shouted, pulling his shield off his belt and waving it high at the crowd, at the same time brandishing the shotgun.

The crowd backed off.

He came to the end of the street. Stopped for a moment and searched the block ahead for Willie.

There he was!

Dal dashed across the intersection, flashing his shield and gun. "Police! Coming through!" he yelled and kept going. Horns blared in his wake. Somebody shouted a curse. But he wasn't about to let Willie get away this time.

Dodging around pedestrians and loiterers, Dal chased Willie down the street.

He saw the little bastard turn around and grin at him, then dash across a big intersection and duck into an opening between two buildings midway down the next block.

"Oh, no you don't." Dal sprinted diagonally across the intersection, vaulting one-handed over the front fender of a compact car that was waiting to make the turn, slamming into the side of another. Brakes were squealing, people were shouting, but Dal was on track again and nothing was going to stop him. Nothing.

"I'm coming, Willie!" he shouted, feeling the air explode out of his lungs and his heart rate soar. "I'm coming, you grinning little shit."

He came to the narrow pocket where Willie had disappeared. Stopped. Looked in. The slit between the two buildings was barely shoulder-wide and dark as pitch. A sense of déjà vu overwhelmed him. He'd been lured like this before, following Cherry that night. He wasn't about to let himself be suckered into that rat trap again.

He stood listening, and in a moment caught the faint sound of running footsteps.

Reattaching his shield to his belt, he raised the shotgun and began moving forward quickly, down the block, keeping pace with Willie's footsteps running along behind the buildings. He'd wait for a larger alley before dropping into that maze.

In a moment, he thought he heard the footsteps coming closer. He paused a beat, listened. Sure enough, Willie popped out of another slit down the way. He swung a look over his shoulder, spotted Dal, and grinned. Then sprinted off.

Dal's finger quivered on the shotgun's trigger as he began running again, his eyes locked on the target of Willie's back. He damn sure didn't intend to kill the little bastard, at least not yet, but the gun in his hand transmitted the thought of how it would feel to jam the barrel up against Willie's soft gut and squeeze the trigger, slowly squeeze the trigger.

Willie ducked into another alley.

"Shit!" Whatever game this little dickhead was playing had gone far enough. There was no doubt left in Dal's mind that Willie wanted to lure him into that hole. Willie wasn't trying to evade him—he was acting like bait.

But that didn't matter now. Right now all that mattered was that he and Willie were on a collision course and if anybody tried to interfere he'd blow them away.

He sprinted over to the alley where Willie had disappeared. Stopping at the edge, he darted a look in, saw a dark shape bobbing away toward the far end. Pale street light filtered into the alley from behind, laying a ghostly aura on the overflowing Dumpsters and jumble of boxes that lined both sides.

"I'm coming, Willie. I'm right behind you," he shouted, and entered the alley.

Trash bins and busted shipping crates littered his path, and Dal had to slow his pace, to duck around the Dumpsters with an eye to who might be hiding on the other side. Empty boxes, refuse that wouldn't fit or that had been pulled out and picked through, formed an obstacle course that further bogged him down.

He wove his way through the litter, still hearing the footsteps up ahead, leading him on.

Just like before. Just like in the alley with Cherry.

This felt planned.

Rounding a sharp bend in the alley, Dal found himself behind the row of buildings. The rear doors of shops and businesses lined both sides, all locked up for the night. No light shone through any of the cracks, though a dim glow came from somewhere, enough to see by.

The dirt and refuse gave way to pavement once more, and Dal realized that he'd come out on a cross street. He swung a left and cut back up to State.

He looked all around him. There was no sign of Willie.

The wind, which had been absent until now, sprang up again. Not as violent as earlier tonight, and hot and dry, rather than cool. Yet it sent a rash of chill bumps crawling across Dal's skin.

"You may as well talk to me, Willie," he called as he began walking down the sidewalk, keeping a sharp eye out for any movement in his path. "I'm not gonna back off until you do. There's a name I want, you know the one. Give it up, Willie, and we're even. I'll let you go." He stopped at a recessed doorway, checked it out, walked on.

"I can make a lot of trouble for you on the street, Willie. Put it out that you've been snitchin' on some major deals. Wouldn't give odds on your lasting too long after that."

A feeling of being *not alone* swamped him, cold, like the play of eyes on his back.

eyes watching him from behind.

He swung around, shotgun leveled. There was nobody there.

For the first time, Dal thought about the extra shells he'd left back at the car. But the big automatic sitting comfortably in his shoulder holster would provide plenty of backup firepower, and he had two extra clips for that.

Dal was coming up on the alley where Coly Dean had met his end—how many nights ago? He wasn't sure. He stopped about ten yards from the mouth. Someone was standing just inside the opening.

He leveled the gun. "You, there! Come on out."

The shadow moved silently, shifting forward into the meager light. It wasn't Willie. It was a big black man, grinning like the Cheshire cat.

"You buy—?" The raspy voice floated on the air, seemed to spin and echo around Dal, like a spider's web, soft and thin.

A street vendor—Christ, they were getting bold. Another time Dal would have reveled in busting the creep.

Another time.

"Pack it in, slimeball, unless you want to get busted. I'm a cop."

The big man didn't move.

Dal's hand tightened on his gun. "I said, back off!"

But the creep just stood there, grinning.

Dal frowned. The dude must be flying on his own pond scum.

Giving the spaceball a wide berth, he walked on down the street. The guy kept on standing there, watching him go.

eyes on his back

Freaking weird. They were going to have to get some more people down here. Clean this place up.

Later. He'd think about that later.

Dal scanned the block ahead for Willie Dee. There was no sign of him. *Where did he go?*

He glanced back up the street. The pusher from the alley had begun walking toward him.

Dal frowned, not sure what to make of that. Was this dude flying his own flight plan, or was he cruising Willie's?

Slowly, Dal started moving forward again, keeping his back to the boarded-up warehouses lining this side of the street. He alternately searched the shadows ahead for Willie Dee and maintained tabs on the steadily approaching space cadet.

"You buy—?"

"You buy—?"

The scratchy voices came from just beyond him, and Dal spun around as another huge black man stepped from a dark slit between two buildings, followed by yet another. Both wore grins that looked neither friendly nor natural in the meager light. Their eyes glinted oddly in the darkness as they fastened their twin gazes on him, and Dal realized they weren't blinking. These dudes were totally spaced.

He began backing away as the pair stepped slowly forward, forcing him into the street.

The first dude was still approaching from his right. Dal aimed the shotgun at the closer pair.

"You assholes better back off, I'm warning you. This is police business. Don't interfere."

They kept coming.

A rustle, off to his left.

Dal glanced toward the new sound and saw another pair of street vendors shuffle out of the shadows and start heading his way. They joined the others, and all continued walking slowly toward him, paying no attention to the gun in his hand, grinning stupidly.

"You buy?" The soft, scratchy voice floated over to him from one of the newcomers, the other one immediately echoing, *"You buy—?"*

These guys were totally stoned. Dal backed away. He might have to kill them all.

His eyes caught flickers of movement in the background, more shadows coming to life. What was this? What the hell was going on? Was this some sort of fucking pusher freak show run amok?

Dal backed toward the other side of the street, still keeping the gun trained on the closest pair, calculating his best move as the ring of street pushers continued to box him in.

He glanced over his shoulder to see what lay behind—and felt a sudden crazy lurch of recognition.

It was the alley. The alley from the photograph.

He was being herded toward it, locked inside a semicircle of spaced-out goons like a rat in a trap.

Sweat burst from his pores.

"You buy—?"

"You buy—?"

The grinning street pushers kept murmuring the question over and over as they slowly shambled forward, the dry rustle of their clothing and shuffling feet blending with the whispery words into a hissing chorus that rippled on the wind. Dal thought if he closed his eyes it would sound like a swarm of insects slithering through dry grass.

He was going to have to make a break for it—*and how had he let himself get into the middle of this? He knew better. Should have never let them back him into a corner like this.*

He felt the dark alley at his back.

Sweat slid down his skin. He kept trying to think, but his thoughts seemed muddled, as though the darkness behind him were sucking at his brain, chasing away thoughts before he could get them formed.

Wind brushed his heated skin, and he raised his face to it, seeing little sparkles floating before his eyes.

He shook his head, trying to clear it. A wave of disorientation washed over him. The voices, the shuffling feet, were a constant buzzing in his ears.

His heel hit the curb and he lurched around, face-to-face with the alley that at once drew and repelled him. Its black-on-black shadows seemed to twist and turn, almost form a pattern, then melt into shapelessness again.

He didn't know how long he stood there.

Behind him the shuffling feet, the whispering voices grew faint. He turned around—*did it seem to take forever?*—and the freak-show pushers were gone, merged back into the shadows from which they had come—*had they ever really been there at all?*

He faced forward again.

The alley lay splayed before him like the grinning jaws of a trap. Black and silent, dark secrets lurked within.

Someone was coming . . .

Dal tensed, searching the stillness for a sign, a movement, that would let him pinpoint the man he was after. His hand felt welded to the shotgun, his eyes glued to the darkness ahead.

What kind of game was this? What kind of brutal, nonsensical game was being played here?

He felt as if someone were watching him. Glanced right.

Two people stood silently about twenty-five feet away. Willie and Cherry Pye. Their figures were silhouetted by the dim street light.

They stood there, watching him. Willie wasn't grinning anymore.

Dal looked away.

Willie and Cherry didn't interest him now. The one he wanted was in this alley, he could sense it. The person who murdered J.J. was waiting for him just inside.

J.J.

Someone is coming to get you.

Dal glared into the center of the alley as he stepped forward. "I'm coming, you motherfucker. I'm the one who's coming."

Darkness reached out to claim him. It gathered him in like a sponge; he was being absorbed by it—eaten alive.

Another step; he forged through the thick air.

Little wisps of fog crawled across the ground to greet him. They circled his feet and gathered into miniwhirlpools as he strode by.

His eyes were beginning to adjust now. He could separate the darkness into varying shades of black on gray: buildings on both sides looming over him, tops lost in the total blackness of the predawn sky; walls stretched behind in a parody of his dream, or hallucination, or whatever it had been. They seemed to reach around him now, close in at his back like giant wings.

Or the folds of a cape?

The death's-head phantom from his most recent nightmare reared before his eyes—he shook his head, the specter vanished.

"I know you're in here." Dal walked farther in. His head felt thick and heavy. He wanted to reach up and massage his neck, it felt so stiff, but he didn't dare take his hands away from the shotgun. Whoever this fucker was, whatever his game, Dal was taking no chances. He'd seen that horror chamber in the house, those severed heads. He'd seen what this bastard had done to J.J.

J.J. His mind still wouldn't accept that fact. The fury of grief rose up in him again at the thought of his friend, and he felt a savage, primitive need to do violence, to assuage his hurt by hurting someone else. Strike back. Lash out. *Kill.*

The need was strong.

A sudden movement of air against skin—*had someone stirred the stillness?*

"Come on, you fucker. Show yourself."

The shadows just beyond him began to shift, *like in his dream, in the photograph, a sudden shifting of perception—*

And there he was. Standing right there in front of Dal—*had he been there all the time and it was only now that Dal could see him?*

The man stepped forward into the shallow light.

A young man, handsome to the point of beauty, and something about him made Dal want to puke.

There was no doubt in his mind that this was the person who'd killed J.J. And the others. Dal didn't know how he knew that, he just knew. There was the feel of death about this man.

Kill him. Shoot him now and have done with it. Don't make a mistake and wait.

Dal's finger hardened on the trigger.

The man smiled.

There was warmth in that smile, and amusement, and a smear of contempt.

Dal squeezed the trigger. Squeezed it again and again. But nothing happened. The gun didn't fire.

Though he hadn't felt his hand slacken, the gun fell to the ground. He bent his head to see it—*pick it up! What's the matter with you? Pick It up!*—but his arm wouldn't respond, his fingers had gone numb. The gun seemed to be spiraling downward, continuing to fall as though a hole had opened up in the earth at his feet.

He felt dizzy.

The man stepped closer—Dal raised his head—close enough that Dal could reach up and fasten his hands around the man's slender neck and snap it like a twig, but something prevented him. Something immobilized his hands and arms and legs.

Fight it. Fight it!

Sweat broke out again on Dal's body, cold and clammy, coating his skin like oil. This was no ordinary killer. This fucker wasn't ordinary at all.

"Who are you?" he whispered, and the man raised an expressively arched brow.

"Does it really matter, Detective Reid? Isn't it enough to know that I killed your friend?"

Dal felt rage boil up in him and break through the paralysis that had momentarily held him frozen to the spot.

This creep had killed J.J.!

His hands shot up and around the man's neck, thumbs digging into the windpipe. It didn't take much to crush a man's windpipe. Not much at all.

With every bit of strength he had, he squeezed down.

The man's smile broadened. White teeth gleamed in the sallow light. Being choked didn't seem to bother him at all.

Dal squeezed harder. Wanting to kill this man. *Needing* to kill him—he'd never needed anything more in his life.

Murderer . . . a little voice in the pit of his mind taunted. *You've always wondered if you could do it, and now you know . . .*

The man smiled, lips peeling back from perfect white teeth, the sound of laughter bubbling up inside.

Dal pressed harder, staring into those dark, smooth eyes and seeing himself stare back; it was like looking at himself in a mirror—

And then the face was changing, becoming something Dal had never seen before, something monstrous, not human. A devil's face.

He gripped harder, fighting the reflex of revulsion that made him want to let go, to turn around and run.

Laughter swelled, as if the sound were buried deep inside the man and its echo was pouring from his grinning, gaping mouth.

The face changed: It was a man again, but not the same man. This was a man who'd murdered a score of women in a cross-country spree three years ago and never been caught; they still had his composite picture adorning their bulletin boards—

Changing once more, this time distorting into a parody of a

woman's face, eyes filled with writhing demon children, mouth gaping open in a hideous infant's wail.

Through all this, Dal managed to retain his grip on the man's throat. His hands kept pressing in, fingers crushing in on flesh, gouging toward bone.

Again the face shifted, became the hard, twisted features of a punk he'd put away last year—the bastard had sworn to get him, get out one day and hunt him down, slit him from groin to throat—

"I'll get you, Reid! I'll get you when you least expect it and that's a promise!" . . .

He could see the vision of that promise in the glassy eyes, like a viewer into the future, the images speeding by: *There was the punk breaking out of prison, hiding in some bushes, lunging out with a knife—*

became the face of the handsome young black man once more, smiling with amusement as Dal continued to bear down with all his might.

It was as if Dal were squeezing against solid marble. He was having no effect. The collar of the man's shirt wasn't even crumpled.

"We'll meet again, Detective Reid. I look forward to it." The man smiled,

and in the space of a heartbeat, Dal's hands came together, clamping in on each other as if he'd been squeezing a piece of tissue paper and it had suddenly collapsed.

Now Dal tried to release his grip—but he couldn't. He *couldn't!*

The man's face was beginning to decompose.

Dal strained to force his hands apart, unlace his fingers and pull them away, but nothing would obey. They were locked around the shrunken neck.

A rotting cadaver now grinned at him. It continued to shrink away, shriveling and drying up like old, yellowed paper. Skin began to crack open and peel, dropping away from bone.

For a moment, it was the grinning death's-head from Dal's dream, an exact replica, eyes burning redly, black cape billowing in the wind.

Then it was only a skull. A grinning, empty skull. And Dal's hands were fastened around the slender white cervical vertebrae of the neck.

The muscles in his fingers suddenly spasmed, and with a tremendous burst of effort, he jerked his hands away. The skeleton crumpled to the ground.

Bones became disjoined as they fell, toppling in on each other, until, with a sharp crack, the skull dropped onto the top of the pile, teetered there a moment, then rolled off to one side and came to rest against the edge of a jutting piece of hip.

The sound had been the collapse of a Lego structure, the topple of a Tinkertoy man.

Dal took a couple of stumbling steps backward, his gaze still locked on the pile of jumbled bones.

What had just happened? It had to be some kind of magician's trick. He'd been fighting with a mirage. He reached an unsteady hand toward the bones, intending to pick one up, examine it, see if it was real—

And in that instant, the bones began to disintegrate. Like time-lapse photography, they crumbled, came apart, reduced themselves to powder until no solid piece remained, nothing was left but a few mounds of white dust strewn across the dark, broken pavement like sand.

Reeling as if he were drunk, Dal backed toward the street. *It couldn't have been real, what he'd just seen—it couldn't.*

But it had been real, he knew that, knew he'd come up against something he didn't want to believe existed. And he'd been allowed to walk away. This time.

"We'll meet again, Detective Reid. I look forward to it." Dal shuddered.

His head was spinning wildly. He could no longer stand. Falling to his knees at the mouth of the alley, he began gulping in air, trying to regain his equilibrium, chase away the nausea that was threatening to force his body to evacuate itself.

He almost wished it would. He felt as if he needed to purge himself, clean out whatever insanity had gotten in. *Was he losing his mind?* He felt as if something horrible—*unclean*—had entered him, strewn nightmare visions through his head.

The wind sprang up. It feathered around him, making him shiver as it stroked cold fingers against his sweat. Then it gusted on by, and he glanced up to see it stirring the white dust particles in the alley beyond him, carrying them into the air.

The dust devil whirled crazily about for a moment, dipping and rising, a little funnel cloud. Then the dust particles began to disburse, spreading out on the wind which carried them away.

Dal dropped his head, giving in to the nausea.

On a slab at the morgue, J.J. opened his eyes.

TWENTY-SEVEN

J.J. felt like a pincushion. For weeks now, doctors and lab techs had been poking him with their needles, drawing blood for their tests—buckets of it, it seemed. A vampire should have such a setup.

He left the cool interior of the forensics lab, went out into the hot, bright June sunshine and headed across the black asphalt parking lot to his car.

He realized he was noticing things more fully now, and smiled, hoping the heightened sense of awareness wouldn't go away too soon. It was a cliché, he knew, but a brush with death really could make you appreciate your surroundings. And the things that truly mattered in your life.

Dal felt it too. J.J. had never seen his friend so subdued. Dal's sudden radical shift to the more serious side of life was a welcome, if unexpected, change. He knew Dal had been shaken by what he thought had happened to his best friend. Not that he'd said much; it had been Agent Swann who had filled J.J. in on most of what had occurred that night.

But it was more than that. Dal was getting some direction to his life. He'd quit the force and was moving to Raleigh, going to work for the State Bureau of Investigation in their deep-cover program. He'd stopped drinking.

Jackie Swann had helped him get the position. She was giving up field work, Dal had reported, and would be training undercover agents at the SBI academy from now on. He said she had a special skill for altering her appearance, and had already given him some valuable pointers.

All in all, it seemed they were all getting over the experience of six weeks ago, getting on with their lives. And if J.J. still had trouble going to sleep at night, or woke up in a cold sweat thinking he was back in that place, caught up again in the dark, silent aloneness that—so the doctors told him—had been some sort of drug-induced coma that simulated death, then time would take care of it.

Time.

He hadn't really been dead, at least that's what the doctors said, though there were times at night, *in the dark, silent empty times of night,* when he wasn't so sure.

But of course they were right. They were running their tests and sooner or later they'd come up with the substance that had caused it all.

There's a new drug in town.

The entire law-enforcement community was mobilizing to find out what had been used. There was talk of a "zombie" drug that had been used for years—maybe even generations—by the witch doctors and sorcerers of Haiti, those self-proclaimed mystics who practiced voodoo, dispensed powders, potions, poisons, dabbled in magic and the forbidden arts. There were reports by respected researchers and institutes of strange incidents recorded in the Haitian culture, people thought dead and buried, later revived by the Bokor, or priest, to do slave labor, or more sinister jobs, for a price.

It had long been thought that a drug that simulated death was administered to the unlucky individual, then other drugs used to revive and control him, keep him in a "zombie" state.

The substances had never been isolated, but it was the consensus at least among the local police, that something of the same sort had been used by the Haitian traffickers to try and take over the drug business city-wide.

Apparently this Boneman person was part of the deal. They'd found evidence at the house where J.J. had been held. The house had belonged to Maurice Martineau, they discovered, and it seemed he'd hired this man, who was considered some sort of High Bokor by the folks back home, to come work his magic on the competition.

The man was pretty good at his job, J.J. could testify to that. So could Dal.

Dal had reported what had happened to him that night in the alley, how he'd come face-to-face with the man who they now thought had done all the killing, or caused it to be done.

"I'm what you fear most. The face of your own mortality."

J.J. shivered in the sunlight.

Dal was lucky to be alive.

Others had not been so lucky. They were still finding apparent victims all over the city, some dead, some as good as. Willie Dee had been brought in in an almost comatose state, as if he'd been lobotomized. Dal said that the hooker who'd been under this crazy guru's spell was even worse, barely alive, if you could call it that. The doctors were doing everything they could, but there wasn't much hope. It was as if their brains had begun to decompose, like metal subjected to corrosion over a period of time.

This is your brain on drugs.

He unlocked his car, stood there a moment feeling the wind brush his face. Dal had told him about the crazy sequence of events that had occurred that night. Hallucination, the doctors said— they'd been sticking Dal full of needles too. The drug could have been given without his knowledge, brushed onto his skin, even inhaled. They just didn't know.

But they'd find out. They were working on it.

J.J. wondered what he'd really seen that night. Had he really gotten up off that bed and gone downstairs, talked to this Boneman person, phoned Dal?

Dal swore it was him on the phone, and the doctors wouldn't commit either way. So maybe he had gotten up and done it; or maybe it had really all been a dream—like a hypnotic suggestion—and the Boneman had simply imitated his voice.

But why? Why would he want to call Dal and expose himself? What had there been to gain?

"A moment's amusement, Mr. Spencer."

The man was clearly insane.

Yet sometimes late at night, when the memories took hold and wouldn't let J.J. sleep, when the fear crept in and sat like a satyr on his chest, he wondered: *Had he really held a conversation with the Grim Reaper? Had he come face-to-face with the Devil himself and walked away? Would the Boneman—in whatever guise—be waiting for him somewhere, someday, around some bend in the road?*

"I'm coming for you . . . coming for you all . . ."

He stood listening to the traffic noise, and the sound of laughter from a group of lab techs walking by. Birds chirping in the trees.

He missed Buddy.

He opened the door, climbed in, and started the car. Pulled out into the street.

Dal's absence was felt on the home front too. Though he wouldn't officially be leaving Phoenix City until the end of the month, he was spending a lot of his free time in Raleigh, getting an apartment, going through a whole battery of preliminary interviews and tests. J.J. actually missed those postmidnight visits, though he doubted the neighbors did.

It got very quiet after midnight.

J.J. joined the string of traffic merging onto the beltline, headed home.

Home. That had a good sound to it. And maybe it wouldn't be quite so lonesome soon.

He had a date tonight with Charlotte Ramsey. The first, he hoped, of many.

Apparently she'd broken off with that guy she'd been seeing

and J.J.'s perseverance had paid off. She'd agreed to go out with him. He had quite an evening planned, starting with dinner at Anton's, then tickets to a jazz concert with the hot group Toys Don't Hate. After that, maybe a little top-off at The Dessertery.

J.J. smiled broadly, feeling better than he had in weeks. Maybe soon he'd even get back into writing—though not the Jehovah Jones stories, he was through with that.

Maybe Dal was right, maybe it had been some sort of *altar*-ego thing coming out, a backlash of living in the Bible Belt and being brought up with the image of God as a cross between Santa Claus and the Terminator. For a while he'd toyed with the idea of becoming a minister like his father, whom he adored. But the more he'd studied theology, the less he'd been inclined to believe.

Maybe the Jehovah Jones stories had been an attempt to bring God down to his own level so he could understand.

Whatever. He just knew now that the stories would never be written, though the questions still remained. What if this was all there was? What if this was the only chance you got, so you'd better make it count—not because of threats of hell or hopes of heaven, but because this was It.

A poser for the philosophers.

But if there *was* something else, J.J. thought as he zipped off the beltline and turned his car toward home, if he had been given a glimpse of what was out there beyond the pale. If the Boneman was really real . . .

then just maybe there was a Jehovah Jones out there too.

He smiled in the sunshine and headed home.

Someone was coming . . .

A cool wind blew down the dark, deserted two-lane road just outside a little town not far from Atlanta, Georgia. It carried dust and the smell of an open cesspool.

Clouds blotted the midnight sky. Except for the sound of a hound dog baying in the distance, all was quiet.

The dust particles rode the wind until it dipped downward, strewing them along the ground. They came to rest momentarily, a scattering of ash on the blacktop road.

An owl hooted nearby. A lonely sound.

The breeze dipped down once more, teasing the dust particles back to life. It spun them into a little funnel cloud that rose above the blacktop.

Slowly, the particles began to merge.

Bones started to form. Long, slender bones. Clean, white bones coming together in a familiar shape . . .

Try, try
Hard as you can
You can't kill me
I'm de ol' Boneman . . .

AUTHOR'S NOTE

The question most frequently asked a writer is: "Where do you get your ideas?" We're asked this so often that many of us have light comebacks ready, such as: "The ACME Idea Company" or "There's this mail-order house in Memphis, where for five dollars and a self-addressed stamped envelope . . ."

But what people are really asking, of course, is: "Where do you get ideas that are good enough to turn into a book that a publisher will want to buy and that people out there will want to read?"

So I thought I'd share with you how *Boneman* happened.

A couple of years ago, I was asked to participate in a program by the Carolina Crime Writers Association in Raleigh, North Carolina. The panelists included a mystery writer, a science fiction writer, a crime reporter for the local newspaper, and myself representing the horror genre. The scenario set for us was: "Your stolen car has been found on the interstate with a dead body handcuffed to the steering wheel and a kilo of coke in the trunk." Each panelist was to take this basic format and develop a story line from it that would show how we would treat it in our respective genres (or as a factual event in the case of the reporter).

We all had a lot of fun—and believe me, if I had ever doubted that several writers could be given the exact same idea and come up with such radically different plots, this sure brought it home. Aside from the basic starting point, the stories were totally unrecognizable as anything akin to each other.

Anyway, I came up with the voodoo angle, treating it tongue-in-cheek style at this point, sort of Zombie Jamboree time. I had no intention of turning it into a "real" novel. After I gave my presentation (and the audience really got into it), one of the other panelists leaned over to me and said: "You've got a book there; you may not know it yet, but you've got a book."

Nah . . .

On the drive home, a couple of friends who'd gone with me said: "You've got a book there; really, you've got a book."

Nah . . .

But the seed began to grow.

I remember exactly at what point that spark of recognition occurred, that comic-book light bulb that goes on in a writer's head when she's "got something." It was when I thought up the name Boneman. From that point on, the novel came alive to me.

As you now know—if you've read the book before reading this, as you're supposed to do—that original scenario never made it into this novel. But it was the seed from which the story grew.

"Where do you get your ideas?" From the Carolina Crime Writers Association. Thanks, guys.

Lisa Cantrell
November 1991